C000069366

THE

BROKEN

ONES

Mark Higgins

Fisher King Publishing

THE BROKEN ONES
Copyright © MARK HIGGINS 2021
ISBN 978-1-914560-04-0

All rights reserved. No part of this publication may be
reproduced or distributed in any form or by any means, or
stored in a database or electronic retrieval system without the
prior written permission of Fisher King Publishing Ltd. Thank you
for respecting the author of this work.

This is a work of fiction. Names, characters, businesses, places,
events and incidents are either the products of the author's
imagination or used in a fictitious manner. Any resemblance
to actual persons, living or dead, or actual events is purely
coincidental.

Fisher King Publishing
The Old Barn
York Road
Thirsk
YO7 3AD
England

fisherkingpublishing.co.uk

Cover image:
Fighting Horses in Nature Reserve Oostvaardersplassen
by Inge Jansen

This book is dedicated to the memory of Laura Manby 10th February 1992 – 14th May 2019 whose spirit is summed up in this poem by Emily Dickinson

If I can stop one heart from breaking,
I shall not live in vain;
If I can ease one life the aching,
Or cool one pain,
Or help the fainting Robin
Unto his nest again,
I shall not live in vain.

Part One

Chapter One

The mustang mare had been in labour for ten hours, having gone off on her own away from the main herd to give birth. Now in the final stages, she frantically pawed at the earth with pain and discomfort. At last a head began to appear, then in two big contractions the foal fell to the ground protected in his amniotic sack.

The mare immediately began consuming the protective cocoon then licked life into her offspring. Like a moth emerging from its chrysalis, the young horse found the strength to push himself up onto his rear legs encouraged by his mother. He stumbled around for thirty minutes before eventually getting on to all fours, albeit gingerly. The mare nosed him in the direction of her teats. He nuzzled around until his mouth connected and he was able to suck eagerly at the colostrum milk, essential as it contained antibodies to bolster his immune system. As the foal suckled, he continually nuzzled his mother, forcing the milk to flow faster.

After a the night on her own, the mare returned to the herd or band. She kept the foal safe, chasing off any of the other older colts that came too close while also seeking the comfort of her sisters and the mares. They were a fifteen-strong mix of mares, young colts and the stallion. The popular belief that a stallion rules the herd is a common misconception: he is in charge regarding protecting the herd and servicing the mares, but that is about as far as it goes. Herd politics can be shared but usually the one in charge is an older mare. She knows where the best grazing is at any time of the year, along with the location of the water sources and mineral deposits in their range. Luckily for this young colt, his mother was the band's lead mare and commanded respect from the others, even the stallion.

As the weeks and months passed, the foal grew stronger and learned his place in the herd. At around a year old, sometimes more, sometimes less, a young horse has to fit in and become a productive member of his band. His mother will still keep an eye on him but she and the other members of her herd set out the rules. It was a confusing time for the youngster who up until that point had done whatever he pleased regardless of the consequences. Now he would start to spend a lot of time with the other young colts, where their play-fighting would hone the skills needed for them to survive.

It was now spring near the Wyoming–Montana border where the winters can be incredibly harsh. There was also the problem of bigger bands which would move into the area and disrupt a small herd's headcount. The stronger invading stallions could drive out the male colts, dethroning the lead stallion and taking all the mares. And of course, there were the predators: bears, mountain lions and even wolves in some parts, always on the lookout for a meal.

At this time resources were plentiful and life was full of play. The youngster was still all legs but had started to lose his fluffy foal tail, his coat gradually lightening to a pale cream with four white legs and a broad white strip between his eyes. Life was generally peaceful but sometimes the band would hear strange sounds off in the distance; the screeching of a coyote or the sharp thuds of a thunderstorm. They would then move off and put some distance between themselves and the worrying noises.

Spring rolled into summer and all the time the young colt was learning how to stay safe in his environment. He was becoming more independent and his mother was now in foal again, so he only looked to her when he needed comfort. Their range at this time of year was the high prairie and, although it was hot, there was plenty of grazing and water which sometimes they shared with the bison.

After one particularly humid day, they spent the night on a high hill overlooking the vast expanse before them. A weather front came in from the west, big thunderheads at its leading edge. The storm was massive: wave after wave of thunderclaps followed by sky-splitting bolts of lightning. The horses were on edge but they stayed together. Crack! A bolt of lightning split the herd sending them into a panic, horses running for their lives out on to the open prairie below.

In the morning, something smelled different and the colt followed the scent trail until he found its source. The lightning had claimed three of the herd and one of them was his mother. Her body lay in the morning sun, its shape changed due to the lightning strike and the start of decomposition. He nuzzled the corpse trying to get his mother to rise but eventually nature took over telling him he had to leave. Not long after, the colt was pushed out of the herd by the band stallion and was left to fend for himself in the wilderness.

Chapter Two

Billy Higgs lost his mother as she gave birth to him. His father took an overdose and died when he was five and none of the extended family claimed him. Since that time, five years ago now, he had been living with foster parents. Most were okay but the family he'd now been sent to felt different. Even on the trial placement there was a coldness to them which made him feel ill at ease. Being a foster child, he felt there was no choice but to give things a try, but this decision would cost him dearly.

His new foster family, the Brents, lived in the suburbs of Denver. They comprised Johnny Brent senior, his wife Rebecca and Johnny junior, their only offspring. Johnny senior was a long-haul truck driver and could be away for weeks. Rebecca – or Becky – was a housewife and full-time foster carer mum, while Johnny junior had just started college and, like his dad, would be away most of the time.

When Billy visited with his social worker, he was shown the room in which he would be living. In reality, only two weeks into the deal, he found himself sitting in the basement on an old mattress, hungry and nursing bruised ribs courtesy of Becky's tough love.

He soon found out that Becky had a very different take on the whole foster mum deal. Basically, she just took the cheque each month for whatever child was snared into choosing the Brents as their temporary mum and dad. Over the past two weeks, Billy had already suffered plenty of physical and mental abuse, and had lost hope of finding a way out of his predicament.

Billy looked around the basement wondering how many other kids had gone through this misery. The only luxury was a busted-up radio set thrown down there with the rest of the junk that was lying around: boxes, bikes with flat tyres and a couple of storage racks with a plethora of unused household goods, all just sitting there, forgotten and gathering dust. He had found the radio on one of the racks and was surprised when it crackled into life when he plugged it in. Every time he finished listening or thought someone might check on him, Billy carefully replaced the radio on the dusty shelf.

As Billy sat in what he came to refer to as the dungeon, he could tell where his foster mum was by her routine and distinctive footfalls. On this day, Becky was heading for his lair.

"C'mon you, get up these stairs. We have to clean you up, it's time for a visit to your new school."

His mind was racing. Could it be true? Could he be going to meet other kids?

Becky yanked him up the last two steps and into the kitchen where Billy could see a set of new clothes and a backpack for keeping all his school stuff in. He was excited until his foster mother made him strip naked in the middle of the kitchen. She had a full basin of water with a cloth, a scrubbing brush and a large block of coal tar soap with an antiseptic smell. Becky rinsed out the cloth a couple of times then rubbed the soap hard against it.

"You get your skinny ass over here. I ain't sending you to school smellin' like a dawg."

Although Billy knew this was not going to be pleasant, he could only comply with Becky's order. To say his guardian was rough when she bathed him would be an understatement: she would have been quicker and gentler throwing Billy in the washing machine. She rubbed his face almost raw with the cloth and used the scrubbing brush on his elbows, knees and feet, drawing blood in several places.

"Better keep your mouth shut about what goes on in this house," she ordered.

Billy stood in the kitchen recovering from this rough handling. His clothes fitted him, just, and he had a basic pencil case, a lunchbox containing a single sandwich and a bottle of tap water.

St Brigid's grade school was like any small education establishment: kids went in at one end and older kids came out at the other. The old school that had stood on the site since the turn of the century had been demolished in the late eighties and replaced with a modern structure, but it was still a big grey box that the children either loved or hated.

Becky pulled into the car park in her old station wagon or as she loved to call it, Old Faithful. She leaned across Billy to undo his seat belt and at the same time, with a smile on her face, warned him: "Remember what I told you in the kitchen."

Looking up at Becky, Billy nodded in compliance.

As they stepped out of the air-conditioned car, a blast of heat engulfed them.

"It's a hot one today," Becky said, "Bet you're glad I put that bottle of water in your bag."

Billy had only said a few words to his foster mother since he first arrived but he now plucked up some courage.

"Thank you, Mrs Brent, it was really thoughtful of you to know it would be this hot." Billy forced a smile for her but meant none of it, just playing the game he had to in order to survive.

Becky walked him towards the school building but there was nothing pleasant about her. Billy knew he would have to sit tight and trust to luck.

The only good thing on entering the school was the air-conditioning. Billy had been to a couple of other schools in his time and they all smelled the same; sanitised. As they walked along the main corridor, Becky looked for the principal's office. About halfway along on the right-hand side there was a hatch with the word 'Reception' printed on the glass of the small window. Just as Becky reached out to press the buzzer, a slim woman with red hair appeared at the hatch.

"Hi, my name is Karen. How can I help you this morning?"

In a flat tone Becky told Karen that she had an appointment with the principal.

"Here we are, Mrs Brent, and this must be…" Karen let her sentence tail off. After a small but awkward pause, Becky spoke Billy's name. Karen leaned out of the hatch stretching her hand towards Billy.

"Hi there, my name is Karen," she repeated pointing

to her badge, "Welcome to St Brigid's, Billy. You're going to love it here." Billy shook her hand but didn't believe her.

"Hello, hello, hello, come in, please take a seat." Principal Margaret Campbell was a self-confessed large woman and had no intention of changing that. She sat at a suitably impressive desk. The office was sparse: nothing hung on the walls except a family tree of the Clan Campbell, as Principal Campbell was immensely proud of her Scottish heritage.

She looked over the desk, her eyes locked on to Billy.

"And you must be William." She reached across and shook his hand. This was familiar ground for Billy, who had been to quite a few schools in his short time in the education system. He took the principal's hand.

"Yes, that's correct ma'am, but most people call me Billy." Margaret looked at Becky.

"What a well-mannered young man." Becky ruffled Billy's hair.

"Yes he is, we are so lucky to have the chance to be a part of his life and give him stability, so important in a child's development."

Becky and the principal exchanged smiles.

"Well now, if it is okay with Becky," – more smiles – "I'll take you and get you settled into your class. How do you feel about that?" Billy put on a brave face. This was the part of moving to a new school he disliked most; being the new kid.

"Okay," he said, "I hope I make some new friends." Of the things he had said to the principal, this last statement was the one Billy meant most. At one of his other schools Billy had been given a hard time just because he was in care.

After saying goodbye to Becky, Billy and Principal Campbell walked along the corridor in silence until reaching the door at the end.

"Here we are," the principal said as they entered the small classroom. There was a buzz of activity that stopped as the pair walked in.

"Good morning, children," the principal said. In unison, the class replied.

"Good morning, Ms Campbell."

"We have a new pupil starting today, his name is William. Ms Drake will be your teacher while you are here."

Ruth Drake could see that Billy was nervous so she kept things short.

"William, welcome to our class. We would like to know a little about you." Billy stood motionless for what felt like hours but was only a few seconds. When he spoke, his voice was barely a whisper.

"Hello everybody, my name is Billy Higgs. I am originally from Estes Park in the Rocky Mountains but now live with the Brents, who are my new foster parents." His gaze dropped to the floor.

"I think William deserves a big hand for that," Ms Drake said, "It's not easy being new in a strange school." Everyone clapped then the teacher showed Billy to his desk.

At the day's end, Billy sat in the empty playground waiting for Becky to pick him up. Old Faithful pulled into the car park, the passenger door popping open as

Becky glared at him.

"Well, what are you waitin' for, an invitation? Get in."

All the way home neither passenger nor driver spoke. Becky listened to the radio not once enquiring about Billy's first day at school, while Billy just sat quietly knowing that when he got home things would change and not for the better.

First came Becky's interrogation which took place in the dungeon. Then came the retribution, on this occasion in the form of being suffocated until he was almost unconscious with a few knocks to the ribs and no proper meal. The only food Billy got that night consisted of scraps that his new mother left after dinner.

In the cold and damp basement, Billy sat on his mattress sobbing. He was thinking about his father and his drug addiction. Even in the worst of times, and times had often been tough, his father had never laid a hand on him even though he sometimes deserved a spanking. His father had never really recovered from the death of Billy's mother and gradually his life had spiralled out of control due to heroin.

One of the most precious things Billy possessed was a photograph of his father and mother taken at the beach. His parents seemed so happy that day; it was sunny and his dad tipped Billy's mum's nose with an ice-cream cone as a beach photographer snapped the shot. Over the years Billy had come to gradually blame himself not only for the loss of his parents but also for the fate their deaths had placed on his own shoulders.

In the darkness of the basement, Billy began running

an escape plan over in his head. He knew that life with the Brents would only get worse and he made the decision that no matter what the consequences were, he had to get out.

Chapter Three

High in the Wyoming wilderness the young colt's condition was suffering due to his solitude. His coat was matted and dull, he had lost quite a lot of weight and his general demeanour was one of submission. Over the past week or so he had wandered aimlessly, calling out then listening for any reply: there was none. As a herd animal, his being excluded could be a death sentence as he and he alone would be responsible for his day-to-day wellbeing and safety.

On this day he had been grazing in a small bluff next to a river when he came across some fresh horse dung. Immediately he began again to call out into the wild. Nothing. He called again more frantically. Nothing. He was about to call for a third time when the faintest of sounds on the light breeze caught his attention: it was a horse. With a burst of adrenaline and running as fast as could, he set off in the direction of the sound. It came again, this time more clearly, and calling out as he ran the colt's legs burned with the build-up of lactic acid. He slowed his pace then he saw movement ahead: it was a bay horse and, by the sound of its call, a mare.

They moved cautiously toward each other, each reading the other's body language for any tension or possible aggression but there was none. Unknown to the colt, the bay mare had recently lost her youngster to a bear. On hearing his calls she had worked purely on instinct: there was still a need for her to be a mother to someone and luckily for the colt that someone could now be him. As they came closer, she nickered softly to him the way only a mother horse would do. He replied in kind, then they were together. They rubbed muzzles for a while before getting down to the serious business of mutual grooming which would cement their bond. If only his passage into her herd could work out so easily.

The herd was twenty strong, one of the biggest bands in that area. There was the usual mix of mares and youngsters and of course colts. This band had a larger than normal group of young colts and these would eventually be ousted by the lead stallion, but for some reason he was tolerant of them at this time.

As the mare wandered back to the herd with the dun colt in tow, the lead stallion flew at them charging, kicking out as he tried to hamstring the young horse. The mare did all she could to position herself between the colt and the ferocious attacks. After what seemed an age the attacks stopped and the stallion moved off having made his point. The mare stood next to the colt who was nursing deep wounds to his neck and legs but had survived.

The mare now shadowed her new charge as he met some more members of the herd. The mares were more forgiving as they realised he was just a youngster but the colts acted as they had seen the stallion do; charging, biting and kicking out at the intruder. After a while they calmed down and moved off to graze on their own.

Over the next few days the bay mare and the dun colt stayed on the fringes of the band. There were still occasional scuffles but these grew less frequent and not as intense as time moved on. The fall grew closer. After that, winter would raise its head and the real battle for survival would come. This would sort out the weak from the strong.

Chapter Four

It was Billy's third day at school and, as on the previous two, he sat alone at one of the outdoor lunch benches. Today, however, someone sat down at the same bench on the opposite side. Billy looked up from his half-eaten sandwich to discover a boy staring at him.

"Hi," the boy said, "My name's Sam, Sam Quinn." Billy looked around then realised Sam was talking to him.

"Sorry, I'm Billy. Have you been at this school long?" Sam smiled.

"Just about a year, after I got adopted. My new parents brought me here so I know how hard it is trying to fit in." As Sam stretched his hand across the table, Billy mirrored him and a friendship was born.

It had been a while since Billy had talked to a kid his own age and although both he and Sam were young in years, they were older in life experience. They sat talking until the end of lunch, although Billy stayed clear of saying too much about the Brents, mentioning them only briefly. But Sam knew that Billy had held back on the details. He had been in Billy's shoes and knew that things could be tough for a kid who drifted through the care system so he didn't push him on the subject.

Just as they were about to go back inside for afternoon lessons, a bigger boy who was a class above them called out to Sam.

"Who's your new boyfriend, Quinn?" The older boy and his friends had a giggle then disappeared into the building.

"Who's that guy?" Billy asked Sam, "And what's his problem?" Sam was still looking in the direction of the building.

"That's Eddy Thompson, just your average school bully. I'm sure you've had a few of them, I know I have." A heavy weight sank on to Billy: that was all he needed, another dictator in his life. He just nodded in reply but it was enough to let Sam know that, yes, he did understand him on the subject of bullies.

The 'get your ass back in the class' buzzer sounded and it was time for afternoon lessons. Sam said they should meet at the same bench tomorrow and Billy gave him the thumbs-up then headed for Ms Drake's class.

That night, Johnny Brent senior returned from one of his long-haul runs. From down in the basement Billy could hear the party atmosphere above. On returning from school he had been formally introduced to his new father.

"Skinny little fucker, ain't cha!" All Billy could do was nod. "What's wrong with ya, boy? Cat gotcha tong?" Again, Billy nodded and this time his eyes found the floor.

"Becky, you did not tell me that this here boy was deaf, do we get more money for that?" Billy didn't like the way Johnny senior smelled, all stale sweat and booze. At this point Becky appeared in the kitchen.

"He ain't deaf Johnny, dumb maybe but not deaf.

Ain't that right boy?" She glared down at Billy until he uttered a near-imperceptible reply.

"Y-y-yes, ma'am." Becky exploded into laughter.

"But he do stut-stut-stutter sometimes!" She pulled a Happy Meal off the table and handed it to Billy who almost thought it was an illusion.

"Take that," she said, "and don't say we ain't good to you. Now git down those stairs before I change ma mind." Billy half-snatched the bag out of Becky's hand but had the good manners to thank her before heading downstairs to tuck into his feast. It was a disappointment to find half the meal missing and the remainder cold, but he ate what was left and it tasted delicious.

The coming-home party went on into the small hours but although Billy had little sleep there were no surprise visitors that night. Thank God it would soon be the weekend and he could start making his escape plan.

As promised, Sam was at the bench waiting for Billy the following day. He was quiet so Billy asked if he was okay. Sam paused then told Billy of a run-in with Eddy Thompson and his friends.

"Did they hurt you?"

"Nah, just called me names and all." Sam seemed far away as he said this, like he was running the incident over and over in his head. Billy in turn started to talk about what had been going on at the Brents.

"Ain't ya going to the police?" Sam asked.

"I can't. They won't believe me and then I'll be in even more trouble." Sam could see the strain this was putting on his new friend.

"I promise not to say a word to anyone about what you told me," he said, "Cross my heart and hope to die." He stood up and with his right hand drew two diagonal lines that made a big X in the middle of his chest.

Sam then told Billy of having started a karate class and on hearing this Billy perked up.

"You gonna kick Eddy Thompson's ass, then?" Sam laughed.

"Damn straight I am, dipshit needs a wake-up call." The boys were in hysterics when Thompson and two of his gang suddenly appeared beside them at the table.

Eddy was quite a lot taller than the other kids and he knew it.

"Is that all you got for lunch, newbie?" Eddy had picked up Billy's lunchbox and tossed it on the ground before turning his attention to Sam.

"Hey Quinn, you got any goodies?" Eddy did the same thing with Sam's box only this time he picked up the two chocolate bars that Sam's mum had given him for lunch.

"Thanks, Sam," he said, "New kid, you better have something better for me next week. See you later, suckers." And with that Eddy and his sidekicks were gone. The two boys sat in silence until Sam started to collect their scattered lunches.

"What are we going to do?" Billy said. Sam shook his head.

"We'll just have to do what he wants for now, don't you think?" Billy shrugged.

"Becky won't give me anything and I'll get my butt kicked!" The pitch of Billy's voice rose almost to the point where Sam was worried he might have a panic attack.

"Calm down, Billy," he said, "I'll get you something from our house, my mom won't mind and she spoils me anyway." The school bell sounded breaking the boys out of their thoughts.

As the children returned to the classroom, Ms Drake noticed that Billy was looking tense and decided to try and pick a moment later on to see if she could learn why the boy seemed so troubled. Although quite young for a teacher, Ruth Drake was a natural. She was good at focusing on small changes that occurred in children who were potentially suffering from abuse, and in Billy she could see a child with tell-tale signs of some sort of trauma. She would make it her mission to find out what was troubling him.

When Billy got home Johnny was gone, back on the road again. Becky for once was in good spirits and Billy soon found out why as his foster mother took a big draw on a joint. Billy headed down to his own personal suite at Château Brent. After changing quickly he took a chance on Becky being stoned enough to let him outside for a while. As he entered the kitchen she lit another joint. He walked up to her.

"Mrs Brent, could I go outside to play?" He took a step back as he asked this in expectation of a torrent of abuse or worse, but Becky was so stoned she just gestured in the direction of the back door.

Without hesitation Billy headed out into the street. Since moving in with the Brents he had only ever travelled back and forth to school so scarcely knew the surrounding area at all. He ran down to the railroad tracks where he stood, catching his breath, as the crossing bell began to ring and the barriers dropped behind him, stopping traffic as the train approached.

Billy watched almost hypnotised. In the darkest part of his mind a voice spoke.

"You would have so much peace, just step forward and all the pain will stop." He was edging out on to the tracks. The ground around began to vibrate and the train was sounding its horn but Billy noticed none of this, still listening to the voice in his head.

"You have brought all of this misery on yourself, it's all your fault that Mum and Dad are gone and you are at the mercy of the Brents."

Tears flowed down Billy's face. "No!" he shouted then stepped back against the barrier just as the train hurtled past the spot where he had been a moment before. The airflow caused Billy to turn and grip the barrier just to stay on his feet. Then the train was gone.

As he walked back to the Brents, he felt a sense of relief and his head felt clear for the first time in a long while.

Opening the kitchen door, he stepped inside just as Becky launched her first punch.

"Where have you been, you little shit?" Billy was winded, bent double, but this only made Becky more furious. There was another punch, then another, and another. Finally, she picked up Billy by the scruff of his neck and threw him down into the basement.

"You better start to give me some answers, think about that. I'll be back later."

Something was different, however. Instead of being

scared, Billy was angry. He knew that things were going to change for him and it was just a matter of time before he would have a better life. He sat waiting for Becky to return, vowing to tell her it was she who had told him to go outside.

Chapter Five

The dun colt stood by the bay mare. The leaves had started to fall and the goodness was starting to drain out of the grass they were both eating. It was at this time of year that the herd matriarch would come into her own: she was the one who knew where and when was the best time to move to new pastures. But even though the autumn had started there was still good heat in the sun.

As the horses ate, they kept the length of their bodies facing the sun. This allowed warmth to heat their muscles without them overheating. If they became too hot they put their short side to the sun, usually their rear. So they grazed and changed from one side to the other, letting their bodies enjoy the morning rays.

Over the past days the colt and mare had become closer and were always near one another, even when the other colts or the stallion came calling. The assaults from the stallion had lessened to a degree but the colts were a different story.

When a sorrel colt introduced himself to the dun colt, their meeting was very low-key and lethargic at first. They did the usual foot-stamping and squealing, nipping at each other's shoulders, chasing one another until they wearied. Then as they stood grooming, two rogue colts charged, catching the dun colt off guard. He managed to turn enough to escape the full force of the kick but still took most of its power on his flank.

Reeling from the aggression, the dun colt ran and kicked out, but both the rogue colts were close by and dodged his attempts to fend them off.

It was at this moment that something unexpected happened. The sorrel colt blindsided one of the chasing colts and kicked him square on his jaw which, if broken, could mean the end for the colt, such are the narrow margins between life and death for a wild horse. The remaining colt kept up his pursuit as they ran through a coppice and here in the trees the pace slowed, though only a degree. With teeth tearing at his quarters there seemed only one fate for the dun colt, but he caught the movement of a diamondback rattlesnake just early enough to avoid its strike.

His pursuer was less fortunate. The snake's fangs sunk deep into its foreleg instantly bringing the horse to a halt. As the snake released its grip, the colt pawed it until there was no movement from his foe, but the venom had already started its work.

Exhausted from his confrontation, the dun colt sought comfort from his surrogate mother. He found her by the river grazing on some clover and she gave out a low whinny at the sight of him. The youngster stopped about ten metres away, gradually working towards her as horse etiquette dictated. Once close enough he, being the subordinate, initiated grooming and the mare responded by nuzzling him where she wanted grooming. He duly complied.

That afternoon they enjoyed each other's company and all the warmth an autumn sun has to offer. Later on their way back to the band they paused to examine the bloated carcass of the colt that had been bitten by the snake, congealed blood oozing from every orifice. Nature told them to move, leaving the body for whoever came calling.

Chapter Six

Becky kept good on her promise and made her way down to the basement.

"Now boy, you can make this hard or you can make it easy, it's up to you. But I want to know why you went off on your own without me telling you." Billy waited till she was about to explode before he let her know the truth.

"You wanna know, Mom? You told me it was okay and that's a fact. The other fact is you were too stoned this afternoon to remember what day it was, let alone why I left the house."

His heart raced but he now felt a kind of freedom that had been missing for so long.

"Don't you talk to me like that, ya little bastard!" Becky's fist caught Billy on his already painful ribs and he let out a yelp. This seemed to please Becky so she hit him again.

As Billy lay on the floor she pinned his arms with her knees, then ever so slowly pinched his nose and covered his mouth with her other hand. His body was screaming for oxygen and his lungs were convulsing but he did not struggle as he had previously. Instead, he surrendered himself to unconsciousness.

When he came round Billy didn't know how long his blackout had lasted but Becky was gone and his shoes were missing. I guess that's one way of keeping me from running, he thought.

Johnny junior returned from college on Saturday afternoon. His mom was in raptures that her golden boy had come back to visit his parents. Most of what was left of the weekend Becky spent with Johnny leaving Billy in the basement, his only company being the old radio. He had very little to eat or drink that weekend, only the food and water he had squirreled away through the week, and that was not much.

By the time Billy met Sam at school on Monday he was not only hungry but also looked pale and drawn. This was not lost on Sam, whose first words were: "Man, you look like shit". Billy managed a smile for his friend.

"You're telling me," he said.

Sam reached into his bag and handed Billy half a dozen chocolate bars. "Not all of these are for our friend Eddy." Billy put four bars into his lunch box and hurriedly ate the other two. He thanked Sam and they headed for their respective classes.

Ruth Drake noticed the change in Billy as soon as he walked into the classroom and she made a note to speak to him later. She then began the class by asking each pupil to bring out their daybooks so she could check their work. As she looked through Billy's book she was surprised by the quality.

"This is good work, Billy," she said, "Your handwriting is very good and your tables are well above average."

"Thank you, Ms Drake," Billy replied, "I've always liked schoolwork as it helps me to stay focused."

This last statement seemed rather odd so Ruth quizzed him on it.

"In what way does it help you focus, Billy? Do you have anything you are worried about?" And there it was; an opportunity for Billy to get out of the situation he was in. But no, he thought, this is not the right time.

"Nothing, Ms Drake. I just have trouble staying on track and I find that the work you give us stimulates me." The teacher did not believe a word of this but knew by the way Billy spoke that there would be no real answers today.

"I am glad you find my work helps you," she said, "If there is anything else you need help with don't hesitate to come talk to me."

Watching Billy walk back to his seat, Ruth felt that at least she had offered something. If he was as smart as she thought he was, then the door was open.

Chapter Seven

Winter came hard and fast that year as it had done previously. The band members had bulked up during the autumn to give themselves good fat reserves to help stave off the worst of the weather. Their coats had grown in thick and along with the natural grease in the hide it had created a thermal barrier against the elements that would stalk them in the cold months ahead.

There had been a steady fall of snow for a several hours and the band spent most of their time sheltering on a western slope of evergreen forest that covered this side of the mountain. Even though the weather had deteriorated, it did not stop the dun colt from being challenged by the remaining members of the colt bachelor group. His surrogate mother did her best to assist him but there was only so much she could do. With every encounter the dun was burning precious reserves meant to see him through the winter.

There was one downside to staying so close to the forest and that was that you didn't know what was in residence there: bears, cougars and so on. In winter the band had to take chances and with a good head count there were always extra eyes to keep lookout just in case. At this time of year, the horses reverted to their ancestral roots and took to browsing trees and shrubs as well as the usual grass diet. The basic rule was to survive for another day.

The dun colt stood next to his bay companion eating what was left of the grass. Both stayed close to the main herd as it was safer under their current circumstances. They would eat here during the day and move out into the open at night when the herd members would take turns at being windbreaks for their fellow horses. There were some rules in the herd that were set: never attack a horse on the ground, and every horse takes a turn on guard duty. Every horse.

The harassment of the colt had not gone unnoticed by one individual. He had been watching the herd for some time waiting for the right opportunity. After all, every animal has to eat to survive. Studying the herd, he had selected an individual that looked weaker than the others. He watched for a lapse in concentration that would give him the advantage he needed.

The snow had stopped during the night. As a low mist rose to expose the treeline, the horses started to make their way upward to continue yesterday's grazing. Soon the herd would have to move down from the slopes and search for pastures at a lower level. At the back of the band one of the rogue colts that had attacked the dun stood on his own. The kick he had received to his jaw had not broken it but two of his molars were damaged and infected, making it difficult to feed. He ate what he could but with all that was happening to his body it seemed like a losing battle.

The other horses saw the movement first; a flash of tan hide. An opportunity like this did not come along often for the cougar, especially with prey this size. He had waited nearly a full day for the colt to move to a position that was the most beneficial to him. Even though he was a full-grown male cougar, there were risks involved in taking on the colt.

Finally, leaping from some high boulders on the edge of the forest, the cougar caught the colt off guard, sinking his claws and teeth deep into its body as he landed.

The colt knew nothing until the cougar was on him then writhed in agony as his attacker bit hard into his flesh. Holding the colt in his forepaws, the cougar used all its power to bite through the flesh of the young horse's neck in an attempt to shatter its spine. Running blindly, the colt quickly used all his own energy to try and fend off his adversary, rolling over and over to partially free himself.

After nearly losing his grip, the cougar changed his angle of attack: this time, he took the colt by the throat. Almost in slow motion, the great cat brought this struggle for life and death to an end, only releasing its hold when the colt's body went limp. He stood over his victim breathing heavily from the exertion, steam rising from the bodies of both victor and vanquished.

The snow turned crimson as the cat feasted. He would eat his fill and hopefully more before the day's end but, as ever in the wilderness, death attracted attention. First to spot the fresh kill were the ravens and their calls would alert every scavenger within earshot. The cougar ate till he was bloated then reluctantly left the kill hoping to return later.

Next morning, however, there was nothing left but a red stain leading all the way back to the woods. With a token lick of the snow the cougar moved off into the trees.

The band had run for about a mile before slowing down and looking back to where the attack had taken place. They would be on alert for the rest of that day. As if prompted by the loss of one of their own, the lead mare headed towards the valley floor. It was time once again to move on.

Chapter Eight

There's a starman waiting in the sky
He'd like to come and meet us
But he thinks he'd blow our minds
There's a...

David Bowie's *Starman* whispered out of Billy's radio as he sat completing his next work assignment for school. Suddenly there was movement upstairs and footsteps were heading his way. He grabbed the radio, putting it back on the dusty shelf where he had found it. Returning to his mattress-bed, he was just in time before the basement door creaked open.

"Billy... Billy... are you there?" Surprisingly, it was Johnny junior calling his name.

"Over here, Johnny," Billy replied, wondering what it took for him to be graced with Johnny's company. Johnny made his way over to where Billy was sitting.

"Jesus Christ man, it stinks in here." Billy did not know what Johnny was talking about and looked around to see where the smell could be coming from until he remembered the piss bucket. He had become so used to the smell that it no longer registered.

Becky did not let Billy use the main bathroom but gave him an old plastic paint container to use as a toilet. Every second day she made him empty this down a drain in the back yard, the only time now that Billy was allowed out of the house except for going to school.

Getting up, Billy moved the bucket out of the way.

"What brings you down here, Johnny?" Billy's tone was flat as if he already knew what Johnny's response would be.

"I've brought you these." As the older boy reached inside his jacket, Billy waited for some cruel punchline but none came. Instead, Johnny handed him a bottle of diet cola then from his other pocket he produced a packet of biscuits and two chicken sandwiches.

Billy looked at Johnny before opening the sandwiches and devouring both.

"Guessed you might be hungry," Johnny said, "Mom used to lock me in here when I was younger but just overnight, not like this. Has she beat on you yet?" Tears welled in Billy's eyes and he nodded yes to Johnny's question.

"Figured so. She used to beat on me till I got too big for her then she stopped."

Wiping his eyes, Billy thanked Johnny for the supplies. The boys spoke for a while then Johnny had to go. On leaving, he paused at the bottom of the stairs then turned towards Billy.

"I'll do what I can to bring you food but I'm going back to college next week so..." The older boy's words tailed off and he started his ascent back to the land of the living. As he reached the top steps, Billy called out another thanks then the door clicked shut and he was alone again.

True to his word, Johnny brought Billy food for the rest of that week before he returned to college. To be extra careful, Billy hid the wrappings from his illicit stash so that Becky would not find them. Then it was back to his usual routine.

Eddy Thompson was doing his rounds in the playground like a hummingbird flying from flower to flower collecting nectar from the helpless students chosen to be this year's victims. As he stuffed his pockets with extorted bounty, he spotted Sam and Billy in conversation and headed their way.

Sam had been watching Eddy and was, to put it mildly, pretty pissed off. As he sat speaking to Billy, he kept one eye on Eddy going about his business.

"You know something, Billy," Sam said.

"What?"

"They say all bullies are really cowards, did you know that?" Billy stared across the table at his friend, who by now had turned to face the oncoming bulk of Evil Eddy.

"Yes, I've heard that, but maybe it's just a theory that some scientist came up with and not something to test in real life." The words had barely left Billy's mouth when Eddy reached their table.

"Okay losers, what have you got for me today?" In almost super-slow motion and without saying a word, Sam rose to his feet and stood looking up at Eddy's scowling face.

The next thing he did would live on in St Brigid's history. He stepped backwards into the first forward stance in karate, his hands held out in front of him on guard and his legs moving back and forth ready to spring into action at any moment. As he did this, Eddy looked at him quizzically then laughed.

"What's this loser tryin' to be, some kinda Bruce

Lee? Give me the goodies."

Eddy's first mistake had been to underestimate his opponent. His second had been to talk too much. And his third, well, there was no time for that. Sam stepped through with his back leg and kicked Eddy hard between the legs like he was kicking a field goal. Everyone who was watching winced at the mighty blow. The action of Sam's first kick caused Eddy to fold over double, at which point Sam kneed the tyrant on the chin, knocking him out cold.

There was silence then mass applause and cheering as Eddy lay flat on the ground like the giant who had fallen from the beanstalk. The celebrations did not last long, though, as Ms Drake came running to the aid of her unconscious student. Billy was still sitting at the table frozen in disbelief. Sam re-joined him and they sat in silence finishing their lunch.

Of course, there were repercussions for Sam. "Students cannot just go around hitting other students," Ms Drake had said to Mr and Mrs Quinn. Sam had to do a couple of detentions and speak with the student advisor about anger management issues. Ms Drake in turn thought that she had got to the bottom of why Billy was so distant but how wrong she was. And finally, Eddy Thompson never again took advantage of another child at St Brigid's.

It was a week after Sam's martial arts demonstration when Billy arrived home from school to find the old radio and the wrappers from the food Johnny had brought him scattered across the kitchen floor. He froze, the door swinging shut behind him. As he stepped into the kitchen Becky exploded.

"You lying sack of shit, where did you steal this from?" She punched Billy on the jaw, knocking him back against the wall. As he tried to regain focus she struck out again, this time bursting open Billy's mouth. He fell on his back, the warm taste of blood swilling around.

His backpack slipped off as Becky continued her assault. She yanked him to his feet then slammed his head against the radio sitting on the worktop, sending it spinning and falling to the floor. She still had Billy by his hair and forced his face into the scattered wrappers.

"Where the fuck did you get all this food, you little bastard?" As she pushed Billy down against the floor, rough parts of it tore at his face. He tried to think of a way out of the situation but his foster mother's attacks were coming so fast that his focus was gone.

She threw his small body so hard against the basement door that Billy lost consciousness for a few moments, which was just as well so that he would not feel what Becky did next. Pulling Billy to the side, she opened the door and threw him down into the basement. Becky then ran down the steps just in time to catch Billy regaining consciousness.

"No fucking school," she yelled, "No fucking food, no fucking radio. I'm gonna let you fucking rot down here, forever."

She pinned Billy again as he came round as she had done so many times before, suffocating him until he passed out. Billy would know nothing of what happened next until he woke later. Becky punched his head until her hand hurt then started on his torso and legs. She did not stop the beating until there was no more energy left in her body, but even then on getting up Becky gave him a final couple of stomps with an audible crack coming from Billy's ribcage. Becky then climbed the stairs, closing and locking the door. She took a pot of ice-cream from the refrigerator and sat watching TV as if nothing had happened.

Chapter Nine

The lead mare walked ahead of her band as only she knew where to go when times were tough. As the horses reached the lower ground their grazing became sparse, winter having bitten hard, even here where food was usually plentiful.

The heavy snow made life difficult for them on many levels. Walking in this weather was very strenuous, not only physically but also as it used up their precious reserves of body fat. Digging down to graze was a lottery and most of the time they only ate what they had expended the energy to find. There had already been a couple of casualties: two of the older horses had lost their fight to survive but in turn had provided a lifeline for the others.

As always, the bay mare and the dun colt could be found not far from each other. At this time of struggle there was a reduced drive for the colts to compete. They focused on surviving and less on the normal rough and tumble found in the other seasons.

As if spoken to by some invisible voice, the lead mare strode out toward the far end of the long valley floor. She knew of only one other place that would offer them refuge from the rigours of this winter, but the journey there would take the herd along a treacherous pass, up and out of the valley which was becoming a death trap for all of them. Only stopping every now and then, they made their way through a beautiful but deadly landscape before finally heading up to the pass itself.

The dun colt was beginning to struggle, partly because of the harsh conditions but mostly due to his exertions fighting the other colts during the late autumn. His body had taken a lot of punishment and had little time to heal itself before winter set in. This, added to the herd's present predicament, meant that the young horse was slowly fading away. If things did not soon change for the better, he would perish before the spring.

The path over the pass would be treacherous for all, though especially for the older horses and the youngest ones. Although it started with less snow, the way up was boulder-strewn and the threat of an avalanche was ever present. The horses moved in single file, picking their way through the massive rocks that had been forced free by erosion from the cliffs above.

As they climbed higher, ice became a problem with more than one horse losing its footing and tumbling backward into the one behind. To make matters worse, the snow had come on heavily, blasting straight into their faces and making an already hard task almost unbearable. But they moved on. Then on reaching the midway point there was a crack of thunder muffled by the snow. Some of the horses, mostly the older ones, became restless. They started trying to push their way past on the path as if influenced by some unseen force.

There was a low rumble high on the mountainside: a large slab of snow had detached itself from the main overhang. Gathering momentum, the slab broke up into smaller pieces speeding downward on its collision course. Now at its maximum velocity, the avalanche was travelling at close to 100mph, the cascading snow pushing a wall of air ahead of its leading edge. This acted as would a shockwave after an explosion and unleashed a similarly destructive force.

Fear spread through the herd. In a panicked state, a horse's flight instinct takes over and the struggle to survive overrides all cognitive function. Some younger horses were trampled in what had become a stampede while above them the avalanche loomed like a curtain of death. In its initial blast it wreaked devastation on all in its path. Its shockwave tore horses from the steep slope like they were matchwood, casting their bodies onto the rocks below.

As the main wall of snow approached, horses were trying to salmon-leap over any of their companions that stood between them and safety. The bay mare and dun colt were squeezed together near the front of a group of horses that had broken away and now had no option but to move forward.

The wall of snow roared down like a massive white hand that reached out and erased them from existence. Almost a third of the herd were gone in those few fatal moments. Some lucky ones, partially buried, managed to pull themselves out and join what remained of the herd further on. Fortunately for the mare and colt, they were among a mixed group of horses high enough up that they only caught the edge of the deadly slide. Horses called out and were met by silence, but one remnant of sound was an echo of what had passed, a distant rumble rolling down the valley.

Again, the lead mare walked on with what was left of the band tucked in behind her. The falling snow blew hard straight into their faces and muffled all sound around them. They zigzagged upward as the pass increased in gradient, all the horses scrambling to keep good footing on an almost vertical slope.

It was always likely they would lose more members on such a perilous climb. When an older mare tried to turn and go back down, she slipped and knocked another couple of horses off the rock face and down to their deaths.

As they neared the top there was one last obstacle: a small river which at this time of year had frozen over. Pausing at the edge, the band gathered and waited for one of their number to make a move. Once again it was the matriarch who took charge and after cautiously taking a few small steps, she strode out and across to better ground. The band took heart from her initiative and made their way over to where she stood.

Now on firmer footing but still following their guide, they crossed a small rise. What appeared in front of them seemed completely out of place in this frozen landscape and very different from where they had come. The valley below was lush and green due to a thermal spring that ran along its full length.

On seeing the vegetation, the band rushed forward as if they had not eaten for weeks, which was not far from the truth. As she stood enjoying grass in her mouth again, the lead mare knew that she had brought most of the herd to safety.

The bay mare and dun colt stood together grazing.

Already they had forgotten the arduous journey to what would become their home for the winter.

Chapter Ten

It had been two days since Becky had beaten Billy. He had at least one broken rib and still could not see out of his right eye. He had had very little sleep and when he did doze it would only be for a few moments before he moved, sending a fresh wave of pain shooting though his body. Surviving on some scraps that Becky had not discovered, he started to think about what might happen next.

Sam sat looking at Billy's empty desk. Although he had sworn a solemn promise to Billy not to mention what was going on at the Brents, he now felt compelled to tell someone, and who better than his teacher?

Ms Drake had also been wondering where Billy was and why she had not been told why her student was absent. Just like Sam she found herself looking at Billy's desk. The more Ms Drake thought about him, the more an uneasy feeling grew.

"Ms Drake?" The sound of her name being called brought her focus back to the classroom. Turning to see who had called out she saw Sam, who looked up at his teacher unsure of what to do.

"Ms Drake, can I speak to you?"

"Of course you can, Sam," she replied with a smile on her face.

"I'm worried about Billy," Sam said. As the words left his mouth, the teacher's smile vanished.

"In what way are you worried, Sam?"

"Well, Billy told me a secret and I swore not to tell anyone but now I'm afraid something bad has happened to him." Alarm bells were going off in Ms Drake's mind but she tried to keep things calm and continued to let Sam speak.

"What has you so worried?" She spoke softly, trying not to worry her student who was clearly distressed.

"Well Ms Drake, he told me that Mrs Brent had been really mean to him," – the alarm bells were getting louder – "and she does not feed him enough and keeps him in the basement and sometimes she hits him."

Ruth Drake had now joined together all the pieces that had been worrying her over the past weeks. Looking at Sam she could see the relief on his face. She reached out and touched his shoulder as a way of letting him know he had done the right thing.

"Thank you, Sam. I think Billy would be very proud of you trying to help him." Sam's face beamed with relief and then, with a quick thank you, he turned and took his place back at his desk.

Ruth sat alone in the dining hall lost in her thoughts. She had spent a greater part of the morning trying to work out a course of action that would extract Billy from his predicament. The only thing that stopped her going straight to the authorities was that Sam, being a child, was not a reliable source of information. As she sat running all the variables through her mind, she came to the conclusion that her only choice was to pay Mrs Brent a home visit.

Lying in the darkness, Billy was cold and suffering the effects of dehydration. Occasionally he would hear movement from upstairs but had seen nothing of Becky since the day of his beating and for that he was thankful. He was thinking of the picture of his mom and dad when they were young and happy. His being brought into this world had cost them so much. Maybe that was what Becky had seen in him and also why he had to be punished.

Waves of pain engulfed his body each time he moved, sometimes so bad as to cause him to vomit. He was giving up both mentally and physically as he could see no way forward that would bring him the happiness and stability he craved. Billy closed his eyes and waited in the dark, his body cold and sore. He let the darkness slip over him with its comforting embrace.

Bang, bang, bang, – his eyes snapped open startled by the noise coming from above. He could hear muffled voices gradually becoming louder and he recognised who was talking to Becky. It was Ms Drake.

Ruth had got Becky's address from the office and had gone there directly after school. Driving down Hoover Drive, she squinted in the late afternoon sun and slipped on her sunglasses as she looked for number 1966. "Here we are." Ruth did not even realise she had spoken out loud.

Pulling up behind the old station wagon, she looked at the exterior of the house and as she so did her body shivered in a spasm. Rubbing her arms in self-comfort, she walked up to the screen door and rapped on the frame three times.

Mrs Brent came to the door with a cigarette sticking out of her mouth.

"Can I help you?"

"Hello Mrs Brent, my name is Ruth Drake and I'm Billy's teacher." Ruth could see Becky become tense at the mention of Billy's name.

"He's gone to visit an uncle he knows that lives near here." Becky was lying and Ruth knew it.

"Let's cut to the chase, Mrs Brent," she said, "I want to see Billy right now." Ruth was mad.

"I told you that he ain't here, now if you don't mind..." Becky went to close the door but Ruth stopped her.

"Listen to me, you piece of shit. I know what's been going on here. Now where is Billy?"

The colour drained from Becky's face.

Ruth stepped inside the kitchen and smelled the acrid scent of ammonia coming from the basement door. Ruth caught the movement out of her peripheral vision and instinctively put up an arm to block the punch that Becky had thrown. Spinning around, she faced Becky.

"Bring it on, bitch." Ruth spat the words at her.

Becky rushed at Ruth trying to catch her off guard again but unbeknown to Becky, Ruth had studied aikido and easily moved out of the line of attack. This caught Becky off balance, allowing Ruth to take her attacker's momentum into the nearest wall, which in turn knocked her unconscious.

Ruth opened the basement door and gagged at the smell. "Jesus," she whispered, then descended with a handkerchief over her nose to filter the stench. She reached the bottom step, pulled out her phone and switched on its torch.

The scene would stay with her forever. Billy lay in a foetal position on an old mattress, his face unrecognisable. She called out his name half expecting him not to reply.

"Is that you, Ms Drake?" Billy's voice was barely a whisper. Tears flooded down Ruth's face.

"Yes Billy, it's me. I've come to take you away from this place."

She moved over to where Billy lay, gasping out loud on seeing the extent of his injuries. She switched off the torch and dialled 911 then after speaking to the operator she returned her attention to her pupil. Switching the torch back on, she reached out to comfort him but he flinched away. Again, Ruth stretched out an arm and spoke softly.

"It's okay Billy, I've called the authorities. They should be here in a moment. If it's okay for me to touch you, I'd like to look at your wounds."

Ruth had seen many things as a teacher but this was by far the worst. It was unbelievable to her that someone, a mother, could be so cruel to a child. She ran her hand through Billy's hair, the simplest gesture of comfort that she could do for him while they waited for the ambulance. It was at this point she noticed Billy had soiled his pants. The pain of his injuries must have been such that he could not even make it to the bucket that stood at the bottom of his mattress.

There was a commotion upstairs. Billy was sure he heard Ms Drake's voice but in his present state that could have been a delusion. Everything had gone quiet then the basement door was opened and Billy could hear footsteps coming down. He heard his name being called but assumed it was Becky and when she tried to touch him he shied away, fearing more punishment. Then he could hear Ms Drake's voice telling him that everything was going to be okay. As she sat with him stroking his hair it was the best feeling in a long time. It was at this point that he passed out.

Ruth was worried when Billy slipped into unconsciousness.

"Where is the goddamn ambulance?" Just as she muttered this, she heard a siren in the distance.

"Hang in there Billy, they're nearly here," she said as she looked down at his battered face.

It was at this moment that Becky appeared at the basement door.

"What the fuck are you doing?" she yelled. Ruth had been so focused on Billy that she had forgotten about Becky until she started shouting at her.

"You're a fucking disgrace," Ruth shouted back, "Call yourself a mother? You're nothing but a monster. I've called the police and an ambulance: can you hear it, you fat piece of shit?" Ruth's anger was boiling to the surface. "You're going away for a long time. If it was up to me you'd rot in a hole for the rest of your life for what you've done to this poor boy."

At that moment Ruth heard a voice at the door: it was the police.

"Down here in the basement, quickly!" Two officers appeared next to Becky and Ruth shouted up to them again. "Arrest that piece of shit standing next to you, look what she's done to this child."

The woman officer pulled out her night light and the beam landed on Billy's battered body. The officer took a hold of Becky's arm.

"Ma'am, we would like you to accompany us down to the station." Becky complied without saying a word and was placed in the back of the patrol car just as the paramedic crew rushed indoors. The two paramedics looked down at Billy and then at each other, their expressions saying everything.

"How long has he been like this?" one of the medics asked. Ruth threw her hands in the air.

"Too long, I don't know. I just found him like this and called you guys."

The paramedics placed Billy on a spinal board as a precaution then asked the police officers for help in getting him upstairs and outside.

Ruth held Billy's hand in the ambulance. He had a drip in his arm and was conscious again. Ruth told him she would follow him to the hospital in her car and make sure they took the best care of her star student.

Billy looked up at Ruth.

"Sam," he whispered, "It was Sam who told you." Ruth squeezed his hand.

"Yes Billy, it was Sam."

For the whole journey to hospital, Ruth sobbed uncontrollably as she drove. She vowed that Becky would never touch another child again, not on her watch.

Chapter Eleven

In the high valley the dun colt and his surrogate mother were doing well. The thaw had started and it was nearing time for the herd to move to their spring grazing lower on the plains. All the surviving members had come through the winter well and were in good condition. A few of the mares were in foal and would soon give birth.

The dun colt stood with the morning sun glinting off his new summer coat. He had grown considerably in the months of winter isolation, becoming stockier and more mature. Although there were still occasional fights with the other colts and the lead stallion, these were nothing like the previous encounters. It was a time of plenty for the band. Warmth had spread across the land and penetrated the soil, trees and grasses were showing signs of life and the valley was alive with birdsong.

It was late morning when, once again, the lead mare struck out as if pulled by some invisible force and the others grouped together as they made their way back to the head of the valley. Although still dangerous, with the trail now free of snow and ice it made conditions underfoot much more favourable than had been the case on their previous journey. Lower down in the gorge the band came across the carcasses of those lost in the avalanche. They walked through the remains as if they were just another part of the landscape.

Lower still they would stop occasionally to graze and take on water before following their leader as she walked off in a manner that was a combination of instinct and years spent surviving in the wilds. The younger horses took every chance to stretch their legs, running in groups or play-fighting in preparation for when they would strike out alone. Although still wary of some of the older colts, the dun would join in whenever he could. Each time he did, it made him a little less dependent on the bay mare.

After two days of almost constant walking, the band stepped from the shadow of the mountains out into what would be their spring and summer grazing. One by one the mares dropped their foals and thus the band's number started to increase. It was as if the herd had been released from forced exile and could savour life again.

The biggest difference at this lower altitude came in how much hotter it was through the day. There had been plenty of sunshine up in the valley but there was always a cool breeze which kept the full power of the sun in check. It did not take long for the horses to acclimatise to their new home, however; their success as a breed was linked to their adaptability.

With the passing of days, the dun colt and his bay mother gradually went their separate ways as if some unspoken voice had given them permission to annul their convenient relationship, although they would still call out as if to let the other know they had not been forgotten. As spring moved into summer, the colt found friendship with two other youngsters of the same age. One was a pinto or tri-coloured horse and the other a sorrel or chestnut-orange. This was more like the company young adult horses should keep, where they could hone their fighting skills in games of rough and tumble while finding the companionship of like-minded beings. Life on the plains was working out well for the orphaned youngster, who had now been accepted as a full member of the band.

As the sun rose higher in the sky on a morning in mid-June, the herd was restless. The older members constantly tasted the air as if they could sense that trouble was coming. This nervous energy spread through the rest so much so that they began moving west away from an unseen foe. Far off they could hear what sounded like a giant swarm of bees. This noise then split out beyond both flanks of the herd and travelled parallel to it. Then another sound started to dominate, louder than the bees and coming at them from above. This new beast grew closer and closer, roaring like some prehistoric dragonfly as it zigged and zagged at the back of the herd, forcing them ever forward.

In the confusion, the herd was in full flight mode. Their bodies moved closer much like a shoal of fish, the individuals coming together to form one massive living being. They were forced down a narrow channel by their pursuers who were coming ever nearer. The young horses had never seen this new predator before but some of the older ones knew what the outcome of the hunt would be.

They ran, mares screaming for their foals, older horses collapsing with exhaustion, colts galloping wide-eyed in panic, on and on into the ever-narrowing canyon. Here they were forced through a small passage that led nowhere and so the herd was trapped. They circled trying to find a way out but there was none. The dun colt caught a glimpse of one of their pursuers: this new predator had two legs and made strange sounds that brought more confusion.

Steam rose from the horses' bodies foamed with sweat. The mares with foals were being separated from the main herd and put in a metal holding pen. Then it was the turn of the colts. Forced into a chute, the herd jostled for room, occasional fights breaking out through fear and confusion. The channel narrowed until there was only enough room for one horse between the fencing as they moved forward in single file towards the sorting gate.

The dun's senses were on overload as his captors moved him to his destiny with the gate. He was forced into a pen that contained all the younger horses, who were in turn sorted into male and female pens. By the time all the noise died down it was early evening. The colts took it in turn to drink from a trough but were spooked every time it was refilled, the hissing sound driving them to the other side in terror.

They were given hay through the night and when morning broke things had settled to a level of normality that was only disturbed when their captors appeared with more hay. Just as things seemed to have calmed down, a cattle truck reversed up to the far end of the colt pen and sent all the youngsters back into a frenzy of activity. Two of the predators drove them down towards the truck, shutting a series of gates as the colts moved forward and into the belly of the beast. Once again, the horses were lathered in sweat and faeces ran out of them making the footing treacherous. As the great beast roared into life and eased itself away from the catch pens, more panic spread through the colts. They bunched together trying to find support from the touch of others.

It took four hours to reach the auction facility, where once again they were forced through a maze of gates and pens until finally they found themselves in a pen with fellow inmates. One by one as the colts settled into their new home, they dropped to the ground and rolled trying to dry the heavy sweat that had matted their coats. There was a lot of mutual grooming as the colts tried to displace their anxiety in a purposeful manner. As before, they had a water trough and were given forage when needed. Occasional fights broke out over hay but this was mostly down to a few unsure horses showing aggression to mask their insecurities.

As the days rolled on, the colts developed a routine at the holding facility: eating, play-fighting and rest. The dun colt was kept in a pen that had horses deemed suitable for adoption. This allowed members of the public to take a wild horse or burro for $125.

Each of the horses was taken into a chute and the dun again became agitated at his confinement. In a sudden bid for freedom, he managed to rear up and turn in the chute then pushed all the horses behind him back into the holding pen. This seemed to anger the two-legged predators who rushed in and pushed them all back into the chute before closing the exterior gate.

It came time for the dun to be branded and his captors forced him into the crush at the end of the chute. Every part of his being told him he must flee but there was nowhere to go except inwards to his own mind. Initially there was not much pain involved in the branding but later there would be discomfort. The horses rolled around in the dirt trying to relieve the irritation.

Days grew into weeks and the date for the auction was set. As he scrolled through the auction website, Walter Dawson looked for a new horse to replace one he had lost recently to old age. Picture after picture appeared and almost as they flicked up on screen Walter dismissed them. Then the dun colt's profile came up. Walter hesitated, took in the horse's overall conformation and stature, and jotted down the number next to the photograph: 1961965.

The dun was standing at the east side of the pen with his long side to the sun allowing maximum absorption of the morning heat. When he eventually opened his eyes, he could see one of the two-legs at the far side of the pen. He had seen many of these over recent days but this two-legs smelled different from the others and, more important to the dun, he felt different as well.

Their eyes met for the briefest of moments but it was the two-legs that shifted his gaze first. This simple gesture did not go unnoticed by the dun and he moved closer, halving the distance between them. Now it was his turn to offer something to the two-legs. Letting out a long breath and turning his body slightly off-line, the dun flashed a glance at the two-legs then looked at the ground just in front of where he stood. As he did this, the two-legs let out his own breath, mimicking the dun's behaviour before turning and disappearing into the main building.

The dun was separated from the other horses in the auction pen. One by one his fellow band members disappeared down the chute, never to be seen by him again. The colt felt very vulnerable and ran in circles, calling out for his companions but there were no replies save for some horses in distant pens. Several two-legs then entered his pen and quietly guided him back towards the chute where a transport wagon had backed up.

Again, the colt was forced into the chute but this time, instead of being held in the crush, he was manoeuvred to the farthest end and secured there. He thus had only one option when the gate was opened: to keep moving forward. Once he had crossed the threshold at the rear of the wagon, the door was quickly but quietly closed behind him. He was trapped.

The noise in the back of the truck was almost unbearable to the dun. His whole body was in sensory overload and his being alone only added to his tension. After what seemed like an age, they turned off the main highway and rattled down the track towards Dawson Ranch. The reversing siren beeped incessantly until with a final hiss from the air brakes it all went quiet. The colt could hear muffled sounds coming from outside and strong sunlight penetrated the depths of the truck as the door opened. Without hesitation, the colt ran towards the light and freedom.

Freedom proved to be a round wooden pen thirty feet wide with a water trough at one end and a metal hay dispenser at the other. He ran a few laps of this small corral then settled enough to take in his new environment. A few horses were standing looking at him from their own pen which was closer to the main buildings. The colt called to them and they returned the call. This had an almost instant calming effect on him.

The truck disappeared down the track and as the plume of dust settled, the dun could see one of the two-legs leaning on the gate to his pen. It was the two-legs from the holding facility. He looked at the colt for a moment then rubbed his bare hand on the top rail of the gate before heading towards the buildings. Cautiously, the colt walked over to the gate and took a deep breath, letting the fresh scent of the two-legs linger in his nostrils.

Chapter Twelve

As Sam stood at the hospital reception with Ms Drake, all he could think about was Billy. Ruth had warned Sam that his friend was badly bruised around his face but it was not until Sam entered the ward that the full extent of Billy's injuries became apparent.

He was sitting up in bed with a drip in his arm.

"Sam, oh Sam, it's so good to see you." Billy's voice was barely a whisper. His friend smiled as he sat on the edge of his bed. Ruth stood by the door and watched as the boys greeted each other, a soft smile breaking across her face as she saw how much their friendship meant. She almost failed to hear Billy as he called her name.

"Ms Drake, Ms Drake?" She looked across the room where Billy held out his arms to her, which had the immediate effect of making her cry uncontrollably.

As she held Billy he whispered "thank you" then Ruth broke free and took a handkerchief from her bag.

"Look at me," she said, "and I'm supposed to be the adult." They all laughed. Sam stayed on the bed next to Billy and Ruth pulled up a chair.

"How's the food? Are they looking after you properly?" Billy smiled.

"I'm fine, they feed me small meals at regular intervals because I'm so thin and they have to watch how much I eat."

Ruth nodded. Although she did not want to broach the subject of Becky, she felt her pupil had to hear some information.

"Billy, you know Becky is going to jail for what she did to you?" Now it was Billy's turn to nod. "For that to happen there has to be a trial." He nodded again. "You are going to have to testify against her so that she can never do this again."

The tears began running down Billy's face and Sam gave him a hug. Ruth once again had her handkerchief out and was dabbing her eyes.

"I am sorry for upsetting you, but you have to know what's ahead of you." Billy nodded then sat up as best as he could.

"I know there's going to be a trial, the police have already talked to me. They said I can give evidence by video link if I want." Ruth nodded.

"I think that may be a good idea, Billy, then you don't have to be in the court with that… thing." Ruth's last word hung in the air for a moment before Billy continued.

"The police are going to speak to me more when I'm better." He smiled in an attempt to put Ruth at ease. Sam had listened to the conversation and his next words had them in stitches.

"That bitch deserves the chair!"

Ruth managed to stop laughing for a moment.

"I cannot condone your choice of words, Samuel, even if you are right." There was more laughter. The duty nurse popped her head around the door.

"I see you're feeling better, Billy Higgs, and they do say laughter is the best medicine."

They sat for a while longer before Ruth said to Sam, "I think it's time that I got you home, young man."

Sam let out a long breath. "Okay."

Ruth reached across the bed and kissed Billy on the head then Sam gave him a hug. As they turned to the door Billy spoke.

"You saved my life. How can I repay you?"

"Have purpose in your life, Billy," Ruth replied, "Have a purpose."

In the months that followed, Billy grew stronger each day. The doctors, nurses and physiotherapists looked after him well. The day of the trial came and went. He gave his evidence by video link and it was enough to put Rebecca Brent away for a long time. Ruth and Sam continued to visit frequently, which always made Billy happy.

Although Billy recovered physically, he still bore invisible scars from the abuse Becky had rained upon him. These were so deeply embedded that Billy developed night terrors and other psychological problems: panic attacks and claustrophobia. He was sent to a special unit that dealt with such issues but even they had not seen a case so severe as his.

Dr Anne Rea called a meeting with all the counsellors and staff assigned to Billy's case as she was exasperated at the lack of progress.

"I think what we have to take into account," a psychiatric nurse named John said, "is that it's still early days for Billy. We know he will suffer from posttraumatic stress disorder, so I would like to see if there is anything we can do to help him with his night terrors."

"Anyone else have any ideas?" Dr Rea asked.

Janice the clinical hypnotherapist chipped in. "I've tried but you get so far with Billy then he just pops out, shutting the doors so to speak."

Dr Rea took the bull by the horns.

"Nothing that we have done so far, in my opinion, has helped this boy. but there is a program I'm familiar with that may just be the right thing for him. The people who run it have gotten good results in the past and I think that right now, if everyone agrees, it could be of benefit here."

As Anne briefed the others on her proposal, Billy sat in his room listening to the radio, a habit he had retained from his time in the basement. He sat upright on the bed with his eyes closed trying to let his mind rest while he listened to the music. He always left his door wide open from a fear of again being imprisoned.

Before she even entered the room, Billy spoke out.

"You can come in, Ms Drake."

"Billy Higgs, how did you know it was me?"

"It's your perfume, gives you away every time." He opened his eyes and gave his teacher a welcoming smile.

"I just thought it would be good to drop in and see you," she said.

Ruth had visited Billy regularly but today he could sense there was something different.

"Is there anything wrong, Ms Drake? You seem sad today." His teacher and saviour broke down in tears.

"I've been offered a job in Los Angeles. It has better pay and the package that comes with it… well, I could not refuse!"

Billy looked Ruth straight in the eye. "That's great, Ms Drake. It's not that we won't ever see each other again and we can always write." Ruth sobbed and Billy also started to cry.

"I'll never forget you, Ms Drake, you saved my life and I only wish you could be my new mom, but things will work out for me, you'll see."

"I'll write to you, Billy," Ruth said, "and if I could be your mom I would, but I'm just not ready for that responsibility."

Billy sat in his room that night and cried himself to sleep. When he woke the next morning, he felt quite alone in the world.

Dr Rea looked around the table.

"I know some of you have reservations about this type of therapy, but I've used these guys in the past and they have made big changes in some of these kids' lives." There were a few heads nodding while others just sat quietly. "If everyone is finished, I'll give Billy the news tomorrow."

As the meeting broke up, Anne made her way to the elevators wondering if she had made the right choice.

Billy was still trying to get over the news of Ms Drake's departure when his thoughts were broken by a knock on his door. Dr Rea's timing could hardly have been worse.

"I don't want to move again," Billy said, "I'm happy

here." Dr Rea started to feel exasperated once more.

"Billy, you've already told us you hate it here so we are only trying to do what's best for you. Being here is not working out, can't you see that?"

"I just want to be left alone," Billy said, "I've caused enough trouble, can you not see that?" He turned away from the therapist and faced the nearest wall.

"We just want to let you see that there's more to life than suffering," Anne said with a sigh, "We can't help you anymore, Billy. If things are going to change then that decision will have to come from you." She walked out of Billy's room and took the elevator up to her office, where she again sat worrying whether her decision was the right one.

Billy lay down and sobbed into his pillow. After he had stopped crying, he started to think about the offer. What did he have to lose? He pressed the buzzer next to his bed and a nurse appeared.

"What can I do for you, kiddo?" she said with a smile.

"Could you let Dr Rea know that I said okay? She'll know what it means." The nurse disappeared. Sitting on the edge of his bed, Billy ran all his options through his mind to see if there were any alternatives. There were none. His fate was sealed.

Chapter Thirteen

It had been Anne's decision, she took it upon herself to drive Billy to the new facility. He slept for most of the journey, occasionally waking to find out where they were. He insisted on having the car windows down given his confinement issues and Anne felt she had no choice but to comply with this.

They drove from the city through towns and into a more rural setting. Billy had never seen so much green and began wondering if Dr Rea was just going to drive him into the middle of nowhere and kick him out of the car. These thoughts vanished as she turned down a dirt road that led to a farmhouse.

As they got out of the car the screen door creaked and Walter Dawson and his wife Margaret came out on to the porch.

"Hi Anne, did you guys have a good trip?" As he spoke, Walter descended the five steps that separated them. He gave Anne a big hug then turned to Billy.

"And you must be William or do you prefer Bill? Or Billy?" Billy stood frozen to the spot for a moment then replied, "Billy is okay."

Walter reached out his hand for Billy to shake and Billy instantly noticed two things. The hand felt rough (from heavy work, Billy surmised) and Walter was careful with the amount of pressure he put into their handshake. Anne greeted Margaret with the same joy as she had with Walter then introduced her to Billy.

Margaret took his hand.

"Hey there little man, do you like cookies?" He looked at Anne as if to seek permission but she just laughed.

"Cat got your tongue, Billy?"

"No ma'am, and yes I do like cookies, thank you."

"If you don't mind, Anne," Margaret said, "I will show Billy his room and of course those all-important cookies." Anne could sense a change in Billy already.

As they disappeared into the house it gave Anne a chance chance to talk with Walter.

"My god Walter, I can see a difference in him already," she said.

"What can I say? It must be the voodoo!" Walter laughed. "He seems like a nice kid, you would not believe he'd been through so many traumas in his short life." Anne reached into the car and gave Walter a copy of Billy's case file.

"You'll be staying the night?" Anne knew that Walter was not asking.

"If you'll have me?" As she reached into the back of the car for her bag, Anne thought that this was one of the things she liked about Walter: he was old school in his manners.

Margaret and Billy climbed the stairs which made a squeaking noise with their every step. On the first floor Margaret showed him the bathroom then they walked along to the next door.

"And this is your room, Billy, I hope you like it."

They were greeted by a cascade of sunlight that flooded the space. Billy walked in slowly and placed his bag on the floor at the foot of the bed. Fresh flowers sat in a vase on a low table next to the large windows, which were flanked by pale blue curtains held open with blue tiebacks.

"There's a chest of drawers here, Billy." Margaret pointed to the side of the bed. "And you can use this wardrobe if you have anything that needs hanging."

"Thank you, ma'am. What's that for?" Billy was pointing to an object that hung above the headboard of his bed.

"That, young man, is a dreamcatcher. The native folks who make them believe they can hold on to good dreams and make them come true."

"I tend not to have good dreams," Billy said, "and I hope it doesn't hold on to the bad ones because they're scary." Billy searched Margaret's eyes for an answer and when she spoke it seemed to put him at ease.

"Hopefully you'll start having good dreams that you can save right here. Now, what about those cookies?"

On the way downstairs Billy took Margaret's hand, a simple gesture but it felt to her like a good starting point. They entered the kitchen and were met by Walter and Anne who had a pot of coffee on the stove.

"Hey you guys, is everything okay with the room?" Walter's inquiry was met by a thumbs-up from Billy.

"Well that's great. Maggie, we were going to have coffee, do you want one honey?" Margaret nodded then got Billy seated at the kitchen table.

"Here you go young man, one glass of milk and some homemade cookies."

Billy could not contain himself.

"Whoaw! You made these yourself, ma'am?"

Margaret again nodded. Billy picked up a cookie and took a big bite. "Mmmm, that's the best cookie I think I've ever had." The others could only laugh at his enthusiasm.

As they all sat at the table, Billy could feel a warmth that had not been there since his father was alive: it felt comforting. He watched the adults chat and reminisce. Before long it was time for him to go to bed and Margaret let him take his glass of milk and another cookie up to his room.

"Ma'am?" he said as Margaret closed the drapes.

"Yes, Billy?"

"Would it be okay if I left my room door open? I don't like to be locked in." Margaret took him by both hands.

"Billy, you can do whatever makes you most comfortable." With that she ruffled his hair and said goodnight.

Billy finished his milk and cookies, got into his pyjamas and curled up under the blankets. When he switched off the bedside lamp, the room went completely black and stayed that way even after his eyes had adjusted. He put the lamp back on and breathed a sigh of relief. He reached under his pillow and pulled out the photograph of his mother and father, looked at it for a few moments, then said, "Night Mom, night Dad" and slipped it back under the pillow. It only took him a couple of minutes to fall into a deep sleep.

Back in the kitchen, Anne sat scribbling notes in her diary.

"Walter's just gone to check on the animals," she said

as Margaret sat down. "You know something Anne, I still cannot understand why these kids ever trust people again." Anne could feel that Billy had touched a nerve in Margaret.

"Yes I know," Anne replied, "Billy's such a nice kid. I think it's a miracle that he's turned out as good but there's still a long road ahead. All we can do is support him as best we can."

Walter came back in.

"There's a bite in that wind tonight," he said as he took off his jacket and shoes and put them by the back door. He stood in front of the stove trying to get some heat into his bones then picked up the coffee pot.

"Anyone like a refill?"

"Of course," Anne and Margaret replied in unison, giggling like schoolkids. Walter just shook his head and collected their mugs.

Everyone was up early the next day. You don't get to sleep long on a ranch as livestock is nature's alarm clock. On his way downstairs, Billy was greeted by the smell of Margaret's cooking.

"Good morning, Billy, how do you like your eggs, over easy?"

"Yes ma'am, that will be fine."

"Now if it's okay with you Billy, I would like you to call me Maggie, sound okay?"

"Yes ma'am, oh sorry, yes Maggie."

"See, we're getting to know each other. Now, do you like bacon and hash browns?" He nodded. "Good, now remember to leave some room for your pancakes and maple syrup." Billy was dumbfounded.

"You sure have a big breakfast if you don't mind me saying." This time it was Walter who responded.

"Well you see Billy, out here on the farm we have big breakfasts so that there's plenty of fuel in our tanks when it comes to doing the chores. Sometimes an animal will get sick and you miss lunch but because you get fuelled up in the morning, well it don't really matter that much."

Margaret brought over Billy's breakfast and it smelled amazing. Anne sat across the table and all she could do was smile. Then it was time for them all to say goodbye. Walter carried Anne's bag to the car then gave her a hug.

"Don't be a stranger."

"I won't," Anne said as she kissed Walter on the cheek. Next she turned to Margaret and hugged her the way old friends do. Margaret handed over a small tin.

"I know how much you love my cookies so this should keep you going for a day or two." Anne then turned to Billy.

"Now young man, I will be back in four weeks." Billy nodded. "And in that time I would like you to keep a record of all your adventures and feelings." She took a pencil and a lined notepad from her pocket and handed them to Billy, who said he would fill it cover to cover. Anne kissed him on the forehead.

"Now remember and behave yourself. I have spies everywhere!" With that she set off on her journey home, giving a honk on the car horn as she waved them all goodbye.

Margaret headed indoors as Walter and Billy made their way to check on the livestock.

"Billy, do you have any allergies that we need to know about?"

"No sir, none that I know of."

"Good. Another thing we have to straighten out is that you don't have to call me sir, not now we know each other. If I get to call you Billy, you can call me Walt, how does that sound?" Billy smiled.

"That sounds fair to me, Walt." Walter stuck out his hand to seal the pact. Billy took it and the deal was done.

He wasn't the first kid Walter had shown round the farm but he was the first who had connected this quickly. There was something personable about the boy which Walter liked. They went and fed the chickens and a few head of cattle, mostly black Angus crosses. Then they headed for the pen that held the horses.

"You ever rode a horse, Billy?"

"Nope."

"Well there's something special about being around horses that gets under your skin. When you get a good bond with a horse it's almost like they can read your mind."

The horses were pacing around because they had heard Walter's voice and seen him pull up the hay cart.

"See how they are all jostling for the best seat thinking that may get them more hay? Well, they know that I won't go in there while they're running around like fools, it's too dangerous. Not that they would hurt you on purpose but accidents happen, know what I mean?" Billy nodded. As if by magic, all the horses stopped their pacing and stood still.

"Now that they're settled," Walter went on, "I'll give them their hay." He entered the pen and laid out the hay. None of the horses made a move for it until he had left and closed the gate. Billy was amazed.

"How'd you do that, Walt?"

"It's just time, that's all. If you let the horses get into some sort of routine then they like that, making the next part a little easier." Billy was captivated.

"Can you teach me how to do it?"

"Of course I can, but it takes time and commitment. For all that a horse gives you, you have to give the same back, kinda balancing the books, if you know what I mean." Billy nodded again.

"Now Billy, would you like to see a wild horse? A genuine wild horse who lived out on the plains?" Billy laughed.

"That would be cool!"

Walter asked him to bring the cart and they walked over to a pen set in against the trees at the far end of the yard. As they approached, Walter motioned to walk more slowly. Billy could see a small cream-coloured horse at the far end of the pen, just about as far away from them as it could be.

"Now, I call this little guy Ronin," Walter said, "Do you know what a ronin is, Billy?"

"No, but it sure is a funny name." Walter chuckled.

"Do you know what a samurai is?"

"Aren't they warriors from China?"

"Nearly," Walter said, "They are from a country called Japan. Samurai means 'to serve' and in their case they served their masters or lords. Sometimes a samurai would fall out of favour with his master and they would get rid of him, so they would become a master-less samurai or ronin. Do you understand, Billy?"

"Yes sir, I mean, Walt."

"Good. Ronin means 'wave man' or 'a man cast upon the waves of life'. Some made a living as bandits, some as mercenaries. Others would spend their entire life trying to right the wrongs that they had done. I called this little guy Ronin because he must feel like he'd been cast out of his herd, a bit like the samurai who were banished by their masters."

After Walter had finished his explanation, he let Billy toss some hay into the pen.

"I have a little chore for you," Walter said, "I would like you to be in charge of Ronin's hay, which is one leaf every couple of hours, unless we're busy, then you can give him two leaves to keep him going. Think you're up to that?" Billy felt excited about being given something to do.

"I think that would be fine," he said.

Margaret had watched them leave in the morning to start their work. Almost as soon as Billy had arrived, she could not believe how much he reminded her of her son Daniel, who had taken his own life after a long battle with alcohol addiction. Daniel had only been seventeen and it was because of him that Margaret and Walter had trained to become counsellors, specialising in childhood trauma and addiction.

The placements they offered centred on equine therapy, using horses as something positive for children to relate to and care for. The courses also simply gave the kids meaning in their day-to-day lives, letting them work on the farm and providing them with an array of skills that could lead down a better path than the one they were currently on. Margaret was also a trained teacher and thus able to look after children long-term, keeping them on track with their education.

But Margaret and Walter were also human beings with feelings the same as everyone else. On this morning, Margaret had let her feelings bubble to the surface, for which she berated herself. "No emotional ties," she said to the quiet of the kitchen. She then sat and re-read Billy's case file. It was not the worst one she had seen, but what surprised her was Billy's ability to mask this difficult time in his short life. Margaret hoped that working with the horses might allow him to let go of the hang-ups he must have. Time would tell.

Chapter Fourteen

It had been a few weeks since the move from the stock
yard to the ranch. Initially the colt felt quite unsettled in
his new surroundings but things seemed to settle down.
The two-legs gave him food throughout the day and
a little at night to tide him over until morning. There
was clean water kept free of the algae which tended to
build up in the warmer months. Sometimes the two-
legs would come to watch him, occasionally making
soft tones that had a comforting effect. For the most
part, however, he was left on his own, having only
vocal contact with the rest of the horses and sometimes
the cattle.

One day the two-legs brought a younger one with
him. They stood staring in from the far side of his pen.
After a few moments, the dun colt picked up something
different from the smaller two-legs: his energy felt out
of balance and not as stable as the older one's. They
soon left but that strange feeling stayed with the colt for
most of that morning.

After lunch, Margaret went into town while Walter
and Billy fixed a fence in the big pasture before they
could let the horses go out there later that week. Walter
explained that sometimes deer or bears became caught
up in the fencing; this time it looked like it had been a
bear.

"Are they big bears, Walt?"

"Yeah, some can be, but it's usually small black bear we get around these parts."

The wire was okay and the posts just needed to be repositioned to the side of their original holes. Walter asked Billy to hold a post while he slipped the post driver over the top.

"That looks easy," Billy said after the post went in, "Can I have a try?" Walter laughed.

"Okay Billy, but let me get the next one started first then I'll hand things over to you."

As Billy took over, the first thing he noticed was that the driver weighed more than he expected. Then, when he raised the driver and brought it down on the post, it did not budge. He tried again, and again, and again. All the while he was attacking the post, Walter stood with a big grin on his face. Billy dropped the driver on the post one final time then leaned over it, puffing like he'd just run the 100 metres. Walter gave Billy a pat on the back.

"You sure showed him who's the boss," he said, letting out a belly laugh. Billy looked at him in frustration.

"You make it look so easy, how'd you do that?"

There were a lot of things that Walter could have said. but he only spoke one word:

"time". Billy asked what he meant with a look of confusion on his face.

"You have to be doing this thing a long time before you get good at it," Walter said, "It's not about strength, although that does help some. Technique helps as well, but if you want to get good at anything then you're going to have to spend a lot of time refining what you do till it becomes a part of you." He left Billy thinking about this while he drove the post into the ground with half-a-dozen good hits.

They returned to the ranch to put away the fencing equipment before feeding hay to the animals. After a coffee break with milk for Billy, they headed out to the small round corral where Walter wanted to work with Toby, a dark brown horse with a black mane and tail: a bay, he told him.

Billy looked up at Toby, who seemed enormous.

"Let him smell the back of your hand," Walter said. Toby dropped his head and touched the boy's right hand with his whiskers. At the same time, Toby took in Billy's odour with deep inhalations. Touch and smell are the ways in which a horse builds up a picture of what something is, Walter told him. After a few sniffs, Toby returned to eating from the hay net that Walter had hung up in the corral.

Taking a brush from the grooming kit, Walter handed it to Billy.

"This is called a 'dandy' brush, looks kinda like something you would clean the floor with, but seeing as horses live outside this type of brush will clean them without removing the grease in their coat that keeps them waterproof."

Billy ran his thumb through the bristles, which were made of stiff plastic.

"There are different ways of grooming a horse," Walter said, "and each person has their own way of doing things, but I start at the top and work my way down. You want to follow the natural way the coat lies." Walter ran his finger through Toby's coat the wrong way, which made it stand up. "If you go against it, well all that happens is that."

With his tutor's words fresh in his head, Billy approached Toby and as if by magic the horse dropped his head. Billy took this as a sign that it was okay to start. He began quite softly, especially around Toby's face, but soon got the hang of how much pressure to put into the brush to remove the dirt.

Once Walter had shown him how to brush the horse's body, he went on to comb the mane and tail, learning where to stand and how to check the feet for any stones or injury.

"Grooming a horse is the best way to get to know them," Walter said, "It's something they do in the wild but they just use a different brush: their teeth." Walter let out a chuckle. "We're not trying to replicate their behaviour but we can use grooming to connect to them on a similar level."

With the grooming finished, Walter asked Billy to step outside as he wanted to show him how he would work with a horse. Walter took down the hay net and placed it outside the corral, then he fetched the halter and the long rope that were hanging over the fence. He walked over to Toby and asked the horse to lower his head as he slipped the halter over his nose. Toby complied. Walter then walked Toby to the centre of the corral before walking backwards until the rope was stretched to its fullest extent between him and the horse.

Toby stood quietly in the middle of the corral until Walter stepped to the side and took the slack out of the rope. As if some silent signal had been given, Toby moved to the outside and along the fence-line of the corral. Billy stood transfixed as he watched the man work with the horse: to his eye there was no communication apart from the changes in position that Walter took up and which seemed to influence where Toby would go.

Walter stopped suddenly, signalling to Toby that they were finished. He walked up to Walter, who rubbed him all over while telling him what a good boy he was. Walter and Billy returned Toby to the corral where the other horses were.

"Walt, that was amazing, do you think I could learn to do that?" Walter looked down at Billy.

"Sure you can Billy, all it takes is a little time."

That last word made both of them burst into laughter, thinking back to the hammering the poor post had taken earlier.

"You fuckin' little bastard, I'll teach you for lying to me." Becky punched and kicked Billy as he lay on the basement floor. All he could say in retaliation was "No, no, no".

Margaret heard the shouting coming from Billy's room. She found him lying on the floor next to the closet, his whole body in spasm as his subconscious ran untethered in his bad-dream state. She stood transfixed by how contorted the boy's body became as his mind re-enacted what his foster mother had done to him.

Eventually Margaret could stand it no more. She reached down to touch Billy's shoulder and softly called his name.

"Billy, you can wake up now. Billy, you can wake up, everything is going to be fine. Billy you ca..."

"Noooo!" Billy's eyes flew open filled with panic and terror.

"Billy it's me, Margaret, you're here at the ranch and you're safe." This brought Billy partially out of his nightmare and he reached up to Margaret.

"Save me, Mommy, save me." Margaret burst into tears.

"You're okay my darling, you're okay". She sat on the floor and held Billy until he woke then kept telling him he was safe. She hoped his subconscious would pick up on the key word so she could overlay a more positive image in his mind than the ones that were causing the night terrors.

Billy's pyjamas were wet with urine and he too started to cry.

"Billy, it's okay," Margaret said again, "This will happen from time to time but gradually it will go away. Now let's get you cleaned up, does that sound like a deal?" Billy looked Margaret straight in the eyes and smiled, then he went to the bathroom to wash while Margaret fetched a pair of old pyjamas.

"These belonged to my son Daniel. They should fit you." They were indeed a perfect fit. Billy held Margaret's hand tightly as they walked back to the bedroom and she tucked him into bed.

"I'll leave the bedside light on for you, okay?" Then rather than disturb Walter, she made herself a coffee and sat alone at the kitchen table, lost in her thoughts.

Ronin stood in his paddock eating the hay left for him by the two-legs. It had been so long since he had felt the proper companionship of another horse. He would call out to the other horses and they would nicker back, but he yearned for the feeling of being part of a herd.

As the two-legs again approached from the far side of the yard, Ronin could sense there was something different about him today, noticing the rope in his hand. On entering the corral, the two-legs gathered up what was left of the hay and placed it outside then stepped to the middle of the pen, waiting in silence. Ronin watched every movement that the two-legs made, his muscles twitching with anticipation of any aggression from his captor but there was none.

Every now and then, the two-legs would lift his eyes and catch Ronin's then quickly look away. He became curious about this, as every time it happened – for longer each time – he felt as if he was being drawn to the centre of the pen not of his free will. He wheeled away and ran as fast as he could, round and round, watching the two-legs for any reaction. Once again there was none.

After several laps of the corral, Ronin found himself back where he had started. Still, every now and again, the two-legs would catch his eye then look away. This went on for a good thirty minutes before he found himself walking toward the two-legs in centre of his corral. When he got about a body length away, the two-legs slowly moved his limb close enough for Ronin to touch with his whiskers. With that the two-legs walked away out of the corral then tossed the hay back in as he'd done many times before.

Ronin stood for a long time trying to process this new information. When he had reached a satisfactory conclusion he went back to eating his hay.

A warm breeze came into Billy's room through the open window. He lay in bed letting the different scents pass one by one, guessing what they were as each lingered in his nostrils. Then there was the sound of a car pulling into the ranch. He got out of bed just in time to see Dr Rea step out. Billy shouted excitedly to her as he leaned out of the window. Anne looked up and was glad to see Billy's smiling face.

"Tell me you're not still in your bed, Billy Higgs?"

Billy laughed.

"Sorry, guilty as charged."

Anne climbed the steps to the front door where she was greeted by Margaret with arms outstretched as if she had not seen her in many years.

"Careful, honey," Anne said, "You'll break a rib!" Billy came careering down the stairs.

"Dr Rea!" He too flung his arms around Anne.

"I see the fresh air is doing you well," she said.

They all went into the kitchen where Walter had been seeing to the coffees. Anne looked across at Billy.

"So how are you doing, young man? If the welcome was anything to go by, I'd say you were doing great." Billy took a sip of his milk before answering.

"I can feed and clean the horses and groom them and fix fences, but I need practice at putting the posts in." He flashed a grin at Walter.

"And Ronin is a real wild horse and we're going to train him."

Anne laughed. "Well, it looks like you've been busy!"

They spoke for a while then Walter and Billy went to do the chores.

"How's he doing?" Anne asked Margaret, even though it seemed obvious that everything was turning out as she hoped it would.

"Well, Walt and I have spoken," Margaret said, "and we want to adopt Billy. Now I know you think that it's a crazy idea..." But before Margaret could finish her sentence, Anne had come around the table to hug her friend.

"I could not think of a better environment for Billy to grow up in," she said, "Does he know yet?"

"No, we thought it better to run things by you first." Anne could see there was some concern in Margaret's face.

"Well I for one would support your application one hundred per cent. After all that Billy's been through and how quickly you guys have clicked, the authorities would have to be crazy not to say yes."

Margaret's face softened on hearing Anne's words.

"Do you think we should tell him now? I so desperately want to let him know he has a home." With that Margaret broke down in tears. All Anne could do was to sit and let her friend purge her body of all the pent-up emotion.

Margaret told Anne about the night Billy had his bad terror and how she had given him Danny's old pyjamas. That had made up her mind: adopting Billy would be a good thing for all involved. Just then, Billy and Walter appeared through the back door.

"The workers have returned!" Billy said in a jubilant voice.

"Have I missed something?" Walter asked on seeing Anne and Margaret's smiles.

"I was telling Anne about our surprise for Billy," Margaret said. A grin spread across Walter's face and he turned to Billy.

"Take a seat, buddy. Margaret and I have something to tell you."

He sat facing Walter, Margaret and Anne, wondering about his big surprise. Walter looked at Margaret and gave her a nod. Taking her cue, Margaret looked at Billy.

"Now Billy, you've been here for almost a month and we can see a big difference in you." Billy began to panic. He did not want to go back to the halfway house: he'd grown too fond of Margaret and Walt, not to mention all the animals.

"I don't want to go back," he said. The others could hear the despair in his voice and Margaret put her hand on his.

"Billy, let me finish." The softness of her touch eased Billy's worry but only a little. "Walt and I have grown very fond of you in the time you have been with us and we wondered if you would like to stay longer." Billy's heart was pounding.

"How much longer, another month?" Margaret started to cry and she ruffled his hair.

"No Billy, not for just another month. We want you to come here to live with us, we want to adopt you as our son."

It seemed like a dream to Billy. This was the best surprise he could have wished for. He started to cry and reached out for Margaret and Walter.

"Yes, yes, yes, I feel the same way."

Chapter Fifteen

Walter did not know how Ronin got out, just that he was not in the yard. Margaret and Billy helped in the search but came up with nothing on their side of the farm. As a last resort, Walter and Billy jumped into the pickup and headed for the main pasture while Margaret phoned round the neighbours asking them to keep an eye out for the dun colt.

Walter and Billy drove down the rumbled old track that led to the pasture, man and boy looking for any sign that the colt had come this way.

"There!" They let out the exclamation at the same moment. Just off to the side of the track, a set of fresh hoof-prints led straight towards the main pasture and beyond.

"We'll walk the rest of the way," Walter said as he parked the truck, "No point in spooking him."

The prints led to just before the gate then stopped abruptly. Walter stood for a moment scratching his head then walked up to the gate and peered over. On the other side the tracks began again.

"This way, Billy, the damn horse can jump, I'll tell ya."

Billy walked up to where Walter was standing.

"Look at this Billy, see how he gathered his stride in preparation for the jump?" Billy looked down and saw a set of hoof-prints in a configuration similar to that of rabbit prints he'd seen in some mud on the farm.

"Can you see him yet, Walt?" There was an anxious tone in the boy's voice and Walter immediately put him at ease.

"Sure can, he's right over at the far side filling his gut with all that fresh pasture, he'd better watch he don't colic himself!" Walter reached down and lifted Billy on to the top rail of the gate. As he did so, Billy asked what colic was.

"Well, that's a good question Billy. The simplest answer I can give you is it's like an upset stomach that could potentially kill him." At the mention of death, Walter mentally kicked himself. He quickly followed up with, "But I don't think he's been out that long", at which Billy let out a breath.

They sat watching Ronin for a while: it was nice to see him out of the corral. In due course, Walter turned to Billy.

"Well, I think it may be time for Ronin to meet the other horses, whatcha think?" Billy jumped down off the gate and grabbed Walter's hand.

"Come on Walt, we're burning daylight." The two of them chuckled as they headed back to the truck.

On the journey back up to the summer pasture, Walter had roped some of the horses in what was called a string. Each horse had been tied to its neighbour, which allowed the handler to quickly move a sizeable number from one place to another. Billy's main job was to open and secure any gates that lay between the farm and their destination, but he carried a couple of old halters in case any horses needed to be taken back to the farm. He also carried a basic first aid kit.

It was a lovely day to be out in the sun and once they got on to the track there was enough cover from the trees to give some respite from the heat. As they approached the field, Ronin was still in the same spot but he had stopped eating and had his head up, looking in their direction.

"Billy," Walter said, "Once you have that gate open come and take one of these guys off me, okay?" Billy nodded and followed Walter's instructions to the letter. One by one they released the horses and they immediately ran over to see who Ronin was. They all took off at the gallop with plenty of threats and squeaking, especially from the mares, but things soon calmed down and they all got on with the most important job; the eating of summer grass.

Walter and Billy stood back to watch the ballet of movement that the horses performed so beautifully.

"He sure moves well, Walt," Billy said.

"Yup, it's been a long while since I've come across one so well put together." Walter then hunkered down next to Billy and what he said brought the young boy to tears.

"He's yours, Billy. I've wanted to tell you for a while but today seemed to work out just right." Billy hugged Walter as he tried to regain his composure.

Walter stood up and looked down at Billy.

"Now, having your own horse is a big responsibility and until Ronin's old enough to ride I'll teach you on one of the older ones, deal?" Walter stuck out an open hand and Billy shook it vigorously then looked up at him.

"Walt, I never thought my world would turn out like this, you and Margaret have been so kind. I just wanted to tell you how much you guys mean to me."

Again, they hugged and now it was Walter's turn to speak.

"When we lost our son, something so precious was taken from us." Tears ran down his face. "We always hoped to raise another child but things just didn't work out that way. Sometimes when you want something so bad it kinda gets farther away from you. I'm a great believer in fate, Billy, and we were fated to meet." Walter paused for a moment. "Now let's get back and give your mom the good news."

Billy was trying not to hold on to the saddle horn, remembering what Walter had said: "You ain't gonna learn to ride grabbing leather whenever you feel off-balance". At this particular moment, however, Poppy – the horse Walter had chosen for teaching Billy – felt like a bucking bronco beneath the young boy's rear. Walter had Poppy on a line and led her around the corral at a nice walking pace.

"You have to get with the horse," he said, "Let your pelvis swing to her steps and try to relax."

Billy clenched his teeth and made a conscious effort to relax. Gradually, over the next few minutes, he began to match the horse's natural movement with his own.

"Good, Billy," Walter tried to encourage Billy from the ground, "That's it, but you have to keep a good posture to keep you centred, relax too much and it will unbalance the horse and get them worried."

After his lesson, Billy took Poppy back to the stall

where he removed her tack as Walter had shown him, paying careful attention when taking the bit out so that he did not knock the horse's teeth. He checked if Poppy had fresh water then left her for a while to eat her hay, his way of saying thank you for the lesson.

Walter had gone into the house so Billy gave the yard a quick tidy and filled Ronin's manger with a few leaves of hay. Walter had brought Ronin in for some work: he was more confident now and came right up to the fence, peering through. Billy did one more check of the yard then headed into the kitchen. As he came through the door, Walter and Margaret had huge smiles on their faces.

"Hey Billy, come and take a seat, we have something to tell you." Margaret pulled out a chair as she spoke and Billy sat down a little anxiously.

"We have had a letter from the adoption agents." Here it comes, Billy thought, more bad news. "And they have accepted our application and all we have to do now is go to their office and make everything legal." All Billy could do was look from Walter to Margaret and back again. Everyone seemed to be holding their breath. It was Walter who broke the silence.

"Welcome to the family, son." Margaret burst into tears. Billy grabbed both of them and they hugged for what seemed like an age. Then, as if in receipt of some unseen command, they all took to their chairs at the table and sat quietly reflecting on the moment. In due course, Billy felt he had to make a little speech.

"I cannot tell you both how much this means to me, or properly express how I am feeling right now. You have given me a chance no one else has had the heart to do." Margaret took Billy's hand.

"We hope this is a new beginning for us all." Then she broke down again.

"Don't cry, Mom," Billy said as he held her tight, "We're going to spend forever together."

"Well that's it, Mr and Mrs Dawson, you are now the legal parents of this fine young man." The magistrate reached out his hand and Margaret and Walter beamed with pride, as did Billy. They left by the huge interior doors of the courthouse and as Billy entered the main hall, he looked across at one of benches on the far wall. Seated on it were Ms Drake, Dr Rea and his school friend, Sam Quinn.

"Sam!" The boys rushed to meet one another, closely followed by Ruth and Anne.

"Hey you guys, we want a hug as well!" Billy ran to his teacher.

"Thank you, Ms Drake, thank you. All of this has happened because of you."

"No Billy," Ruth said, "It was Sam, Anne, me and your new parents, but most of all, you, for enduring what you did for so long." Now it was Anne's turn to embrace Billy.

"I had an idea you guys would get close but never thought it could lead to this. I'm so happy for you, Billy." She pulled a handkerchief from her pocket and dabbed her eyes. Sam took the opportunity to get Billy on his own.

"Walter tells me you're helping him with the animals and especially the horses. And he also told me you have your own wild mustang that one day you're gonna ride!" Billy nodded.

"Man, that's way cool, wish I had my own horse." Sam looked a little sad.

"Well Sam," Billy said, "if your parents are okay about it, you could come out and see the place and maybe Walt will let you have a sit on one of the older mares." Sam's face lit up and both boys ran over to Walter and Margaret to tell them of their plan.

"Sure Billy, if it's okay with Sam's folks," Walter said. He had a grin on his face as he watched the two boys run around excitedly. Margaret called out to them. "Billy, Sam, you guys ready for some food?" The boys shouted out "yay" in unison and they all walked down the steps of the courthouse toward the local steakhouse.

Chapter Sixteen

That Ronin had begun to feel comfortable in his environment was in part due to the length of time he had been there, but mostly because of the routine that the two-legs used. The thing Ronin most craved was contact and the close bond that horses form from social interaction. He would call to the horses in other pens and they would call back to him. If the wind blew in the right direction, he could taste each individual scent, collecting them in his Flehmen gland on the under-side of his top lip.

Occasionally, the older two-leg would come into the pen and move him around and he would comply, much like as he had done with the stallion in his wild herd. Each session brought him closer to seeking out the contact of the two-leg as a surrogate form of social bonding. One constant in his world was a connection to the younger two-leg who would stand on the outside of the pen. Ronin felt some kind of kinship with this one: he could feel how his energy would change watching the older two-leg during the work sessions. The horse could feel a sense of loss much like his own at the death of his mother.

It was after one of the work sessions with the older two-legs that Ronin made his bid for freedom. Strong winds had blown in from the west down from the mountains. Ronin had padded around in his pen reacting to the sounds of the other horses milling around in theirs. The wind caused the horses to lose their sense of hearing, with their other senses going into overdrive by way of compensation. They all held their heads higher to use vision as their main survival system.

Ronin trotted around in the pen knowing he had no other horses for support or to help fight off any predator. Dust blew around the farm as the wind grew stronger, blocking out whatever light there was. This was the final straw for Ronin. As his muscles twitched and fired uncontrollably, a sheen of sweat built up on his coat. Finally, he could stand it no longer and with a burst of power and speed he ran at the fence and jumped.

Clearing the top rail of the pen by some margin, he landed on the other side and trotted across to the neighbouring pens seeking comfort from the other horses. To his surprise, the lead gelding charged out of the dust cloud to protect his herd from the stranger. Ronin continued looking for an option to join the others, even contemplating jumping into the pen, but the aggression of the gelding stopped him from doing so. Instead, he made his way out of the yard looking for an open piece of ground which would allow him to at least see any potential predator and flee if necessary.

Making his way along a dirt road, he walked until a metal gate barred any forward movement. His nostrils filled with the smell of fresh grass, something he had longed for over the past months. Without even having to run at the gate, Ronin popped over as if it was not even there and immediately started gorging himself on the succulent grass.

Almost as quickly as the squall had started it blew itself out, but Ronin barely noticed. He continued to fill his gut until dawn tipped over the horizon. As the sun grew higher, Ronin eventually took a break from eating and turned his long side to the warmth to rid his body of the early morning chill.

A sound at the far end of the pasture made him raise his head, bringing the image of the two-legs into view. They were both there but kept their distance, coming no nearer than the gate while standing watching him. Ronin continued eating the grass but with less and less vigour. Even at this distance he could feel a connection to the young two-legs. He had noticed a distinct change in him over the past months. With this thought in his mind he looked once more to the gate, but the two-legs were gone.

It was about forty-five minutes later that Ronin's eye caught movement at the far gate. This time he turned and gave it his full attention. The older two-legs appeared in the field leading some horses, followed by the younger two-legs who had opened the gate and now stood watching as each horse was released. It was not long before the new horses noticed Ronin: they flew at him, squealing and aiming kicks which he manoeuvred around.

After a few such challenges, an older mare broke away from the others who by now were more interested in grass than in the stranger they had found in their pasture. The mare approached Ronin moving her head to the side to show she was no threat. He mirrored her movements until they almost touched noses. Each horse breathed in one another's scent in an effort to work out where the other had come from, reminding Ronin of the surrogate mare who had adopted him in the wild.

The mare in turn recognised that this was just a young horse who needed some social contact. She knew that he was the horse she and her companions had called to in the pen back at the farm. Although she was sympathetic to his needs, the mare put Ronin in his place when he moved into any part of the field that was for known herd members only. Then after a few more squealing matches, both horses settled down to eat, the mare allowing Ronin into her safe area.

Ronin's spirit was filled with joy at being back in the company of horses: it had felt as though he would never know that comfort again and now he savoured every moment.

The two-legs returned again with more horses. This time the lead gelding was among them and once free of his halter he made a direct charge at Ronin. He did not fight back, instead keeping out of range of the assault. This quickly defused the situation and the gelding moved off to take charge off his younger mares.

Over the next few days Ronin got to know some of the herd members, all except the lead gelding's mares to whom he gave a wide berth. There were a couple of quarter horses, a pair of ex-racehorses and a Clydesdale that towered over every creature in the pasture.

Gradually over the course of the week, the horses settled into their new environment and bathed in their freedom. The days were now long and the grass was lush. It was on one of these long days that the two-legs reappeared at the gate having brought something with them.

Chapter Seventeen

It was the day after Billy's court appearance. He lay on his bed staring at the dreamcatcher lost in thought. Never in his wildest imagination had he seen things turning out like this. There was a knock on his bedroom door.

"Are you awake yet, Billy?" It was Sam: he had stayed the night on the farm and Walter had promised him a sit on one of the horses.

"Come on in," Billy said as he swung his legs out of bed. Sam was dressed and ready to go and had a look of impatience on his face.

"We'll get to the horses soon enough, Sam," Billy said, laughing, "but we need to get breakfast first, sound good?" Sam nodded his head and sat on the edge of Billy's bed.

"What's that up there, Billy? Looks like a spider's web!" Billy saw his friend had noticed the dreamcatcher so he told him of its origins. Sam sat transfixed.

"You know something, Billy? I think I'm going to get me one of those dreamcatchers, maybe I could get a pony too and we could ride out together." Sam rolled his eyes and both boys laughed at Sam's plan.

At that same moment, Margaret, Anne and Walter sat at the kitchen table. In the quiet of the house they could hear Sam and Billy's laughter meandering its way downstairs. Margaret had tears in her eyes: it had been so long since she had heard the type of innocent laughter made only by happy children. Walter broke the silence.

"Never thought we would hear that sound again. Well, not for us." His voice broke at the end of his sentence as he walked across to where Margaret sat and placed both hands on her shoulders. Margaret reached up with her right hand and rubbed the back of Walter's left hand.

"You know something," Anne said, "when I first thought of placing Billy with you guys I knew it was a gamble, but I never in my wildest dreams imagined that by trying to help him heal it would end up helping you heal, too." Walter took a seat next to Margaret and listened as Anne continued.

"In our line of work the success rate is marginal, but every now and again you hit a home run and here I feel like we've won the World Series." Brushing their tears away, the friends sat up just in time to greet Sam and Billy as they entered the kitchen.

"What's up guys," Billy asked, "has one of the horses died?" There was genuine concern in his voice and Sam stood alongside waiting on the answer.

"No, no, nothing like that." Walter stood up and walked over to the boys. "We were just reminiscing about old times but that's in the past now, you can't live in two places and you've just gotta keep moving forward, yes?" The boys nodded and relaxed.

Walter carried the saddle out of the barn, leaning it against his hip as he walked. In his other hand was a simple single-joint snaffle bit bridle. Reaching the pen, he swung the saddle over the middle rail and hung the bridle over the top of one of the posts. Billy and Sam had already been put to work cleaning and harrowing the pen ready for Walter's arrival. They now took the wheelbarrow and emptied it out before leaning it back against the barn.

"You fellas ready to hike up to the horses?" Walter asked, to which the boys shouted

"yes!" in unison.

"Okay then, let's go." The three of them headed out of the yard and along the track that led to the summer grazing paddock.

As they reached the gate the horses turned to them, scrutinising their every move. Ronin took a particular interest and gazed for longer than the others. Walter opened the gate and motioned for the boys to stay where they were. Once he was about twenty yards into the paddock he stopped and called out for Toby, his older teaching horse. The bay gelding lifted his head, turned slowly and walked in the direction of the gate where his old friend was waiting.

Walter rubbed the horse's forehead as he had done thousands of times before. Billy and Sam stood mesmerised by the interaction. Walter slipped the head collar on to Toby then walked towards the gate, with Billy pushing the gate open wide then closing it as Walter moved through. The boys walked at Walter's side trying to contain their excitement at the lesson to come.

Back at the farm, Walter took Toby into the pen then slipped off the halter and gave him some time to acclimatise to his new environment. Toby wandered around the pen eating what was left of the previous occupant's hay. Walter knew Toby would settle to the pen but he was teaching the boys how to work with all horses. After a few minutes, Walter asked Billy to catch up with Toby, which he did with some proficiency. Then Walter introduced Sam to Toby in the same way as he had with Billy. Sam was taken aback by the size of the horse but grew more confident with some persuasion from his companions. Once Sam felt comfortable being around Toby, Billy brought out the grooming kit and showed Sam how to use it.

"This is a 'dandy' brush," he said, "It's used for getting the dirt off your horse without taking the protective grease out of it. All you have to do is follow the nap of the horse's hair, like this, see?" Sam took the brush and started to groom Toby tentatively. Within what seemed like just a few moments he was grooming like he had been doing it for years.

Walter was impressed.

"Looks like we have a natural cowboy here with us, Billy!" He winked at Billy, who winked back.

Once Sam had finished, Walter asked the boys to step outside the pen while he tacked up the horse. He had a very specific routine when doing this, always putting the saddle on first then cinching it tight enough to keep it in place. He would then put the bridle on, taking care not to knock the bit off the horse's teeth. Then he would go back to check the cinch and tighten it if necessary before walking Toby around to let the cinch settle into place. Walter would then lift Toby's front legs one by one, letting them relax back down to the ground to release any tension. The boys looked on, taking in every detail.

As he always did before putting a child on board, Walter got on Toby first just to see where the horse was that day, especially since he had been out in the pasture. Toby was fine, so Walter showed the boys what to do when they were 'up in the pilot's seat'.

With the safety briefing over, the boys put on hard hats and entered the pen.

"So, who's first?" Walter looked at Billy, who turned to Sam.

"I've been up there and, since you're our guest, it's only proper that you go first." Sam almost burst with excitement.

"Thanks, Billy," he shouted over his shoulder, then walked over to where Walter stood. After adjusting the stirrups, Walter fetched the three-step mounting block that he used for kids when he ran the courses, as he disliked just throwing them on to horses like some of the dude ranchmen would do. After placing the block in the centre of the pen, Walter gave Sam some guidance.

"Okay Sam, these things you're standing in are your stirrups, and those things you have in your hands are the reins." Sam nodded. "You can steer the horse with the reins or with your legs and you can do both together. Just for today, you're gonna use your legs to ask Toby to move forward, then use your reins to point him in the direction you want to go, okay?" Sam gave Walter a big "yes sir!" and Walter stood laughing at Sam's enthusiasm.

"Now, if Toby decides to get to running, you just hang on in there: he'll run out of energy soon enough.""Really?" Sam replied in a nervous tone.

Walter laughed and looked at him.

"No, Sam, I was only pulling your leg. For your first lesson you'll be on a line so don't you worry about anything." Sam visibly relaxed in the saddle, which was what Walter had hoped for.

"Good luck, Sam," Billy called from the edge of the pen. Sam gave him a thumbs-up then Walter asked him to squeeze with his legs, giving Toby the signal to move forward. Sam rolled back in the saddle slightly as Walter had seen many people do as they failed to anticipate the first step and get behind the movement. As he watched Sam go around, Walter asked him to sit straighter to match the motion of the horse's pelvis with his own.

It took Sam a few laps but he gradually got in sync with Toby.

"That's it, Sam, do you feel how smooth that is?" Sam had a massive smile on his face and nodded his agreement to Walter. Sam's evident enjoyment was testament for him as to why horses were great facilitators for change in humans. It was one of the reasons why he and Margaret used them in their therapy courses. After a few changes of direction and a little bit of trot, Walter asked Sam to pull back on the reins, softly bringing Toby to a smooth halt.

"Now Sam, that was the best halt I have seen in a long time." Sam dropped down off Toby and Walter gave him a high-five. "Good job."

Sam seemed to have grown a little as he walked back to where Billy stood. Once Billy was on board, Sam and Walter went outside the pen. The sound of the gate clicking shut made Billy realise that Walter had left him alone with Toby. Walter spoke to him through the fence.

"Now Billy, you know what you're doing, I hope." Walter had a little chuckle to himself but Billy did not even smile. Walter then took charge, getting Billy to focus on the task.

"Get Toby walking out," he said, "Do a few changes of lead, work on your soft halts." Billy uttered just one word in reply: "Cool."

On the horse, his mind was racing. Walter had never let him ride in the pen on his own before. Picking up the reins and making a soft contact with the bit, Billy asked Toby to move forward. There were so many things Walter had taught Billy but at this moment he was struggling even to remember the walk. On realising that he had been holding his breath, he told himself to "breathe, breathe, breathe" as he remembered Walter's advice: "Billy, you can stop a horse by breathing out and likewise move them out by inhaling." Almost instantly Toby softened internally, then externally.

"That's it, Billy, you're doing great." Walter's voice had an immediate calming effect on Billy. After making sure Billy was in a better place with Toby, Walter watched how good his riding had become. It was obvious to Walter that Billy was a natural, not only in the saddle but also in his work ethic and general manner around the horses. They were drawn to him like a magnet attracts a piece of iron. He watched as Billy slipped Toby into a nice little trot that was soft and sweet, the rider's movement matching the motion of the horse perfectly.

As Billy rolled Toby back down to the walk and

stopped in the middle of the pen, his whole being was coursing with excitement.

"Did you see that, Walt? I trotted Toby!" There was so much joy in Billy's voice that it took Walter a few moments to realise it was the first time he had asked Billy to trot. Billy had an eye for detail, a gift which many people spend all their lives trying to acquire, especially around horses.

By the time Billy's feet hit the ground, Sam and Walter were making their way to the middle of the pen. Sam slapped Billy hard on the back.

"Man, you looked good up there." Sam's broad smile spread across to his friend. Then it was Walter's turn to offer congratulations.

"I remember the first time I trotted my first horse, Bo," Walter said, "and it felt like flying, still does. Don't remember teaching you how to trot, though." Walter stood scratching his head as if the act would elicit some sort of instant recall.

Billy had now unsaddled Toby and taken off the bridle. Then he went to the shed and fetched a leaf of hay and a bucket of fresh water: Toby's reward for a job well done. The three left Toby and walked back towards the house, Sam and Billy still full of energy from their lesson. But Walter's focus was on a trail of dust heading up the road towards the ranch. A large four-wheel drive Nissan pulled in through the gates, and before Walter could ask who was coming, Sam headed towards the car shouting, "Mom! Dad!"

Barbara and John Quinn had travelled from Denver the previous day, staying overnight in a local hotel. The

Quinns had tried for years to have a child naturally but it was not meant to be. When they decided to adopt, Sam was the first and only child they saw. He wanted for nothing, as John had a top job as an investment banker and Barbara was just born to be a mom. Now as they stepped out of the Nissan, Sam hit them like a baseball zipping into a catcher's mitt.

"Hey there, did you miss us?" John ruffled Sam's hair as Barbara engulfed him in her arms.

"We missed you so much, baby!" Barbara said. The separation had been a bigger deal for her than she had at first thought.

John shook hands with Walter then turned to Billy and repeated the gesture.

"This place is beautiful, Walter, and way bigger than I expected." John spun round taking in the view as he spoke. Walter took pride in everything he did so when someone complimented him, he usually had a smile of satisfaction on his face.

"Thanks, John. We do try our best to keep the old place in good order."

"Sure is some place," John said, "Sorry Walter, you've met Barbara before?"

"Sure have, nice to meet you again, ma'am." Barbara managed to tear herself away from Sam long enough to exchange pleasantries.

"Sam tells me you're training him to be a cowboy?" Walter looked at Sam then back at Barbara.

"No ma'am, but what I did say to Sam was he'd make a good bull rider." Everyone was laughing except Sam, who had a slightly stunned look on his face. "Small bulls," Walter said. "Right, Sam?" This was said with a wink and Sam could breathe again, realising that the old man had been having fun with him and his mom.

Margaret had stepped out on to the porch on hearing the commotion in the yard. "Walter Dawson, you had better not be telling everyone about my cooking! If you are you'll be sleeping in the barn tonight" Everyone laughed as she ushered them inside for coffee.

While the adults talked in the kitchen, Sam and Billy slipped upstairs with their milk and cookies to the sanctuary of the bedroom. They were about go back down when there was a soft knock on the bedroom door: it was Margaret.

"Billy, Sam, someone's here to see you." When Billy asked who it was, she just smiled and said, "I don't want to ruin the surprise for you both."On hearing the word surprise, the boys ran past Margaret, pinning her to the door frame as they charged at breakneck speed down the stairs and into the kitchen. On arriving with a thump at the end of the kitchen table, Sam saw Ruth Drake standing there with a smile breaking across her face.

She was in the doorway, backlit by the late morning sun and wearing a plain green shirt neatly tucked into the waistband of a pair of faded denims: just the right attire for visiting horse folk. As if both boys had been practising their harmonies, they called out in unison: "Ms Drake!" then ran to her as if she were a long-lost family member. Ruth took a step back to look at them.

"Is it me, or have you boys grown from the last time I saw you? It seems that fresh air and old-fashioned country cooking does wonders for young bones."

Chapter Eighteen

"What's his name?" Ruth looked at Billy for a moment then switched her gaze back to the horse standing under the aspen tree that grew over the side of the pen.

"Ronin. Walter is going to show me how to work with this type of horse – wild, I mean." As Billy spoke, he never took his eyes off the horse, watching the subtle changes that Ronin's body made even when he was resting. Ruth asked what Ronin's name meant and what was its origin.

"Japanese," Billy said, still watching the horse, "His name comes from a term given to samurai who had fallen from grace and had to live their lives cast on the waves of life. It can be translated as 'wave man'." Ruth was looking down at Billy. He looked back at his teacher with a broad smile on his face.

"Well, Billy," she said, "I never knew that. You're full of hidden talents." She ruffled Billy's hair, which made him giggle in protest.

Ronin had turned around to see what all the commotion was about. The interactions of the two-legs had caught his interest and he moved across to get a better view of their position.

"Look, Ms Drake," Billy said, "He's watching us. Never seen him do that, not while I've been here." They both watched the horse intently and as he came closer Ronin froze. The two-legs had gone quiet and were now staring straight at him, so in response he mirrored their behaviour. Billy turned to Ruth and motioned for her to move closer so he could speak quietly.

"He's gotten kinda stuck and I think it would be best for us to walk away, it takes the pressure off of him." Ruth nodded her agreement. As the two-legs moved away, Ronin paused for a moment then walked back to his safe spot beneath the aspen.

Later, everyone gathered outside Ronin's pen but at a distance that would not distract or put unnecessary pressure on him. Walter and Billy had walked across from the tack room and as they reached the others, they gave polite smiles and continued towards the pen. Billy opened the gate to allow Walter in then closed it behind him and stayed on the outside as he had done previously.

During the time Ronin had been out to grass, Walter had managed to get him halter-broken using the small square holding pen at the summer field as a makeshift work area. All the work Walter and Billy had put in back at the farm had paid off, as Ronin now only gave token resistance to being tethered. Although he accepted the halter, Walter still ponied him, leading him behind a ridden horse to and from the field.

Walter walked to the middle of the pen and stopped at a right-angle to where Ronin stood under the aspen. It took the colt the best part of five minutes to make a move towards Walter but he was becoming more and more confident around the two-legs due to the consistency of their actions.

"There we are." Walter rubbed Ronin's forelock a few times before slipping the halter over his nose and securing it with a single knot.

Stepping back, Walter stood about twelve feet away, allowing the colt a good view of anything he might do and taking the pressure off what was still a semi-wild horse with a heightened survival mechanism. After what seemed quite a long time but was actually only around a minute, Walter directed Ronin off to the right along the fence-line of the pen. Ronin followed his instructions and after a few rein-changes Walter halted him and called out: "Billy!"

As he stood watching Walter and Ronin's every move, Billy failed to realise that Walter was calling him until he did so a second time. He looked behind himself then pointed at his chest as if to confirm he was the only Billy in the vicinity. Walter gave a chuckle then nodded at Billy who almost leapt the fence before realising he should use the gate to enter the pen.

Walter handed him the rope attached to the horse before giving just one piece of advice: "Remember everything you have learned."

As the gate closed with a metallic click, Billy was struck by a sudden and terrifying amnesia. He could feel everyone's eyes on him but did not dare turn and look their way. His mind raced. It was Ronin who took the lead and walked away from Billy who seemed to be lost, which for a horse was not good.

"Don't lose him, Billy!" Walter was trying to prompt him into action and it worked. Billy remembered what to do and repeated all the work that Walter had taught him. At the end of the session he stopped in the middle of the pen and waited for Ronin to come away from the fence, which he did.

Rubbing the colt all over, Billy whispered, "You did well, you did well." As he slipped off the halter and turned toward the gate Ronin, instead of going under the aspen as he usually did, followed Billy, tucking in behind as he would when on the pasture with the other horses. It was a simple gesture of acceptance and trust that Billy did not miss. He did a lap of the pen then rubbed Ronin one more time before opening the gate and stepping out.

Everyone clapped as Billy and Walter walked back to the kitchen, such was the impact of what they had seen happen between Billy and Ronin. It was Ruth Drake who spoke first.

"William Dawson, I have never, ever seen anything like that!" She gestured in the direction of the pen. "And what just happened out there will live with me forever." Billy turned bright red at the plaudits and there was another round of applause, at which point Walter called out

"maestro, maestro!" in an attempt to take the focus off Billy, who seemed uncomfortable.

As things settled down in the kitchen, Sam's parents started to say their goodbyes.

"We have a long drive ahead of us," Sam's father said. "C'mon buddy, we've gotta go."

"I'll help you pack," Billy said, putting a hand on Sam's shoulder. "You know you're welcome back any time." Billy looked at Walter and Margaret for approval and they nodded. With that the boys headed upstairs.

"It's never easy leaving a friend," Ruth said after they had gone. She looked calm but she too was dreading saying goodbye to Billy. Being there for the adoption had been an event she could not miss, but now the realisation that she would not see him for a long time was looming large and uncomfortably.

"We will bring Sam back down to see Billy soon, if you guys are okay with that," John said. Margaret quickly put his mind at ease."Yes, that would be fine, any time." Sam and Billy reappeared at the top of the stairs, Sam having an air of disappointment about him as he descended to the kitchen, his bag dragging across the floor.

"Sam," his father said, "we've been talking to the Dawsons and you can come and visit Billy any time you want." Sam immediately dropped his bag and ran to where John and Barbara were standing. He then ran over to Billy, hugged his friend and asked if he could say goodbye to the horse. Billy put his arm around Sam's shoulder.

"Sure you can!" They headed outside.

The dust trail was all that was left of the Quinns' departure. An air of loss hung over Billy as he stared off into the distance at the last glimpses of the car, then went upstairs and flopped on to his bed face-first.

"Do you think I should go up and have a word with him?" There was anxiety in Margaret's voice and she looked at Anne for some kind of answer.

"You know, Maggie," Anne said, "sometimes it's better to let kids deal with things on their own." Margaret knew that Anne was right, as she herself had done so in the past when running the therapy courses, but in this situation it was more personal. Ruth meanwhile was quietly contemplating having to head back to Los

Angeles.

"When is your flight home, Ruth?" She looked at Anne as if she were some mystic who had read her thoughts.

"It's at 9pm but I'll need to return the rental so I'll have to think about leaving at 3pm at the latest, less stress." Margaret sat down next to Ruth and took her hand.

"Billy is going to miss you so much. Why don't you spend some time with him when he comes back downstairs?" Tears welled up in Ruth's eyes and Anne slid a box of tissues across the table. "If you keep on crying, you'll dehydrate."

"Why are you guys upset?" Billy had appeared in the kitchen as if beamed in from some spacecraft that just happened to be passing. Margaret gestured to him to come over for a hug.

"You should take Ruth and show her the summer pasture and I'll fix you a little picnic, sound good?" Billy looked over to Ruth who nodded, then back to Margaret.

"That would be great, Mom." Every time Billy called Margaret 'Mom' her heart filled with joy.

Billy and Ruth sat on the picnic blanket. They had picked a spot in a small clearing in the wood next to the pasture where the horses grazed. The sun's warmth filtered down through the branches and Ruth finished setting out the goodies that Margaret had packed into the basket and the cooler.

"This is a beautiful spot, isn't it?"

"Sure is," Billy said, but he already had a sandwich

in his mouth so it came out more like "Shoorish". Ruth laughed.

"You are so lucky to have landed here and Margaret and Walter are wonderful human beings." Billy had now finished his sandwich and was able to give his full attention to what his old teacher was saying.

"None of this would have been possible without you and Sam," he said, "You guys saved my life." Ruth could feel the tears welling up again but fought them back as best as she could.

"That's very kind of you, Billy, but you deserved some stability after all that you'd had to endure." They then sat in silence for what seemed like an age before Ruth crossed her eyes and stuck out her tongue at Billy, who burst into laughter.

The sun had changed position in the sky. Ruth and Billy were leaning on the fence that surrounded the pasture. Billy was explaining about herd dynamics and their place in the horses' world.

"It seems such a long time since I found you half-dead in the Brents' basement," Ruth said, "You have come so far in a short time." She noticed Billy's body tense ever so slightly at mention of the Brents' name and his eyes fell to his feet, so she decided to change the subject.

"Come and sit down for a moment. I need to talk to you."

Reaching out with her left hand, Ruth led Billy back to the picnic blanket where they sat cross-legged facing each other. There was a sense of dread hanging over Ruth. She had a dry mouth and there were what felt like a thousand butterflies in her lower abdomen. Just as Ruth started to speak, Billy cut her off.

"I know you're leaving, Ms Drake." His words reverberated in Ruth's head and slid down behind her eyes. The wave of emotion she had been trying to control opened the floodgates and she started sobbing. As she sat head in hands, Ruth felt Billy very gently pull her hands down and wipe away the tears.

"You will always be a very special friend to me, Ms Drake, but I understand that you have your own life to live, as do I…" And I'm supposed to be the adult, Ruth found herself thinking. "But I can write to you and if you have some time you could come here for a holiday, things will be fine." With every word, Ruth's concerns melted away.

Billy threw his arms around Ruth's neck and they hugged each other tightly until a twig snapping caused them to both turn in the direction of the noise. They laughed out loud. They walked over to the fence where all the horses stood looking at them intently.

"Horses are great at reading our emotions," Billy said.

Ruth reached up and rubbed the forelock of the big Clydesdale who was standing directly in front of them and as if by some kind of magic, he dropped his head down into her arms.

"My oh my, I hope he likes water," Ruth said, but she was crying happy tears.

"Well, did you guys have a good time?" Margaret was sitting on the porch bench going through some paperwork.

"Just the best, wasn't it Billy?" Ruth looked down at the beaming face of her young friend.

"We had a great time, Mom, and Ruth wants to come back for a holiday and I can take her out riding up into the hills." As Billy spoke he never took his eyes off Ruth.

Billy headed for his room and Ruth started saying her goodbyes to Walter and Anne who had returned from a trip into town for some supplies. She then climbed the stairs up to Billy's room where she knocked softly on the door and turned the handle. Billy lay face-down on the bed. On hearing Ruth call his name, he could hold his tears back no longer.

"Ms Drake, Ms Drake, Ms Dra…" His words were muffled as he pressed his face into Ruth's body. "You gave me this life, you and Sam. I will not waste a moment of it and I hope someday to make you both proud of me."

When they made their way down to the kitchen, Margaret could see how upset Billy was. She wanted to comfort him but knew she could do that later. Instead, she walked over to Ruth and held her tightly and whispered: "You have given me a son, a son I never thought I would have again, and for that I shall be eternally grateful."

Ruth stepped back and smiled. After a final hug for each of Anne, Walter and Margaret, she walked over to Billy and they hugged for a moment before he ran upstairs. Ruth opened the screen door which protested with its familiar squeak.

She reached the car and put her bag on the back seat, looking up at Billy's bedroom window to see if he was there. He was not. With a heavy heart Ruth sat in the driver's seat and started the engine, rolled down the window and waved goodbye to her friends. Then with a blast on the horn she headed for the gate and was almost gone when she caught some movement in the rear-view mirror. She stopped the car and jumped out as Billy ran up to her. He had something in his hand: the dreamcatcher that hung in his bedroom.

He handed Ruth the gift.

"I want you to have this, Ms Drake. It has brought all of us together and made my dreams come true, maybe one day it will do the same for you." Ruth took the dreamcatcher from Billy but she could hardly see it through tears.

"Thank you. I will hang it beside my bed and dream of the next time we see each other." With a final hug she drove off, leaving only dust and the faint smell of her perfume lingering.

"Coffee's on the stove." Margaret put her arms around Billy and walked him back to the house.

Part Two

Chapter Nineteen

Montana State University had a sprawling campus and a broad curriculum focusing on agriculture and land studies. Billy had enrolled on a land management scholarship and had also, in his own time, signed up for a basic accountancy course. He was sitting in the outside lunch area in a small copse of aspens watching the world go by when his peace was disturbed by a commotion off to his left.

It was Jordan Pope, the local football team jock, who was trying without success to convince one of the female students that his football prowess matched his skill under the sheets. There was nothing subtle about him, he was just your run-of-the-mill bully. Barely a second after Billy had thought this, Jordan became a victim of what would be called in footballing terms a field goal, as the young female student kicked him hard in the nuts. This made Billy immediately think back to the time Sam had incapacitated their school bully, Eddy Thompson.

It had been a couple of years since Billy had seen Sam, not since he had come up to the ranch for a short holiday spent riding the horses and helping Walter with the chores. After letting these happy memories run around in his mind for a few moments, Billy finished his lunch and headed for his class.

Like most of the students at Montana State, Billy's days were split between classroom theory and practical applications of animal husbandry: doctoring cattle and horses, working various types of machinery, creating alternative incomes for rural skills and overall business management. On this particular day Billy was working in the equine section where the horses were being given an anti-tapeworm treatment. The young colts were easy enough to handle except one, a black mustang known to the tutors as El Diablo.

"This one will have to be put in the crush," Frank Hendriks had said as he removed his Stetson and pulled a handkerchief from his back pocket to wipe the sweat from his brow. Normally Frank, the lead trainer, had a very sympathetic manner but the black colt had tested his resolve on this hot afternoon. He handed El Diablo to one of the students and asked them to put the colt in a pen on his own with water and a leaf of hay.

"We'll deal with that knucklehead later," Frank said. There was a burst of laughter from the students, all except Billy.

After they had broken up, Billy managed to get Frank on his own.

"Mr Hendriks, can I have a word?" Frank had picked up a scoop and was dipping it in the nearest trough before pouring the water over his head.

"Billy, how many times do I have to tell you? It's Frank. I like to keep things informal on the yard." He wiped the excess water from his face.

"Now if you say no, I will totally understand," Billy said, "but if it's okay with you I'd like to work on the black colt to see if I can help him with his negative approach to the wormer." Frank took out a small pouch of chewing tobacco, extracted the desired amount and pushed it into the corner of his mouth between teeth and cheek.

"You sure you want to bite off that much trouble? He's pretty hostile, not just about the wormer. I think he's holding on to a lot of the wild side of his personality." Billy listened carefully to what Frank was saying and he never heard the word 'no'.

"Well, Mr Hendriks – sorry, Frank – I've worked with a few troubled horses at my folks' place and I know what's ahead." All the time Billy spoke he never managed to make eye contact with Frank. Frank paused for a moment before replying.

"Now I'm in no way saying that you can't work with the colt," he began, searching for the right words, "but you see, I too have worked with more than my fair share of colts and what I will say to you is it takes a lot of commitment from the human to get the horse past any deep-rooted blocks during their training." There was a silence between the men which unnerved Billy the longer it went on. Frank finally broke it.

"What the heck, son. If you're willing to take full responsibility for that colt, I don't see any harm it will do, not unless he stomps on your head!" Billy was still laughing as he shook hands with his tutor to seal the deal.

"Well now," Frank said, "Let's get back to the rest of those knuckleheads in the far pen." As they walked back, Billy was already formulating a plan of action for El Diablo.

Billy sat on the hay bale watching the black colt's

every move. There were certain aspects to its behaviour that reminded Billy of Ronin and other edgy horses he had worked with back home. El Diablo stood next to the water trough, his safe zone. The breeze blowing across the water's surface became cooled and helped to regulate his temperature, which on a day like this was a blessing.

Having seen enough, Billy picked up his halter with a twenty-foot rope attached in case the colt needed some space to get rid of excess energy. As he stood up, the colt's posture changed from being at rest to one of readiness, every muscle switching on as his natural flight system kicked in. Making a mental note of this, Billy opened the latch and entered the pen quietly before walking to its centre. Taking charge of the middle of the pen and, more importantly, the manner and energy he used getting there gave a clear signal to the horse of Billy's intentions.

Keeping his gaze low and out of direct contact, Billy waited to see the response to his presence and if it would trigger the flight instinct. Watching from out of the corner of his eye, he counted the colt's breaths. They were slightly elevated but still within normal resting levels at around eight to twelve per minute. Billy changed his own breath to match, a simple way to find some common ground and an offering to the watchful mustang.

To anyone looking on it would have seemed like nothing was happening between the horse and Billy, as the subtle nuances of his work had been honed back on the ranch with Walter. Sometimes when Billy worked a horse, especially now that he was older, he could really appreciate his adopted father's skill and how it had been a privilege to learn over the years.

El Diablo's posture changed to a more natural one and Billy took that as his cue to move to the far end of the pen, easing the pressure of close proximity. After a few minutes, he resumed his position back in the middle of the pen but this time shifting slightly to the colt's right, causing it to move to his left. Once Billy managed to move El Diablo, it was vital to keep everything low-energy and not let the colt start to feel defensive.

All the time El Diablo moved around the pen, Billy looked for any conformation issues, injuries and the like. Having completed two or three circuits on the left lead, he moved forward towards the colt's nearside shoulder to block any more movement to the front and initiated a halt. Ideally when asking for a halt, Billy would look for the horse to turn and face him, but the black colt did not do this, choosing instead to stay parallel to the fence.

Billy was thinking back to his time spent watching the colt from outside the pen and realised that he had never obtained a clear view of its right-hand side. He now suspected that the colt might have an old injury or possible damage to his eye that led to this favouring of his left side, which was clearly his strongest side. He knew that injured horses often looked sound but masked the injury to avoid predation or being victimised by other herd members. Again, once Billy had stopped the colt, he backed off to the far side of the pen to give the horse some space and allow him time to work out his next step.

It did not take long to formulate a plan to move the colt over to his left side. Billy's theory was simply to walk toward the horse's head and if he backed up then he would have to turn when they reached the water trough. With the way forward – or rather, backward – now in mind, Billy circled the perimeter of the pen until he was ten feet from the colt's head. In a slow, rhythmic fashion he started to pat the side of his jeans with the halter and rope. This was not an attempt to spook the colt: Billy wanted to create enough energy to initiate movement.

Having done this a few times before, he knew there was a fine line between moving the horse and scaring him. The critical part came when the colt began to turn, as at this point, he would start to lose sight of the human as they shifted into a blind spot. The colt stood his ground and Billy continued the rhythm of the halter, clucking his tongue against the roof of his mouth. This higher pitched noise usually made a horse more aware of the human's position. On this occasion it had the desired effect as the colt started moving backward along the fence.

He backed all the way to the trough, unwilling to take his gaze off Billy until his hind legs hit the trough and he shot forward, tucking his tail in tightly against his rear. Billy stood firm and continued to pat his leg with the rope. Again, the colt moved toward the trough, only this time he eased his legs softly against the obstacle. Billy paused and backed off two steps, giving the colt a little time to process his situation.

Watching him, Billy could see that his breathing had come back down. He continued to move the rope and cluck as he walked forward slowly. With nowhere else to go, the colt began to roll around his hind legs, exposing his right side. Billy immediately stopped moving forward and let the rope hang vertically against his leg. Having completed his turn, the colt looked back in the direction of Billy, who by now had backed all the way across to the other side of the pen.

As he looked at El Diablo, Billy could see there had been a kick to the side of the knee quite recently, probably from when the horses were penned a few weeks earlier. The wound seemed to be superficial and over the next five minutes Billy repeated the exercise on the colt's right side without incident or injury.

"Okay buddy, that will do you for today." He spoke in a low tone to the colt who was now standing to rest his nearside hind leg.

After leaving the pen and topping up the hay, Billy noticed a girl standing against one of the stable blocks looking in his direction.

"I've never seen anyone work a colt like that," she said as Billy passed by, "You have a real nice manner about you." Billy turned to face the girl, a smile breaking across his face.

"Thanks. Most folk miss the small details, but you have a good eye..." Billy left the end of his sentence open waiting for the girl to supply her name.

"Samantha. Sam to my friends." The significance of her name was not lost on Billy.

"Nice to meet you, Sam," he said,

"I'm Billy, Billy Dawson." As they exchanged small talk, Billy didn't miss that Sam was a really pretty girl:

green eyes and long auburn hair with a beautiful smile.

"So are we agreed that you'll show me how to do that, maybe tomorrow?" Billy, distracted, had missed the part of the conversation and tried to fill in as best as he could to save face.

"You mean working with this guy?"

"Sure."

"Er… I think we should maybe use one of the others who is a little better trained, this one's still a bit touchy, if you are okay with that?"

"Great, see you here say four-thirty?" With that, Sam walked back towards the stable block and out of sight.

All the way back to his pickup, Billy was thinking about Sam. He started the engine and the old Ford roared into life as it had done every time since Billy had bought it. It only took Billy ten minutes to reach his apartment. Once inside, he put the pickup keys in a bowl that sat on a coffee table, slipping his backpack off and dropping it on to the floor.

After a quick shower, he sat on the couch still wearing the towel he had used to dry himself. His encounter with Sam had had an effect on him, so much so that he flipped open the lid of his laptop and opened his Facebook account with the intention of looking up her profile page. To his surprise, there was a friend request already waiting for him on the top bar.

Billy clicked on the icon and saw Sam's face smiling back at him from her profile picture. Samantha Hart. After staring at the photograph for a while, Billy hit the accept button and messaged Sam with a thank you. Closing out of Facebook, he was about to get dressed when his mobile buzzed on top of the coffee table. Billy swiped the screen to reveal a Facebook message from Sam.

Hi Billy. Thank you for accepting my friend request. It was really nice watching you work with that mustang today. Can't wait for tomorrow, I'm excited to learn your style of training. C u then. :)

Billy hit the reply button.

Hello back Sam Hart :) Glad you like my horse work. Really nice to meet you and like you I am looking forward to tomorrow, hope you enjoy your lesson. :):):)

Sam replied with *:)* and then she was gone.

Billy put his phone on the table and went into the bedroom to get dressed. On the way to the kitchen, *Starman* rang out from his phone. The choice of ringtone was to remind him that each day was a blessing and to fill it with as much joy as possible. Picking up the mobile, he heard his mother Margaret on the other end of the line.

"Hey Mom, how are things with you? Dad keeping you out of trouble?" As he spoke there was a smile on his face. He loved it when his mother called and he also loved to tease her.

"Aw honey, you know how tight a leash he keeps me on." Maggie was not falling for his game. "Anyway, he's too busy helping me with the latest bunch of kids on the courses."

Billy felt proud when he thought about all the children that his parents had set on a different path.

"When are you guys going to think about retiring?" Even as Billy spoke, he knew what his mother's reaction would be. "Our retirement plan is to have matching urns sitting next to each other on a beach in Hawaii." There was laughter down the phone. "We wanted to know when you will be home next?" Billy could hear emotion in his mother's words. It had been a few months since he had managed to get back home but he had a mid-term break in two weeks.

"I was planning to see you guys soon," Billy said, "say on the…" He glanced at the calendar, "…twenty-fifth of this month." Before Billy could continue, he heard Margaret shouting through into the kitchen to Walter.

"Billy is coming up on the twenty-fifth." Then she returned to speaking into the phone. "Your father wants to know if you want to be picked up."

"Yes Mom, that would be fine, if he's not busy," Billy said.

"We both can't wait to see you, honey," Margaret said, "and I swear that damn horse of yours is pining for you."

On hearing the mention of Ronin, Billy felt a pang of guilt about having to leave his horse at home during his time at university. "I'll make a fuss of him when I get back. Gotta go now Mom, my accountancy class starts in five minutes. Love you, tell that old fart I love him too, bye."

On his way out of the house, Billy could not get Ronin out of his head. Maybe it was because the black mustang had reminded him of his own horse, or maybe it was just the phone call reminding him of home.

Chapter Twenty

The mustang stood measuring Billy's every move with intense focus. It was Billy's day off but he was allowed to come in and work on any horse of his choice as long as he had permission from the tutor. Frank Hendriks had encouraged this, telling all the students to "explore their equine skills" using the schooled horses, unless they thought they could handle any horse that had an issue.

Billy stood at the far side of the pen waiting to see what his next move would be. He did not have to wait long. Having repeated the work from the previous day, he wanted to see what effect it would have on his connection to the colt. El Diablo took a step in Billy's direction, then another, then another. This was a good sign but the bond could be broken easily if Billy moved in a way that got the colt thinking defensively.

As El Diablo reached the centre of the pen, Billy looked up but kept his gaze fixed on the colt's shoulder. This simple change in attitude was enough to stop the horse in its tracks but did not switch him into flight mode: again, a good sign. Without changing the level of his gaze, Billy took two paces towards El Diablo then stopped. With occasional glances in the colt's direction, he walked at a right-angle to its position before stopping again.

The colt, as expected, tracked Billy's movement, keeping his head toward him at all times. After completing a circuit in one direction, Billy repeated the manoeuvre on the other side. Then, having completed this part of the routine, he once again backed off and returned to the far side of the pen. Instead of going back over to the water trough, his safe spot, the colt now stayed in the place Billy had left him.

Taking advantage of this positive attitude, Billy started to move forward slowly. At halfway he paused and switched his gaze to the colt's left side, then to the right. Once again, the colt matched his every move. Standing only two paces from El Diablo, Billy took a step directly towards his shoulder, intensely aware that this was a make-or-break move. The colt's expression, which to Billy meant his whole body, did not change. Billy reached up with his right hand and placed it against the colt's forehead, rubbing softly. This was the real beginning of his connection.

After rubbing El Diablo all over, Billy headed for the gate with the young horse tucked in behind him as if attached by some invisible rope. At the gate Billy stopped to rub him again then collected some hay, placing it directly across from the water trough.

Unknown to Billy, Sam had seen the whole training session. As she walked towards him, he could see she was crying.

"Hey Sam," Billy asked, "is something wrong?" She fished a handkerchief from her pocket, wiped the tears from her eyes and blew her nose.

"No, nothing is wrong," she said in a slightly shaky voice, "I just got caught up in the emotion of your work. I have never seen anything like that before, it was so beautiful and soft." Billy reached out and gave Sam a hug, which she accepted and held for a short while. Taking a clean tissue from his pocket, he handed it to her and said it was quite common for people to get emotional around horses.

"They have a way of getting past the barriers folks put up and they can see straight into you, into the part of you that no one else sees. It's a good place to start, knowing that you can't hide anything, as it forces us to be open with them."

As Billy spoke, Sam never took her eyes off him. She had not even blinked. He looked across to the far pen where the horse he had selected for Sam to work with was waiting.

"Do you want to meet the horse you're going to be working with today?" Sam snapped out of her trance and blushed.

"Sure, sure. Let's get to it. What's the horse's name?"

"It's the sorrel mare over there," Billy said as they walked towards the pen. He pointed to a rust-coloured horse on its own at the far side of the holding area. "She's one of the school horses so you have nothing to worry about."

"Is that the one called Cassandra?" Billy was surprised that Sam knew the mare's name then remembered that she was on the same course as him.

"Yeah, Cassandra. She's a sweet horse and good to teach you some basics." A nervous smile broke out across Sam's face.

On reaching the pen, Billy told Sam to go inside with the halter he had given her but to wait for the horse to make the first move before attempting to put it on.

Cassandra lifted her head from the pile of hay she was in deep discussion with, looked at Sam, then continued eating. Sam stood patiently at the far side of the pen waiting for Cassandra to make a move away from her hay, but she didn't.

After a few minutes, Sam looked across to Billy for some guidance, but all he said was: "Be patient". Rather reluctantly, Sam continued her vigil. Then as if by some unspoken command, Cassandra stopped eating and walked across to Sam, who looked over to Billy with a smile beaming across her face.

Billy gave Sam a thumbs-up and asked her to slip the halter on Cassandra, then to rub the mare all over on both sides before standing back at about twelve feet directly in front. This Sam did in a confident manner.

Having laid the lead rope on the ground, Billy then instructed Sam to move one pace to the side of the horse, and as she did this to start lifting the line off the floor. This would give the horse a clear view of where to go and give a signal that something was going to change.

Walking down the mare's near side, Sam turned to her left. As she did this, the line tipped Cassandra's nose to the inside and her hind quarters moved away to the outside. Once Sam had completed this initial manoeuvre, Cassandra had completed a half-circle and was now directly in front of her.

From the outside of the pen, Billy said that Cassandra now had to walk wherever Sam's feet fell and if at any point the horse moved to the inside or outside, Sam should simply redirect her back into line. In this way, Billy said, the horse had clear guidance on who called the shots.

After a few changes of rein direction, Sam stopped by turning sharply to face Cassandra. This quick movement had the effect of stopping the mare in her tracks. Billy asked her to step back and put some more slack in the line until it was once again lying on the ground.

"Sam, that was great," he said, "You're a natural!" He had a smile on his face. "Now give that horse a big hug."

As Sam approached Cassandra, the horse lowered her head as if she knew what was about to happen. Sam cradled the mare's head in her arms, rubbing her forelock and whispering, "Good girl". Cassandra's whole being had softened and by the look in her eye she was in complete rapture. Billy looked on at the scene thinking that these moments are what being with horses is all about.

He looked down at his watch: 5.30pm.

"Okay you guys, let's break up this mutual appreciation society and give that wonderful horse some hay." Sam turned and looked at Billy.

"Okay boss, whatever you say." She slipped off the halter, gave Cassandra's forelock a final rub, then headed for the gate. Cassandra gave her a soft nicker as she filled the external hay manger before getting back to the serious business of eating.

"Most folks take a while to get the timing on that exercise," Billy said, "Well done." Once again Sam's eyes looked into his and there was colour in her cheeks. She looked down then back up again. "Ah, you know what they say: horses forgive all of our sins. It was

Cassandra who did all the work." Billy and Sam smiled at each other then headed for the main building, leaving Cassandra to enjoy her hay.

"I haven't had any food and…" Billy cut Sam off in a polite way.

"Oh okay, that's cool. Do you want to go straight from here? Steaks?"

Chapter Twenty-One

Chuck's Steakhouse was the closest diner to the university and the best. It took Billy and Sam twenty minutes before they were seated. Their server, Jo, took their drinks order and gave them the menu. Billy had only been in Chuck's once before and opted for his previous choice of a 12oz sirloin with fries, tomato and mushrooms.

"What are going to go for, Sam? The sirloin is good." Sam's head popped up from the other side of her menu.

"Really, have you had it before?"

"Yes and it's amazing." Billy rolled his eyes to emphasise the point. Jo returned with their drinks.

"Are you guys ready to order?" Billy waited for Sam to order first.

"Could I have a Caesar salad to start and a 12oz sirloin, medium rare?"

"And you sir?" Billy smiled up at Jo.

"I'll have mine medium rare also."

"So where are you from," Sam said, taking a sip of her cola, "if you don't mind me asking?" For a moment Billy's gaze dropped to the table.

"I'm originally from a small town in the Colorado Rockies, Estes Park, but I now live with my parents on a ranch near Billings." Nodding her head, Sam continued.

"When did you guys move out here? I can't hear an accent."

At first Billy was going to tell Sam a different version of his past, but he felt that would have been lying and that's never good.

"I'm adopted. My mom died giving birth to me and my father passed away from an overdose when I was five, he never really recovered from the death of my mom. After that I was in and out of foster care before my new parents took a chance on me." There was no reply from Sam's side of the table and for a moment Billy panicked, thinking it was too much information on a first date. "Er, sorry – sometimes I'm too blunt when telling folks about my past."

"No, no, Billy you have nothing to apologise for," Sam said, "I can't imagine what it would have been like to lose my folks and I think myself lucky every day that they are in my life." She reached into her bag, pulled out a tissue and dabbed tears from the corners of her eyes. After an awkward silence, Billy started to tell Sam about his work with El Diablo.

"Yeah, I've worked with a few colts back at my folks' place but he does remind me of my own horse, Ronin."

"Why did you call him Ronan?" There was a puzzled look on Sam's face.

"It's Ronin with an i not an a," Billy said. Sam again stuck her tongue out at him, making him smile. He told Sam about the masterless samurai and their fate, Sam sitting enthralled at the story.

"Whoa, that's an awesome name and story," she said when Billy had finished. "Thank you so much for sharing."

Jo appeared with their salads. As they ate, Sam asked

Billy why the black colt reminded him of Ronin.

"Well, he feels very similar," Billy said, "His what I would call 'presence' reminds me so much of what Ronin was like for a while." He took another mouthful of salad. "I remember when Walter, my adoptive father, showed me how to put a saddle on a young horse that had never been backed and, well, that was a thing of beauty…"

Walter had asked Billy to fetch the backing saddle and halter from the tack-room. This was the big day they had been working towards. Over the last few months, Walter had been teaching Billy how to prep a horse for backing to saddle. In essence, introducing a horse to the saddle for the first time was simply a process of taking your time, which the majority of people didn't do. For most horses, their first experience of the saddle was not sympathetic and, in some cases, downright barbaric. Walter was a firm believer in taking as long as it takes and that was dictated by how the horse was dealing with the groundwork.

As part of the process, Walter would expose the horse to all manner of equipment and challenging situations. This would allow him to gauge the horse's confidence and how it might react to a given stimulus. One of the techniques he used was to put the lead line around the horse's ribcage roughly where the saddle would sit when it was girthed. The line could then be tightened to simulate the girth being done up. If the horse looked uncomfortable, Walter would lessen the tension before gradually building it up again.

Once the horse had accepted the pressure of the line,

Walter would use a lightweight western saddle with its girth and stirrups removed to see how the horse would cope with weight placed directly on its back. If all went well, he would add the girth and tighten it. It was usually at this point that he would find out if enough prep work had been done.

Ronin stood relaxed at Walter's side and watched Billy bring the saddle with its stirrups attached into the pen. He placed it down about eight feet away. Billy took a few steps back and waited as Walter checked the tack then slipped off Ronin's webbed halter and replaced it with the rope one they used in training. All the while Walter reassured Ronin by rubbing his forelock.

With the rope halter now in place, Walter turned his attention to the saddle and pad. Lifting the pad and placing it on Ronin's withers, he slid it into position just behind the shoulder then picked up the saddle. With his hands on the saddle and the lead line draped over his left arm, Walter swung the saddle up and over Ronin's back. It always amazed Billy how Walter could put the heavy saddle over and on to the horses in such a gentle manner.

Ronin continued to stand relaxed while Walter was busy threading the girth through the breastplate, almost as if he had been saddled a thousand times. Billy watched intently, making a mental note of everything his father did.

When it came to the girthing, Walter had always been of a mind that introducing pressure should be done in small increments: today would be no exception. He let Ronin move his feet and get a feel for the saddle and the pressure around his ribs. Then he tightened the girth a little before repeating the process a few times until satisfied that the saddle was fixed in position.

Walter then turned and fixed an eye on Billy.

"Hope you've been watchin' what I've been doin'?" Suddenly there was a knot in Billy's stomach. He knew from Walter's tone that he was about to throw a curve ball in his direction.

"I want you to repeat everything I've just done here with Ronin, okay? After all, he is your horse."

As Billy walked towards Walter his mouth became drier and drier, but he knew there was no backing out; he had to do this. Walter looked down at Billy and handed him the rope. Billy paused and in that fleeting moment it was as if every worry he held on to slipped away into the earth beneath his feet.

"You'll do fine, son," Walter said as he walked to the gate and left Billy and Ronin alone in the pen.

Billy quickly loosened the girth and detached the breastplate. He then reached up and pulled the saddle and pad off in one smooth motion. Not wanting to set the saddle down on the ground, he walked over to the fence and set it down on the middle rail. Billy then fetched the pad and placed it on top of the saddle before walking over to the mounting block and carrying it to the middle of the pen. All the time he did this, Ronin tagged along behind like a four-legged shadow on a hot summer's day.

Once Billy had finished with the block, he returned to the fence for the saddle. Ronin as before just followed Billy around the pen. Holding the lead rope in the crook of his left elbow, Billy lifted the saddle by the nearside shoulder on the horn and the offside panel next to the stirrup. He then swung it back and forth until the correct momentum carried it up and on to the horse's back without landing heavy. Then he stepped off the block, went round to the other side of Ronin and dropped the girth down. He threaded the girth strap though, snugging it up until it was fitted but not too tight.

All the while, Billy was checking Ronin for any signs of tension or discomfort, of which there were none. Now that the saddle was on the horse, Billy moved the mounting block away while at the same time checking how Ronin felt moving around with the saddle on. Once again, he seemed fine. It was common for Walter to snug a girth up a few times until it felt tight enough that it would not slip. Billy repeated what he had been taught.

"Will I walk him for a bit," Billy asked, "or do you want him to trot?" Walter scratched the stubble on his chin as if to seek some divine inspiration from the four days' growth.

"I think you best keep him in the walk, no point spoiling all your good work for the sake of some speed." With that, Walter rested both arms on the top rail of the pen with his left foot propped against the bottom rail.

"Okay Pops, you're the boss," Billy said as he turned back to Ronin and raised his right arm. The horse knew that this was the command to track to his left and duly walked off at an easy pace.

After a few circuits, Billy stopped Ronin and rubbed him, telling him what a good boy he was. He then repeated the process on the other rein and once again Ronin worked really well.

"I think that will do him for today, Pops," Billy said. Walter gave him the thumbs-up then asked if Billy wanted the mounting block so that he could take off the saddle. "It's okay Pops, I should manage fine," Billy said. As if with some prior knowledge of the coming events, Walter just chuckled to himself.

Billy eased the pin out of the girth strap allowing him to slide it up and out of its buckle. He then folded the strap three times into the nearside girth ring before walking to the offside, hitching the girth up to where it sat next to the horn. He then released the breastplate on the nearside and slid the strap over the horn in the saddle to keep things tidy. It was a bit of a stretch reaching up to the horn. That should have given Billy a clue as to what was about to happen.

Standing on Ronin's left side, he reached up on his tiptoes and pulled the saddle. He expected there to be some resistance given the shape of the horse's back but there was none. As he fell backwards with the saddle bearing down on him, he knew that when Walter suggested he use the mounting block he should have taken his advice. Now he hit the ground hard, butt-first, then his back and finally his head. Lying dazed, he did a quick systems-check to see if there was any major physical damage. There was none but his pride was bruised. The saddle then hit Billy square in the chest, knocking the wind out of him. By the time he managed to catch his first breath, Walter had covered the short distance between them, lifted the saddle and helped his still-gasping son to his feet.

"Well, that's one way to get the saddle off," he said with a wry smile, "but I would not recommend it to most folks." He then walked over to the fence and laid down the saddle carefully.

"Yeah Pops," Billy said in a short-of-breath voice, "Don't think I'd wish that little number on someone who I had a beef with." Ronin meanwhile stood stock still where Billy had parked him, a fact not missed by Walter and Billy.

"Well if there was one way to test what your horse will do in a crisis," Walter said, rubbing Ronin on his forelock and down his neck, "maybe this one here passed with flying colours."

"Yes," Billy said as he gradually got his breath back, "he sure is a special horse." He wrapped his arms around Ronin's neck then walked with Walter out of the farm and along the lane that led to the pasture.

"It was a hard lesson I learned about stepping back and looking at the bigger picture," Billy said as he watched Sam wipe away the last of the tears that had rolled down her face from laughing at his story.

"Most horse folk would have kept a tight lid on that," she said, "especially guys." Smiling into her cola, Sam eyed Billy over the top of her glass.

"Getting back to my original point," Billy said rolling his eyes, which made Sam giggle, "El Diablo has a similar feel to Ronin. Although he is a mustang not long in from the wild, the colt is pretty settled in him so he doesn't pull the flight trigger any time you make a small mistake." As Sam nodded her agreement, Jo returned to take away their plates.

"Tell you what," Billy said, "is there any chance we could have some coke in a pitcher? We've been outside all day and have a thirst on us." After Jo left them, Billy turned back to Sam.

"So now that you know my deepest, darkest secrets, where are you and your folks from?"

"Well, my folk's ranch is in Libby and it's been in our family for over one hundred years," Sam said, "Mom and Dad are looking for me to take over managing the ranch, hence the reason I'm on this course. My brother Martin is in the Marines deployed in Afghanistan on his second tour." Pausing for a moment, Sam looked as if she could see her brother sitting next to Billy. "I have two quarter horse colts that are used on the ranch and a young warm blood that I'm looking to compete in dressage at some point. And that's about it, very boring – the life of a country girl."

Jo reappeared with their steaks served with a cheerful "bon appétit". Billy cut into his and took a bite, then shouted after Jo: "Your job is more than safe". Jo laughed and gave him the thumbs-up.

For the rest of the meal, Sam and Billy talked about horses, their love of the land and how much more diverse rural life was becoming. The bustle in the diner died down as the night wore on. Eventually they headed out into the cool evening air.

"Well, thanks for the meal and of course your lovely company," Billy said.

"Billy Dawson, you are very welcome," Sam said with a smile, "and I hope it is not the last time I have the pleasure of your company." Billy smiled too. After they had held each other's gaze for what seemed like an age, he kissed Sam softly on the cheek, then on the lips. It was as if time stood still for a moment and only they existed in the world.

"Well I hope to see you tomorrow," Billy said, "and maybe we can do some more work with Cassandra?"

"Of course, yes. Same time?"

"Cool." They kissed again, then as they parted, both kept looking back, waving.

Billy reached his car. All the way home he had a massive smile on his face, which even made it to his apartment. Almost as soon as he got there his phone buzzed into life with a message:

Nite nite Billy Dawson thanks for a great time xxx

He pressed reply:

Glad you enjoyed yourself, it was an awesome time. The start of many I hope.

Billy wanted to write more but thought it better to keep things low-key. With that he hit the send button, put his phone on charge and settled down for a good night's sleep.

Chapter Twenty-Two

It was a week on from their initial date and Billy had seen Sam on a regular basis, both on campus and off. Today, however, he had put aside some spare time to work with El Diablo. Things had been going along fine: the young horse was showing increasing confidence in his work and was giving Billy more of his trust. It was with this in mind that Billy began prepping the colt for the wormer.

Before the start of the session, he bought a carton of apple juice from one of the vending machines outside the main canteen, then headed to the tack-room and the large metal filling cabinet marked Equine First Aid.

Billy had found the key in Frank Hendriks' desk drawer and opening the cabinet he took out a large plastic syringe. His plan was to introduce the syringe, let the horse become comfortable with it, then add the apple juice. Finally, if all went well, he would be able to worm the colt in a couple of days.

In the past few sessions, Billy was pleased that El Diablo had begun to nicker on seeing him, and today was no exception. This was a clear indication that the horse saw Billy as a point of trust, which given the task ahead always helped. Before entering the pen, Billy set out the two syringes, filling one with the apple juice and leaving the other empty. He slipped the full syringe in his left pocket and the empty one was tucked under his belt. Picking up the halter he entered the pen.

"Hey boy, how's things?" Billy stood as the colt walked over and let the halter be placed around his head. With a customary rub on the forehead, Billy proceeded to the middle of the pen and started some basic groundwork to see where the colt was mentally.

Once he had established that the colt was in a good place, Billy started to work. First, he simply rubbed the colt's muzzle then slipped his thumb inside the corner of the mouth. After a few repetitions of this with no reaction, Billy gave the colt a break before continuing.

Next, he used the lead line in a similar fashion as when putting a bit in the horse's mouth. Again, El Diablo was quiet and almost uninterested. Finally, Billy took the empty syringe, repeatedly placing it in and out of the corner of the horse's mouth as a way of becoming comfortable with the feel of the plastic.

He now stopped for a longer break before haltering the colt once again, this time using the syringe full of apple juice. Almost instantly, El Diablo noticed the taste and Billy quickly depressed the plunger to squirt the warm juice into the back of his mouth.

The colt slobbered and drooled at the introduction of the tasty treat, which to Billy felt like a job well done. He slipped off the halter, brought some fresh hay then headed towards the main building.

"You sure are patient, Billy," Frank Hendriks said, "I don't know if I would have gotten that done so quietly. You have a gift, son." He had been watching Billy work with the colt and was very happy with what he saw. "You know, Billy, I was going to offer you a position on the teaching staff at the end of your time here. You're an exceptional student with a very bright future in the equine industry. This is not just my opinion. I have spoken to the other tutors and they all speak highly of you. Hell, you could teach us all some new skills."

This new opportunity took Billy by complete surprise and he was almost lost for words.

"You've kinda put me on the spot, Mr Hendriks," he said, "but I'll have to decline your offer. I have a good idea where I want to go in the future and I feel that the position you're offering would tie me down to the one spot which was not in my plan." Frank just smiled and stuck out his hand, which Billy shook longer than he should have.

"Billy, I respect your decision," Frank said, "Most of the students in this place don't have a clue what they're doing next week, let alone years from now. You have a way with horses that most horse folk, myself included, would give their right arm for. If things don't work out for you, come see me – there will always be a place here for you as long as I'm in charge." With that, Frank headed back into the main building leaving Billy feeling a little bemused.

Later that day Billy told Sam about his conversation with Frank.

"You mean he offered you a teaching position and you said no? Man, you must have some big dreams, Billy." This was not the response that Billy had expected so he quickly changed the subject.

"I was going to take a trip up to my folks' place next week and wondered if you wanted to tag along?" This had an immediate effect on Sam's thought process.

"Er, um, sure. What day and for how long? I'll have

to let my parents know." Sam joined Billy on the bed and curled up beside him.

"Well, I was going to go for a full week as I haven't seen my folks for a couple of months. We would leave on the Friday afternoon and fly back the following Friday. What do you think?" Sam looked at Billy with a huge smile on her face.

"I think that would be great and I can't wait to meet Ronin." Sam rolled over on top of Billy and kissed him passionately. Billy responded by pulling Sam closer to him and let his hands work over her naked body. They spent the night together and were woken early by the sun penetrating through the bedroom screen. After showering and eating a quick breakfast they headed to the campus in their separate pickups.

Early morning on the equine campus usually consisted of poop-picking and haying the horses that were still in the pens. As they headed towards El Diablo's pen, however, there was a large dust cloud being kicked up from the colt and Billy could hear a familiar voice shouting obscenities. Billy and Sam rushed forward to find Jordan Pope in the pen with a rope around the terrified horse's neck.

"Fuckin' stand still, ya crazy black bastard," he shouted, "or you'll end up in the glue pot."

Billy told Sam to stay back as he confronted the obviously drunk Jordan. There was a broken Jack Daniel's bottle in the pen and as Billy looked at the colt's face, he could see a nasty laceration above his eye. The sight of the injury made his blood boil.

"Hey Jordan, whatcha think you're doing, man?

You know he's fresh in from the wild and could kill you." Billy could feel his adrenaline kicking in so he concentrated on his breathing while waiting for a response, but he got none. He stepped inside the pen purposely slamming the gate hard to draw Jordan's attention away from the colt and fix on him. This worked.

"Hey Billy, this fuckin' horse of yours just tried to bite me so I had to teach him some fuckin' manners." All the time Jordan spoke, the colt danced frantically at the end of the line trying to get away from the human responsible for his current state. Sam had meanwhile run back to the main stable block and returned with Frank Hendriks and a few other students.

As Jordan ranted on, Billy picked up the pieces of glass scattered around the pen then checked the colt's feet for any signs of trauma, but they were okay. With that done he turned his full attention back to Jordan.

"Hey man, I'm gonna take the rope off the horse's neck, okay?" Billy did not wait for an answer but walked over to where El Diablo stood shivering with fear. He lifted the rope from his neck and threw it in the direction of its owner.

After checking that the cut was superficial, he turned and walked straight towards Jordan. Sam and the others watched the confrontation unfolding but it was only Sam who noticed a slight change in Billy's movement. His body and motion had become more fluent as with a ballet dancer.

Jordan threw a punch but Billy slipped inside, taking the arm in a downward arc that sent his aggressor to the ground. Jordan rose to his feet.

"Dawson, you're a fuckin' dead man." Without pause, he rushed Billy in a move more reminiscent of the football field. His attempt to tackle Billy's midsection was met by nothing more than fresh air. As he pondered how he had missed such an easy target, his head connected with a metal support post that gave the pen some rigidity. It knocked him unconscious, which in the circumstance was best for all involved.

The sound of head hitting post snapped all those watching out of their trance. Frank checked Jordan for any serious injuries but there was just a bruised ego, so he got a couple of the other students to carry him to the medical facility. Billy asked Sam to bring the emergency first aid kit from the equine medical cabinet then checked the colt thoroughly from head to hoof. Thankfully the cut over his eye was the only damage.

"How's he doing, Billy?" Sam's voice was slightly shaky.

"He'll be fine," Billy said, "Just a cut, pretty clean but he could so easily have lost an eye." Slipping the halter over the colt's head took a few attempts, unsurprising given what he had been through. Taking a couple of plastic vials of saline, Billy snapped one open and carefully washed the eye, then with the other vial and some cotton wool he cleaned the blood away. After it had dried, he put some antiseptic fly ointment both around and inside the wound. Then with a rub down the colt's neck they left him in peace.

On their way back to the equine centre they met Frank. "Billy, how's the colt doin'?" Frank, a true horseman, spoke with concern. Billy told him it was just superficial but that the experience would have set the colt back.

"You take all the time you need to get that horse back," Frank said, "Jordan will most likely be expelled for that little stunt if it's any comfort." Billy nodded his thanks and shook Frank's hand. As they parted, Sam could see that Billy was becoming quite emotional.

"Hey honey, are you okay?" Billy began to sob uncontrollably and slumped down against the wall of the corridor. After what seemed like an age he spoke.

"I don't really do confrontation, it reminds me too much of when I was a kid." Sam wrapped her arms around him. "I suffer from PTSD, have done for a while. It usually shows up when shit like this happens." As Billy stood up, he pulled a tissue from his pocket and wiped his face.

"Hey, those were some pretty sweet moves you pulled on Jordan," Sam said in an attempt to change the subject, "What was it?"

Billy smiled and replied with one word:

"Aikido."

Chapter Twenty-Three

It was Ruth Drake who advised Billy to take up aikido during a short visit to the ranch a few years back. "It will teach you focus and discipline," she had said. Now, back at the apartment, Billy sat explaining the principles to Sam.

"Translated into English it means 'the way of harmony'", he said, "As a martial art, the technical aspects are to take whatever energy your attacker throws at you and redirect it. At its core, however, is a system of self-refinement that allows the practitioner to reflect on themselves through diligent practice in armed or unarmed combat."

"So are you a sort of ninja or something?" Sam asked. Billy laughed then kissed her on the forehead.

"You do have an over-active imagination, honey. Yes I can take care of myself, but no, I don't creep about rooftops in black pyjamas with soot on my face." It was Sam's turn to laugh.

"So how long have you been studying it?"

"About five years, less so now that I'm at college but I do keep my eye in whenever I can." Sam had a puzzled look on her face.

"And are you a black belt master?" Billy laughed again but louder this time. He reached over and picked up a bottle of water, unscrewed the top and took a quick mouthful before offering it to Sam.

"I'm a first Kyu, which is one belt below black belt.

And as I was taught when you reach Shodan – black belt level – you are only then ready to learn the true art form of aikido." Sam came over and lay next to Billy on the couch. She kissed him softly on the cheek.

"So it's like you're my own personal bodyguard." Billy furrowed his eyebrows and looked as stern as he could.

"Yes ma'am. I will take on the weighty task of guarding your body and if you don't mind me saying, what a body it is." Sam laughed and they held each other. Without turning to look at Billy, Sam spoke again almost in a whisper.

"How long have you suffered with PTSD? My brother knows a few guys that have it from their time in the military but I'm guessing yours is more to do with your childhood." Billy kissed Sam on the back of her head and gave her a gentle squeeze.

"My mom noticed the signs of it early in my teens and she knows a good counsellor who has been a great help to me. It's just something I have to live with and deal with as best as I can. Thankfully I don't have too many days like today so that helps."

As the light of the day faded they both gradually fell asleep, rising only to exchange the couch for their bed where they slept all the way through to next morning.

After finishing breakfast, they drove to the university and headed out to see how El Diablo was faring. On the way there they bumped into Frank Hendriks.

"How you guys doing?" He didn't wait for their answer. "Jordan Pope has been expelled. His parents are not too happy but as we are not pressing charges they accepted our decision, albeit grudgingly."

"Did you ever find out why he attacked the colt?" Frank scratched his chin at Billy's question, as though he was considering not telling them.

"Well you're not going to believe this, but he had a secret crush on Samantha and when he found out you guys were an item he finally blew a fuse and the rest is history. I've checked on the colt's eye, it's drying up nicely and the swelling has gone down some, but I know you're dying to go see for yourself so I'll bid you good-day."

Frank turned to leave and Billy reached out his hand which the older man shook. With that Frank continued his duties while Billy and Sam headed in the direction of the stockyard.

As they approached the pen, the colt stood with his head down as if resigned to some unspeakable fate that lay in his near future. Then on hearing Billy and Sam's footfalls, his head snapped sharply upwards in an almost military fashion. Billy felt a moment of anxiety that eased quickly when the colt gave them a soft nicker.

"Hey fella," Billy said, "how're you doin' today?"

The colt walked over to where they stood, then shadowed them as they made their way to the gate.

As usual, Billy asked El Diablo to back up, which he did without hesitation. The cut on the eye looked fine. Frank having given it a good coating of antibacterial gel with built-in fly repellent. Apart from some superficial rope burns, the colt had survived his ordeal relatively unscathed.

"You know something, Billy?" Sam said, "It always

amazes me how much horses put up with from us. If that had happened to me yesterday I would probably be in therapy for the rest of my life or worse."

"Well, that's what's so special about these guys." Billy unconsciously ruffled the colt's forelock as he spoke. "They are really great at letting go of things, not all the time but most. That's the reason my mom and dad incorporate horsemanship in their courses. The kids seem to relate to some of the stories Dad tells of horses that have been scarred emotionally by humans but still manage to push past that and get on with being a horse." Sam stood listening to Billy intently, fascinated by his insight into how horses operate.

Now that they had satisfied themselves that the colt was okay, they topped-up his hay and with a kiss on the nose from Sam bade him farewell.

As they drove home, Sam told Billy she was really excited about meeting his folks and having some downtime from studying.

"Yeah, I was thinking that given all that's gone on," Billy said, "the colt can have a break till we get back. I'd already asked Frank to keep an eye on him and our time away gives him a rest from his studies also." They both laughed then Billy continued.

"Frank said he would move a few of the school horses over next to the colt, which I think will benefit his mental wellbeing. I've always had a bit of a thing about quarantining horses – yes, it needs to be done, but they are herd animals and need social contact. At least this way if the colt needs company it's there in the next pen, they can groom through the bars if necessary."

Something Billy had said got Sam thinking.

"You know Billy, his name El Diablo kinda gives him a reputation. I've been thinking about suggesting a name change, what do you think?" Billy had not even thought about the colt's name but Sam was correct, it did give people the wrong impression of a horse that was one of the sweetest mustangs he'd ever worked with.

"You're right, honey," he said, "his name does not suit his personality. Any suggestions?" Sam was almost bursting with excitement.

"Yes, I do. When I was a young girl my folks bought me a little black Welsh cross pony, he taught me how to ride and had such a big heart for such a little guy. He was called Raven and El Diablo reminds me of him in so many ways, so I thought could be a fitting name for such a good-natured guy. What do you think?"

Before Billy even answered, he knew Sam had picked the perfect name. His face beamed.

"Raven – what a great name, yes yes yes, it's so him. I'll tell Frank when we get back and it's made me make my mind up about something else: I'm going to ask if I can buy him." Sam let out a scream of joy and reached across to kiss Billy on the cheek. This made him swerve a few times before getting the pickup back between the white lines.

Their flight did not leave until 9am, but Billy wanted to be there by six. As he and Sam settled down for breakfast in the terminal building café, she seemed unusually quiet.

"Hey I forgot to ask," Billy said, "Are you a nervous

flyer?" Sam looked across the table at him with a puzzled look on her face.

"No."

"I just wondered, you've been a bit lost in your thoughts." Sam smiled at Billy then reached across the table to take his hand.

"I'm sorry, honey, I just get worried about meeting new people, that's all. It's really dumb, I know." Billy squeezed her hand.

"Don't worry, my folks are the most relaxed people I know, they're positively horizontal. They will make you feel right at home." Billy looked at the clock on the café wall. "8am. Time to go, gate six awaits."

As they walked towards the departure gate, Billy put his arm around Sam and kissed the top of her head.

"You know you mean the world to me," he said, "I love you, Samantha Hart, I have since the first day that we met." Sam started to sob.

"I looove you too, Billy, you're amazing." They broke away from each other and smiled, then continued to gate six and the adventure ahead of them.

Chapter Twenty-Four

In the time since Ruth Drake had left after Billy's adoption hearing, Ronin had grown accustomed to his new life at the ranch. He felt more settled in the herd and gradually got to know each individual horse, even the lead gelding, though this relationship was tenuous, especially when the mares were in season. The one horse in the herd with which Ronin had a good connection other than the chestnut mare was Toby. When not in the field, he and Toby spent a lot of time back at the ranch where Ronin watched Toby's interactions with the two-legs. These sometimes seemed strange as Toby regularly allowed both the older two-legs and the younger one to sit on his back. This was a sacred place for all horses but Toby accepted them.

On occasion, there would be a group of young two-legs who would run around making noise most of the time, but when accompanied by the older female two-legs they would come individually to groom either Toby or one of the other horses. It was at this point that Ronin noticed something. He felt a change in the atmosphere and the energy of the young two-legs would shift from a high state all the way down to a more settled flow.

It was on one of these days that Ronin was given his first real job in equine-facilitated learning. Billy was at a stayover with his school friend Sam for a couple of days. Margaret had arranged this with Sam's parents as quite a big group would be at the ranch and she and

Walter did not want Billy on site.

As usual, the minibus would arrive and a small group of children of differing ages would be led to the bunkhouse. After a short time Walter and Margaret would bring the kids outside to where two wooden picnic tables were set out. As on all their courses, Margaret first went over the finer points of health and safety or, as she would call them, 'The do's and don'ts of the Dawson ranch'.

All the kids were given a sheet with a list of the rules. Most quickly folded this into a nice compact square then shoved it into the deepest recesses of whichever pocket was most convenient. One kid even made a paper plane out of his, which he duly sent flying into another boy's ear, an act of aeronautic assault met by roars of laughter from all those gathered at the tables, all except from the plane's victim. Margaret told them they would get one warning and after that it would be the bunkhouse and no return visits. They all became silent.

Walter then stood up.

"I have one main rule," he said, "Well, two actually. Number one: don't feed the horses unless asked to. Number two: don't raise your hand to the horses or to any animal on this ranch." Every child at the tables nodded their head. After letting the silence sit on the now quiet group, Walter spoke again.

"If you retrieve the sheet with the rules on it, we'll continue." Once again there was a buzz of activity and the noise of rustling paper as the kids, now desperate to impress, fished out their folded sheets and ironed them flat with their hands.

Walter sat back down and gave the floor once again

to Margaret.

"Thank you, Walt – and that's Mr Dawson to you guys," she said, "If you want to get to call us Walt and Maggie, well that's got to be earned. Now, if we all look at our sheets I will continue."

Most of the morning was spent on orientation, health and safety, and meeting some of the equine coaches. As always, Walter would bring out Toby and let the kids get familiar with being around horses as most of them had only been exposed to cats, dogs and an occasional rabbit or guinea pig. Toby would be tied up next to the pen with a hay bag to munch on and Walter would take the kids up one by one to touch and, if they wanted to, groom the horse. Even this simple exchange brought a change in most of the children: all except one, Mark.

Margaret had noticed almost immediately that Mark was a bit shut off. She knew from having read all the case histories that he had come from a family where his older brother had beaten him regularly since he was young. She had taken her eyes off Mark to see how one of the girls had overcome her initial fear of horses, and when she turned back round Mark had gone. There was a knot of fear that hit Margaret in her stomach. As quickly as it came, it was gone as she spotted Mark standing outside Ronin's pen, softly stroking the horse's muzzle.

Ronin had been quietly munching his hay as the children arrived. With all the excitement going on he had started to pace around the pen, but eventually settled as the young two-legs disappeared into the bunkhouse.

Later as they came back out, he immediately felt a connection to one that sat slightly off to the side of the main group. It seemed to Ronin that there was a deep fear emanating from the two-legs' body and it reminded him of his days of being harassed by the colts back in the wild.

Ronin got the young two-legs' attention by slowly moving back and forth along the fence-line. The colt would occasionally glance directly at the two-legs then change position and start again. After only a few attempts, the two-legs got up quietly and walked across to where Ronin stood and looked deeply into the horse's eyes. Looking down, Ronin could feel a shift in the two-legs' energy. It was at this moment that he dropped his head and let him touch his muzzle and stroke his face.

Mark and Ronin never heard Margaret approaching until she spoke.

"His name is Ronin and he is – was – a wild mustang." Ronin's head flew up and Mark stepped back from the pen as if they both had been caught in some secret plot.

"Hey it's okay, Mark," Margaret said, "I did not mean to startle you. We try to encourage the kids to interact with our animals. Do you want to go inside to meet Ronin?" Mark nodded and a small smile broke across his face. This simple gesture made Margaret beam inside.

She took Mark to the tack room to get his hard hat and on their way back Walter caught Margaret's attention, giving her a wink as if to say 'good job'. She winked back at him.

All the time they were away, Ronin kept his focus on the direction they had gone. When he saw the young two-legs coming back with the hat on, he nickered softly. Margaret laughed on seeing this.

"Well Mark, it seems you have made a friend."

She opened the gate to Ronin's pen and slipped his halter on, then picked up a dandy brush and asked Mark to come inside. Very cautiously he walked through the gate, which Margaret then latched behind him. Ronin had once again dropped his head low enough to allow the boy to touch him and the colt could now feel an even deeper shift in his internal energy.

Margaret watched this with awe. She had seen a few horses do this but never one who had not been through a couple of their therapy courses as a training horse. She asked Mark if he wanted to brush Ronin and instead of his usual nod, Mark spoke his first words since arriving at the ranch.

"Yes, Mrs Dawson, I would like that very much."

Again, Margaret was taken aback. She had been told that Mark did not communicate well verbally and would usually only shake his head for yes and no. She handed him the brush.

"You can start any ways you want, but I usually start at the top and work my way down." She demonstrated by brushing Ronin's face, stopping just behind his ears. "Do you think you could do the rest of him for me? I'll get you the block to stand on for the high-up parts."

Mark nodded and Margaret fetched the mounting block and sat it on Ronin's left side.

"Here you go, honey." She handed Mark the brush, which he took from her hand very carefully before climbing on to the block. By the time he started brushing, Ronin was half-asleep, partly through being groomed – which he loved – but mostly because of the amount of energy released from the young two-legs, whom he felt was now more balanced.

As Margaret watched Mark, she was taken by how gentle he was in the way he groomed Ronin. When he spoke again – "Mrs Dawson, do horses dream?" – she had to think quickly. She knew from experience that boys, and for that matter girls, who had suffered physical abuse to the point that they shut down usually started to speak when they were ready to unburden themselves of held-back emotions.

"Well Mark, that's a very good question," Margaret said after a few moments, "I think we have all seen our pets, especially dogs, go for what looks like a run in their sleep. And I have observed that horses do the same thing, but unlike us they don't have the part of the brain that holds on to information processed in a dream. Does that answer your question?" Margaret fiddled with the lead rope as she waited for the boy's response. When Mark did speak, he never took his eyes away from Ronin's side. It was almost as if he were using the horse as some sort of confessional.

"I wish that I could not remember my dreams," he said as he continued to brush Ronin, "They are very bad and make me cry sometimes. My brother used to hurt me really bad and I never found out why he did it or what I had done to make him so mad." Margaret could hear the tears in the young boy's voice, but rather than console him she simply let him continue.

"My mom and dad did not care, they were never there to protect me from the things he done to me. I still dream about it even now. And now I don't have any family or anyone who would want me anyway."

With that, Mark's emotional dam burst and he sat down on the mounting block sobbing uncontrollably. Fighting her own emotions, Margaret took a tissue from her pocket and was about to hand it over when Ronin's head curled around Mark's shoulder in what appeared to be an act of comfort. Margaret stood watching in amazement as Mark's arms reached up and encircled the horse's neck in reciprocation of its gesture.

Time seemed to stop.

On thinking back to the incident in later years, Margaret never knew how long boy and horse had comforted each other for. It was such a tender moment. Eventually Mark stood up and gave Ronin a final pat on the neck, followed by a soft "thank you". He then walked over to Margaret and gave her a hug.

With his head still buried around her waist, he said, "I don't want to feel this way anymore, can you help me?" Margaret's reply was simple: "Yes".

Once they had composed themselves, they left Ronin in the pen and headed over to see what the main group were doing. Ronin sought the shade of his favourite tree and started to slowly feed on the fresh hay that was lying there. His world was once again back in balance.

Chapter Twenty-Five

A few years after Billy had started college, Walter had saddled up Ronin to go and check on some cattle that were pastured on the highest part of their property. He liked this time away, usually a two-day job, as it gave him a sense of days past before things became more mechanised. Margaret had packed enough food to last him a fortnight rather than two days: "You never know what can happen up there and you are on your own".

With the words still fresh in his head, Walter headed out of the sanctuary of the homestead and rode up into the foothills to the north of the ranch. Ronin had been backed for some time now, knowing his job and what would be asked of him. He liked the time spent with Walter and especially the days like these when they ventured away from the comfort of their home.

The weather was forecast to be good for the rest of the week. As they rode, they passed small coppices of fir and aspen that broke up the barren grasslands and only grew as high as the sagebrush. It was next to one of these coppices that Walter stopped to have lunch. He carefully removed Ronin's tack and haltered him with a long line that would allow him to graze. He was not a big fan of hobbling horses – tying the legs together – to restrict their movement. The colt was familiar with having lines around him on the ground and would not panic if he snagged one around his leg.

Walter sat there looking out at the wide-open spaces

with the satisfied glow that came with feeling connected with everything. He shifted lower to rest his back against the saddle, or what he like to call 'the cowboy's armchair', then picked up his coffee flask and a few of Margaret's oat biscuits. After around thirty minutes of prairie meditation, he called out to Ronin.

"Well fella, you ready to hitch up the wagons?" Ronin turned and walked back to where Walter stood. He had done this often enough to know it was time to move on.

It was about five o'clock when they spotted the first steer and then the others as they broke over a small rise. Every year Walter would go to the local cattle auction and buy in twenty to twenty-five head of cattle, usually Black Angus crosses. They were young steers that he could fatten up and sell on for meat, taking one or two for himself. Although Walter and Margaret were animal lovers, they had no reservation about eating meat or foul. They knew how well they looked after their cattle and chickens and the quality of life given to them before they went for slaughter.

Walter counted the herd. He was one down, which happened sometimes when a steer fell sick and died or made a bad decision that would leave it injured and weak. With that in mind, Walter took Ronin on a wide sweep of the herd's position in case the missing steer had gone down recently, plus Walter's rancher intuition was in overdrive. Most ranchers took dogs for their cattle work but Walter knew that if he used his horse and knowledge correctly and did not push the herd too hard, they would move together and not get spooked.

As he sat on Ronin, however, he had a feeling that

maybe a dog would have been useful on this particular trip as he felt a sense of foreboding. When they rode up a small valley to the west of the herd, Ronin picked up a scent he knew well from his time in the wild: the scent of death. Walter felt Ronin's body tense beneath him and gave horse a pat down his neck. "Yes boy, I smell it too."

They soon found what was left of the steer's carcass at the top of the valley close to the treeline. There were drag marks and bones littered in a direct line toward the trees. Walter's inner sense was telling him to high tail it out of there, but the rancher in him wanted to look at what was left of the steer. He got down off Ronin and slipped the single shot .22 rifle out of its holster which sat on the right side of the saddle. Keeping the reins in his left hand, Walter approached the remains of the steer with caution.

"Looks like a bear had his way with this one, Ronin, and I reckon it was not all that long ago looking at the state of him."

As Walter glanced back at Ronin, the horse's focus was not on him but on the treeline directly in front of them. It was just as Walter said, "You smell something boy?" that all hell broke loose when the owner of the carcass, a black bear, returned to claim his prize and anything else that was going.

The bear ran straight at Walter who was trying desperately to gather his thoughts. It was at this moment that he witnessed something unheard of to his knowledge. Ronin saw the bear running at Walter and going against all his instincts, he ran towards it. As the beast was about to strike out at Walter, Ronin ran between them and caught the great bear square in the chest with a powerful kick from his hind legs. The bear roared in pain and backed away then, as Ronin approached for another attack, it struck at his hind quarters, cleaving a large trench with its claws.

As Ronin lurched forward squealing in pain and the bear tried to press home its advantage, there was a crack like thunder which echoed off down through the valley. The bear lay motionless at the feet of Ronin while Walter stood with the rifle still pointing to where the great beast had stood, a plume of blue smoke drifting upward from the barrel of his gun. He quickly reloaded just in case another round was needed, then carefully approached the bear and prodded it with the end of the rifle. There was no movement.

On closer inspection he saw that his kill shot, as expected, had gone through the bear's heart. Walter also noticed a wire snare around the bear's back leg, which explained why it went after the steer and also why it was so cranky. With the bear dead, Walter quickly turned his attention to Ronin. The horse had been spooked at the sound of the gun but had only run a few strides before stopping.

As Walter came closer, he could see that the wounds on the horse's quarters were fairly superficial and the worst of the bleeding had already stopped. He looked his companion square in the eye.

"Thank you, Ronin, that's one I owe you." Then he tenderly stroked Ronin's neck before reaching inside the saddlebag for the first aid kit. Using his water canteen, Walter washed off almost all the blood from the wound and the rest of Ronin's leg. He then applied a healing balm to each cut before re-examining his work.

"Well fella, you'll live but you'll have those scars for life."

Once again Walter rubbed the colt's neck then picked up the reins. "You deserve a rest, old friend. I think we'll walk down to those steers before I get back in the saddle, sound like a deal?" They headed down the valley and picked up the herd not long after.

It was early next morning when Walter pushed for home. They had rested at an old cattle station, now abandoned but still having a corral where Walter could pen the animals for the night. He had taken hay earlier that week in the pickup and cleaned the troughs which were fed by a natural stream. Ronin spent the night resting in the old barn and come morning Walter tended his wounds and put fresh balm on them.

The best thing to do was head for the ranch as the act of walking would keep any swelling out of Ronin's tissue. With an easy pace they would make it back well before dark. The ride home was uneventful and Walter as usual had prepared one of the bigger pens for the steers. Once that was done, he turned his attention once again to Ronin. He had just finished when Margaret appeared.

"You're a little late, Mr…" She saw the wounds on the horse's quarters. "Jesus Christ, Walt, what happened?"

"A black bear took one of the steers and nearly us," Walter said, "If it were not for Ronin, he would have had me for sure. Margaret, I have never seen a horse put its life on the line to save anyone but that's just what he did for me up there. That damn bear would have killed me if Ronin had not kicked him square in the chest. Those scars on his butt will prove I ain't lyin'!" Walter's voice broke as he released the pent-up emotion.

They left Ronin munching his hay and headed back to the house where Margaret prepared a pot of coffee. For the rest of that night Walter talked about Ronin's heroics until exhaustion finally got the better of him and they headed off to bed. Outside, Ronin lay sleeping peacefully under the star-filled night as if nothing much had happened in the previous days.

Up on the high pasture, coyotes feasted on the carcass of the bear. Very little goes to waste in the wilds of the back country.

Chapter Twenty-Six

The flight only lasted two hours and after they negotiated the terminal, Billy and Sam were greeted by Walter.

"Hey, Dad," Billy gave Walter a big hug, "I would like you to meet Samantha." Walter slipped off his baseball cap before reaching out to shake Sam's hand.

"It is a pleasure to meet you, Samantha, and a complete surprise, too." Walter shifted his gaze to Billy then back to Sam, keeping a broad smile on his face so that neither would take offence at his comment.

"Please Mr Dawson, you can call me Sam, and Billy has told me so much about you and Margaret." The genuine warmth in Sam's words instantly soothed any reservation that Walter might have had about Billy's surprise guest.

"They're all lies, I tell you," Walter said, "We're good God-fearing folks up here and don't let him lead you astray!" They all looked at each other for the briefest of moments before Billy burst out laughing.

"C'mon Dad, stop pulling Sam's leg – the only thing you and Mom believe in is the resilience of the human spirit." To which Walter simply added:

"Hallelujah". When the formalities were over, Walter ushered them on.

"Let's get to the pickup, I'm in a red zone and you know how twitchy these guys are with their red zones."

Margaret was baking cookies when she heard the

familiar sound of the truck pull up at the back porch. Quickly dusting herself down, she opened the door just in time to see Billy step out of the pickup.

"Billy Dawson, I swear you can smell those cookies from all the way out at the airport." She hurried down the steps to greet her son just as Sam slid out of the same door of the pickup.

"Oh Billy," Margaret said, "You never told us you were bringing a guest and certainly not one as pretty as this young woman." She walked past Billy and gave Sam a great big maternal hug before turning back to Billy.

"Where are your manners? Does this fine young girl have a name?" Margaret had already started to walk in the direction of the kitchen arm-in-arm with Sam. Walter laughed and Billy rolled his eyes.

"Yes Mom, her name is Samantha, or Sam if she likes you!"

"And you can call me Mrs Dawson or Maggie," Margaret said. Again, everybody laughed as they headed to the kitchen.

Once Billy and Sam had unpacked, they went downstairs and were greeted with freshly baked biscuits and coffee. Sam took a deep breath and sighed.

"There's nothing on this planet smells better than cookies straight out of the oven. It's like being back home with my mom." Margaret ushered them both over to the table where she had set out placings.

"Do your folks have their own place, Sam?"

"Yes ma'am – sorry, Mrs Dawson."

Margaret took Sam's hand and said to her softly,

"Maggie will do, we're not at school anymore. You were saying about your folks?"

"Thanks, Maggie. Yes, my folks have their own spread, mostly cattle and some horses. They want me to take over and run the place, and that's how we met." She patted Billy's thigh before continuing. "We're on the same course at college. It's pretty tough going but will have benefits for our future – er, the future." Sam blushed slightly at her slip.

"Well I think that it's great that you young folk are trying to keep the heritage alive," Walter said, "You should both be proud of your achievements."

"Thanks, Dad," Billy said. "Hey, I was going to show Sam around the place, are the horses still in the summer pasture?"

"William Dawson, you are just back two minutes and you want to go play with that damn horse of yours." Margaret smiled a warm smile: it was good to have her son home again.

"Thanks Mom, Dad." And with that they excused themselves and walked out through the screen door.

"They remind me of us when we were their age," Margaret said. She crossed the room and slipped her hand around Walter's waist. In return he planted a kiss on her forehead.

"They sure do, honey, they sure do."

Ronin as usual was at the far end of the field when Billy arrived with Sam. They both leaned on the top of the gate as Billy told Sam who was who.

"And the dun fella at the other end of the field is my horse, Ronin." Putting the small finger of each hand into his mouth and rolling his tongue, Billy whistled twice. Ronin's head snapped up in their direction and he came galloping across accompanied by all the other horses. After milling about at the gate vying for any sort of attention, the herd broke away leaving only Ronin at the gate.

Billy climbed into the field and rubbed the colt's forelock.

"Hey buddy, did you miss me?" Ronin nickered softly as he enjoyed Billy's attention. He then switched his focus to Sam, turning his rear so it was pointing directly at Billy. He then put his head on Sam's shoulder and breathed deep into her ear. This made Sam giggle.

"He's a real ladies' man!"

"Yeah, just like his dad," Billy said, at which moment Ronin's rear let go of some gas and Sam laughed hard.

"I won't comment on what he thinks of you but maybe you're full of air, too!" Billy asked Sam to come and get a closer look at Ronin. She hurdled the gate then let the colt sniff her hands and her hair.

"He's a real beautiful horse, Billy, nice nature, too." She stood back and took a closer look at Ronin's physique. It was then she noticed the scarring on his quarters. "Where did he get those?"

"Well, you are in the company of a genuine hero," Billy said, "This fella right here got between my dad and a black bear a few years ago and saved his life. This is a little memento of the occasion." He rubbed his hand over the scarred area in a tender fashion. "My dad says he has never heard of a horse doing that, except in the wild to protect his herd." Sam smiled.

"But is that not what we are to these guys? We have

become part of their herd and he was protecting your father the same way he would drive off a bear in the wild." Billy went quiet for a moment; he had never thought about the incident in that way.

"You know Sam, I think you may have hit the nail on the head. I always thought it was a case of self-preservation, but Dad was adamant that the horse blocked the bear."

He walked over to where Sam stood and wrapped his arms around her for a kiss, but it was not long before Ronin nudged Billy in the back to break up the embrace. With that, the colt wandered off to join the others grazing happily in the warm sunshine.

At dinner that night, Billy spoke about Sam's theory on the bear incident and Walter agreed.

"That dang horse saved me and nobody can convince me otherwise. As Sam says, we are their herd and in a herd we look out for each other, ain't that right, Maw?" Walter looked over his shoulder at Margaret who was putting the finishing touches to their meal.

"Sure thing, honey, and as a senior member of the herd could you please help me serve out this food?"

Margaret had made salad for the starter and a big bowl of chilli for the main course. Walter gave her a peck on the cheek as he placed the chilli in the middle of the table. He then brought a wicker basket full of freshly cut bread.

There was a jug of lemonade beside Billy so he filled everyone's glass as Margaret finished the salad and brought it to the table along with olive oil, balsamic vinegar and four small bowls. She took each bowl and filled it halfway with the oil then added a tablespoon of the vinegar and handed the bowls to Billy to pass to the others. Margaret then broke off a piece of bread and dipped it in the oil and syrup.

"Bon appétit," she said, "Dig in guys, it's a little recipe I got from a friend." Rather reluctantly the others broke the bread and dunked it in the oil. Walter, who was usually a strict meat-and-potatoes man, turned and smiled at Margaret.

"You never fail to surprise me, Mrs Dawson, this is really nice."

After dinner, the men went outside while Sam helped Margaret tidy away the dishes. Walter snapped the padlock shut on the main gate and turned to Billy.

"Samantha's a real nice girl, son. She's got a pleasant nature about her and that's a rare thing in this modern world." Billy laughed.

"It isn't that bad, is it, Dad? The modern world, I mean." Walter thought for a moment.

"Well the way I see it is like this. A lot of younger folks are forgetting about the old ways, their heritage. They forget that this country was built with hard work and sweat. Heck, when I go into town now nearly every kid I see has their head buried in these smartphones, or as I like to call them, fartphones. I can see that they have a value but some of these youngsters don't know how to hold a decent conversation. We see it all the time when we're holding our courses."

They were quiet for a while before Billy spoke. "Yeah, I guess you're right, Pops, but that's what's great about your work with these kids – it gets them back in touch with nature and themselves." Walter nodded in agreement and let out a sigh.

They stopped at the pen and stared into the open space, then Billy turned to look at the house where he could see Sam and his mother talking. "I was thinking about taking Sam up to the old cattle station tomorrow, is that okay with you?" Walter only caught the end of Billy's sentence.

"Sorry son, I was miles away, what did you say?"

"That's okay, Dad. I was saying that I wanted to take Sam up to the old station tomorrow, if it's okay with you guys?" He turned back to the pen.

"Well I know your mother will want to show Samantha around town," Walter said, "but I guess she can do that any time. What I will say is that if you are going up there, be careful and take the rifle. I'll speak to your mother and see if she can rustle you guys up some provisions."

"Thanks, Dad." Billy put his arm around Walter's shoulder and they headed back indoors.

Chapter Twenty-Seven

"It feels great to be back in the saddle again," Billy said. Sam smiled back at him.

"Yeah, sure does." She reached down and stroked her horse's neck. Sam was riding a sorrel quarter horse named Firefly. Billy had warned Sam that, as suggested by her name, the little mare could become a bit hot under the collar sometimes and get squirrelly if you were too handy with her.

"You know Billy, I don't believe this pretty little girl would hurt a hair on anyone's head, she is so cute." Again, Sam reached down, this time scratching the mare's shoulder. For her part, Firefly seemed to enjoy the attention and stretched out her neck in agreement.

It was a warm day but the breeze kept most of the heat out of the sun, the wind kicking up dust devils here and there. About halfway to the cattle station, Billy suggested they stop for a break. They tied the horses to a tree and eased off their cinches. With the horses made comfortable, they unpacked their coffee canisters and some biscuits Margaret had made for them, sitting down next to a couple of large rocks where there was shelter from the wind.

Looking out over the prairie, Sam sighed.

"This place reminds me so much of home, it's so beautiful." She leaned her head against Billy's shoulder and took a bite of her biscuit.

"You're right," Billy said, "I sometimes forget how

blessed I am to be able to come out here and enjoy being in nature. Kinda lets your system reboot, don't you think?" Sitting quietly enjoying the view and the heat off each other's bodies, they rested for a while before packing away their coffee and riding on.

As they came into the station, Billy was explaining what was what. "That's the barn and the main building is over here." He pointed over to his right. "And do you see how the logs are half tongue-and-groove joints but the milk parlour has crown joints?"

"What's the difference?" Sam asked.

"Well the half dovetails are like the joins you would get on a piece of furniture, whereas the crown joins meet in the middle like the gable on a roof." Sam looked from one to the other.

"Yeah, I see it now. And the milking parlour is fed off the natural spring to help keep the milk fresh?"

"Exactly."

They rode up to the main corral and untacked the horses, putting their saddles on the fence. Almost immediately both horses rolled on the ground to dry any sweat patches. Billy and Sam went into the barn to see if there was any hay lying around. There were a couple of leaves left over from the previous cattle run so they took them to the pen and scattered them around.

Billy slipped his hand around Sam's waist and kissed her softly on the neck.

"Have you ever fooled around in a hay loft, Ms Hart?" Sam laughed.

"Why, Mr Dawson, what kind of woman do you take me for?" She waved her hand in front of her face mimicking the movement of a fan.

"Well, Ms Hart," Billy said, "if you don't mind me saying, you look like the kinda horny type of woman, begging your pardon, ma'am." Sam looked at him square in the eye.

"You know, Mr Dawson, you may well be right!" She ran her hand down his body and grabbed Billy's belt, pulling him in the direction of the barn. They climbed up the stairs to the loft, giggling as they went.

At the top, Billy stopped and told Sam he would be back in a minute. He ran outside and got the blanket he had packed to use for the picnic from the saddlebag. On reaching the top of the stairs he was greeted by the sight of Sam sitting on a bale of straw with no clothes on.

"See anything you like, Mr Dawson?" He missed a step and almost fell down the ladder.

"Well, er, I can see a couple of things that I would like to get my hands on, if you're up for it!" Billy had now made it halfway to where Sam was sitting.

"Well, Mr Dawson, I can certainly see you're up for it." Sam looked down then back up to catch Billy's eyes. She rose to her feet and embraced Billy, kissing him hard on the mouth. After a moment, he broke away and laid the blanket on the top of the straw then returned to where she stood to continued their embrace.

Late in the afternoon they lay in each other's arms, a thin film of sweat covering their bodies. Billy heard Ronin nicker and, knowing his horse, he knew something or someone was coming. Dressing quickly, they descended the ladder just in time to hear two male voices talking to the horses.

"Can I help you fellas?" Billy's tone was neutral

but assertive. The men's heads snapped around as their attention was suddenly drawn away from the horses. Both men looked Sam up and down before they spoke to Billy.

"Nice horses you have there, son." There were warning bells going off in Billy's head but it did not stop him from being curt in response.

"I know that. Now as I said, is there anything I can help you with, seeing as you are on my property?" As Billy spoke he gradually made his way over to where the saddles were sitting on the corral fence.

The men's faces dropped ever so slightly as Billy spoke. It was the taller of the two who took charge.

"Well first of all son, there ain't no signs out tellin' folks that this here is somebody's property. And secondly, I don't think either of us likes your tone." The tall guy turned to look at his smaller companion who was nodding in agreement while still undressing Sam with his eyes.

It was at that moment Billy noticed both men were wearing sidearms but they had not undone their safety straps, giving him a small advantage. He knew he had to change tack and allow the situation to mellow if there was any chance of getting out of this unscathed.

"Well I'm sorry for my tone," he said, "but you are on my parents' land and we are up here alone checking on things." He had managed to manoeuvre both himself and more importantly Sam away from the barn and within reach of the rifle that sat on the offside of his saddle.

"Well that's more like it, I knew you were the type whose parents taught him to respect their elders." As the tall guy spoke, he turned his attention to Sam. "Hey girl, are you his sister? Please say yes." Sam knew what Billy was up to. Although she was scared, she continued the conversation with the intruders.

"Why how did you guess? Not many folks see the resemblance!" She managed to keep the quiver out of her voice but didn't know how long it would stay that way.

"See that, Clint," the taller man said, "I knew she was his kin." The smaller of the two nodded in agreement. When he did speak it sent shivers up and down Sam's back.

"Yeah, you sure did Burt, I knew a gal that pure just had to be his kin. Why, you're so fine little lady, with everything wrapped up real tight." Clint was almost frothing at the mouth when Billy cocked the hammer back on the rifle.

"Mister, I don't like the way either of you are looking at my girl and before you do anything stupid, I'd appreciate it if you undid your gun belts and threw them over here." Billy moved the gun back and forth between the pair of what he now considered to be less than human scum.

The sound of the hammer going back on the Winchester got the men's attention.

"Now son, don't be doing anything foolish," Burt said, "We didn't mean no harm and we're both right sorry for any ill we have caused you or your gal, ain't that right, Clint?"

Clint, who was now looking down the barrel of the gun and not at Sam, nodded in agreement. The pair loosened their belts and threw them halfway between themselves and Billy. He reached over with his foot and dragged both belts closer without taking his eyes off his quarry.

It was at this point Billy caught a faint smell of stale whiskey coming from the direction of his new friends. All he could do was shake his head in disgust.

"Pretty dangerous game you fellas are playing, mixing whiskey and the outdoors. You're lucky it was me and not my dad that came upon you, 'cause he's the 'shoot first and ask questions later' type of rancher that you get in these parts." Billy embellished the truth a little but knew that most ranchers would get twitchy with these kinds of critters.

Sam came over next to Billy and retrieved the gun belts, then Billy spoke to the men one last time. "I will be contacting the local sheriff about you pair and if you want your guns back you will have to take that up with him. Now if you don't mind, I'd prefer that you did not spoil the rest of our day and you can go back the way you came." Pointing the gun over Burt's shoulder, Billy showed them the direction he wanted them to take and they hurried off without another word. He and Sam stood for a while as they watched the men go out of sight.

"You okay, honey? I'm sorry you had to endure those horrible bastards." Sam walked over to Billy and kissed him softly on the cheek.

"You were amazing, I thought..." Sam's words trailed off, but Billy knew what she was going to say and finished the sentence for her.

"Now I think the best course of action is we get the hell out of here and back to the ranch, sound like a plan?"

"Best idea I've heard today," Sam said. After saddling the horses and retrieving the blanket from the loft, they headed for home at a brisk pace.

Once back at the ranch and after they had told their tale to Margaret and Walter, Billy phoned the sheriff as he had promised. He came out, took a statement and recovered the guns taken off the men.

"It sounds like this pair came from off-state and they were on a drinking spree," Sheriff Seaforth said as he was leaving, "I'll get my boys to keep an eye on the place for the next few weeks and I'll be in touch if they come back for their guns."

"We are much obliged to you and your men for taking the trouble to come out to see us, and thank you for all of your help," Walter said as he shook the sheriff's hand and walked him out to his pickup.

Back in the kitchen, Walter joked, "Did you really tell those pair of coyotes up there that I would blast them? You do realise you were correct in your assumption?" Everyone laughed and it seemed to get rid of any tension that was left.

"Well if you young ones don't mind," Walter continued, "all this excitement has made me and your mother a little weary." He winked at Maggie.

"Yeah, you're right honey," she said, "Time for us old folks to hit the hay." Sam and Billy both burst out laughing at this, thinking about their own exploits in the hay loft.

Margaret bade them goodnight and followed Walter up the stairs. Sam cuddled into Billy and told him how proud she was of him and that he could now be called a hero for saving her. He blushed then kissed her softly on the forehead.

"I would never let anything bad happen to you," he said; words that would come back to haunt him in the weeks ahead.

Chapter Twenty-Eight

Back in the apartment, Billy and Sam relaxed with a coffee after their trip. Tomorrow they would be at college and into the familiar routine again.

"You know, Billy," Sam said, "I've really enjoyed our time together this week and your parents are awesome." She paused a moment. "The ranch and land are so pretty, a bit like my folks' home. So it will be my place next time, okay?"

Billy kissed her head. "Sure thing, honey." Sam had not told Billy but she loved it when he called her honey.

Later when Sam had headed home to unpack and grab some sleep, Billy called his folks to let them know he had arrived back safely. He had already made up his mind to take Raven and had discussed it with Walter, who was more than happy to have a 'new member' of the Dawson family, as he put it. Next thing Billy would have to do was to speak to Frank Hendriks and see if he would be willing to sell the colt.

It had been a long time since Billy had any nightmares, but that night he woke drenched in sweat and shouting Sam's name. He could not remember much about the dream that had caused this, but there was a part just before he woke when something bad had happened to Sam.

Billy got up and poured himself a glass of water and tried to put the dream out of his mind. Come morning, the first thing he did was text Sam, *Good morning*, to which she texted back, *And a howdy to you xxx*. Billy relaxed and chalked up his nightmare to how important Sam had become to him.

Seeing Frank out in the stock yard and quite far away, Billy had to shout. Frank stuck two fingers up in the air to indicate that he would be with him shortly. As Billy waited, he looked across at the black mustang which he hoped would soon be his. Watching the colt doze in his usual spot next to the water trough, Billy's mind wandered off to thoughts of Sam and their time up at the ranch.

"What can I do you for, Billy?"

"Jesus Christ, Frank." Billy jumped and his startled reply made them both laugh. "Sorry Frank, I was miles away there. I wanted to ask if there was any chance you could sell me that black colt." Frank rubbed his chin, which had about two days' growth of stubble. He pondered Billy's request for a moment.

"Well the way I see it, Billy, is that he is practically yours anyway given all the work you have put into him." Billy smiled. "So tell you what I'll do: to make it legal and all, if you show me some of that fancy horse training you do, then you can have him. Sound like a deal?" Billy was almost overcome by emotion. He dropped his gaze and reached out his right hand, which Frank shook.

"This means a lot to me Frank, and it would be my honour to show you what I do." Billy's voice trembled. It was at this point Frank said something that would stay with Billy for the rest of his life.

"Don't be ashamed of your tears, son. They show your passion for the work you do. It's this that most folks lack: they don't put their heart into it. Your work should always come from the heart." Billy looked back up at Frank with tears flowing freely.

"I know that sir, it's why I do this." The two men smiled as they released their grip and Frank patted Billy's shoulder as he headed back towards the building. Once Billy had regained his composure, he walked down to the Raven's pen and called out to him.

Billy rang his father. "Hi Dad, got that horse I told you about." There was a small pause.

"Son, that's great news." There was genuine happiness in Walter's voice.

"Yeah, I was thinking about bringing him up in a couple of weeks, is that okay?"

"That's great, son. If you can get me a definite date nearer the time, I'll prepare things at this end."

"Thanks Dad, talk soon." He was about to hang up when Walter spoke again.

"Before you go, Sheriff Seaforth came round today and gave us an update on those guys that were up at the old cattle station. They turned up to collect their guns and it was like we figured – they were from out of state, a couple of clowns looking for trouble. Tom put them in the cells for the night and really put the fear in them." Billy smiled. "Then he got one of his deputies to drive them to the state line with orders never to show their faces this side of it again." Again, Billy chuckled.

"Tom Seaforth is a good man. I'll pop up to see him when I drop the horse off. Gotta go, love you and the same for Mom, give her a big hug for me." With that Billy hit the red phone symbol on his screen and put the mobile back in his pocket. He sat for a moment thinking, *That will show those assholes*, then walked to his next class.

That night, Billy told Sam what the sheriff had done to the two men.

"Those bastards had that coming," she said, "and I'm so glad they got their guns confiscated, fucking morons." Sitting at his end of the couch, Billy teased her.

"Samantha Hart, you're nothing but a trash mouth." Sam threw a cushion at Billy and it hit him square in the face, making them both laugh. Billy then told Sam the news about Raven.

"Honey, that's such good news. I think for Frank you are the perfect owner for that horse." Moving to the end of the couch she straddled Billy and they kissed passionately. "Are you taking him up yourself?" she asked.

"Yes, it's usually a two-day drive but if I leave early I could do it in less. I know you have your exams coming up and it's best you focus on them rather than bouncing around the countryside with me pulling a horse trailer." This was frustrating for Sam because she really wanted to go but knew in her heart that Billy was right. She had already lost revision time with their previous trip.

"I hate it when you're right," she replied, kissing him softly on the nose, "It's like living with a goddam oracle." They both laughed. Billy reached up, putting the fingertips of both hands against his temples and closed his eyes.

"I see a night of passion for you…" – he opened one eye then quickly closed it – "…followed by a lovely late supper." When Billy opened his eyes again, Sam was sitting with her arms across her chest.

"Well Mr Oracle, the supper sounds good but the passion is up for negotiation." She picked up a cushion and thumped Billy on the side of his head. He pulled his handkerchief from his pocket and waved it in surrender.

When Sam finally put down the cushion, Billy said, "Food first, then?"

"Okay."

The day before the big move, Billy was hitching the pickup to the trailer which Frank had loaned him. Once it was securely attached, Billy filled two hay bags for Raven then put what was left of the bale up front in a secure locker along with two large containers water and a basic first aid kit.

Just at that moment Frank appeared.

"Ah, prepared for the journey then?" Billy wiped the sweat off his forehead.

"Reckon so, all I need is the horse."

"Thought you might need these." Frank handed Billy a folder containing paperwork. "It's all the documentation for the colt. Good luck with the trip and I'll see you when you get back." With that, Frank turned to leave but Billy called him back.

"Listen Frank, I really appreciate all you have done for me, can't thank you enough." Billy held out his hand to shake with Frank.

"You take it easy on the road, and if you hit any

snags give me a call, okay?" The older man turned and headed towards a group of students waiting at the far end of the yard.

After Frank was gone, Billy parked the trailer next to Raven's pen. "Hey boy," he called out to the colt as he walked round to open the back doors. Billy thought it good practice to see if Raven had any hang-ups about being loaded. Most horses brought to the campus had travelled in some sort of transport, usually the big livestock rigs, with some coming in smaller units. Billy would have to see where Raven was with being in the trailer.

Raven soon came across to inspect it.

"Hey buddy, you wanna go inside?" Raven shifted his gaze from the vehicle to Billy who had stayed next to the gate of the pen with the halter draped over his arm. As the colt walked over, he rubbed his head against Billy's chest and the gesture made Billy smile.

"Yeah buddy, it's for you." As a rule, Billy always had hay for the horses when they travelled even short distances, as seeing hay could give the horse a positive association in an unfamiliar environment. Billy also knew that if the horse was not eating the hay it could show an underlying tension.

He haltered Raven and led him out to the trailer. As a way of setting things up, Billy had given the colt a little less hay previously. This he hoped would make Raven more eager to load as he could eat inside. As suspected, Raven walked in easily and went straight to the bag to eat. After repeating this a few times, Billy returned Raven to his pen where he topped up his hay and removed a few droppings. He stood watching for a while then decided to head for home.

As he walked away he called out, "Big day tomorrow, boy!"

The glow off the sun clock woke Sam, who turned around to look at it: 4.25am. She was always amazed at how the body's natural systems would pick up the change in ambient light in the room. Sam rolled over and kissed Billy softly on the cheek.

"Come on sleepy head, you're burning daylight." Billy woke with a sigh.

"Jesus, I had a really weird dream. I was in a pine forest, really dark. And no matter where I went or how far I travelled there was no way out. I've not had a dream like that since I was kid." Sam cuddled into him.

"It's probably just your subconscious fretting about the road trip with Raven." She kissed him softly again trying to allay any fears.

"Guess you're right," Billy said quietly, "No need to overthink things." He got out of bed and headed in the direction of the bathroom. Switching the light on he turned to Sam.

"Do you want to wash my back?" He winked and switched the shower on but when he turned back round Sam was gone. He stood with a puzzled look on his face until he heard the shower door close with its usual clunk. As he turned he could see Sam's naked form through the mist created by the hot water.

Billy opened the door and stepped inside.

"It's like living with a goddamn ninja," Sam giggled with delight as Billy's hands sent waves of pleasure shooting through her body.

Later as they ate breakfast, Sam asked if she could stay at Billy's place while he was away.

"I'd feel closer to you lying in your bed." Billy reached across the table and took her hand.

"It's only a couple of days, max. But if it makes you feel better, sure." Sam smiled and squeezed his hand.

"I've made you two flasks of coffee to get you started and also sandwiches: cheese, tomato and ham." Billy stood up and took the small lunch bag then kissed the top of Sam's head.

"I'd better be going, you know what they say: the quicker you leave the faster you return. Love you, honey." Sam hugged Billy.

"I love you too. Give me a call when you get there." Hugging her back, Billy said,

"I will", then stepped out into the cold of the early morning.

As he pulled into the campus yard, Billy could see Raven standing with his coat fluffed against the cold. Plumes of mist billowed from the colt's nostrils every time he exhaled. Billy reversed up to the trailer and hitched it with a clunk. He attached the trailer light, lifted the jockey wheel and opened the back door ready for Raven. Billy then cleared the overnight droppings and left the pen in a good condition for the next occupant.

Raven loaded with no fuss.

"Wait till you see your new home," Billy said, "You're gonna love it." With a final pat on the neck, he left Raven munching his hay and closed the doors. Driving slowly out of the yard, he was pleasantly surprised that Raven did not call out to any of the other horses. Billy knew that when moving a horse for whatever reason it generally called out if tense. When this didn't happen, he knew Raven was quite content.

Billy had planned a couple of stops where he and more importantly Raven could have a stretch and get a break from the monotony of the road. At the first of these, he found a patch of grass and let Raven tuck into the tender green shoots. This was something he had done back on campus to help prepare the colt for the trip.

After Raven had spent a while eating, Billy took him back to the trailer and tied him to one of the rings on the side. He then fetched a hay bag and a bucket of water while he tucked into Sam's coffee and sandwiches. As he ate, he thought: 'a third of the way there, we should make it home for six or seven o'clock, just in time for supper'.

Chapter Twenty-Nine

Since Jordan Pope had been expelled from college, his life had hit the skids. After a massive argument with his parents who told him to "come back and see us when you've grown up", things had gone from bad to worse. Jordan had always liked a drink but in his current mental state he hit the bars most nights, drinking himself into a stupor then returning the next day for more. It was during one of these benders that a friend offered him some cocaine. This was like throwing petrol on a fire to put it out. From that point he became more unbalanced, turning to stealing to feed his addiction.

The person Jordan blamed for all his woes was Billy Dawson. As he sat in the bar downing shot after shot of whiskey, he became more and more angry with each drink. The other men at the bar just shook their heads as Jordan mumbled about all the depraved things he would like to do to Billy and his bitch, Sam.

"Fucking Dawson, I'd like to open that cunt up and spill his guts over the floor. And his bitch, I have something here I'd like to stick in her." Jordan reached down with his left hand and rubbed the growing bulge inside his jeans, causing a few of his fellow patrons to move further down the bar, much to Jordan's displeasure.

"What the fuck do you know anyway?" he roared as they moved away, his words tailing off as he downed another shot. Slamming the glass down rim-first,

Jordan got up and headed in the direction of the rest room. He almost fell through the door as he fumbled for something in the pocket of his jeans: a small deal bag of cocaine which he threw on the worktop next to the wash hand basin.

He looked in the mirror and reflected back was a pale reflection of the once athletic freshman. As if to rid himself of the image, Jordan washed his face and wiped his wet hands down the mirror, nodding his approval. Next he turned his attention to the bag of white powder, emptying its contents on to the driest part of the flat surface before using his credit card to separate the small pile into two neat lines. He took out a ten-dollar bill and rolled it into a tight tube, bending over and snorting the lines one after the other, rubbing the leftovers on the gum above his teeth. The effect was immediate. With the drug coursing through his veins on top of the alcohol, Jordan felt almost invincible.

He left the bar, went to the nearest liquor store and bought a bottle of Jack Daniel's. Then he wandered along the main street until he reached a pawn shop where he looked in the window at the goods on offer. The first and only thing that caught Jordan's eye was a 9mm Colt pistol. He stared long and hard at the gun then entered the shop where he spoke to the man behind the caged counter.

"I'd like to see the Colt you have in the window." The silver-haired shopkeeper went to the window, returned with the gun and placed it on the counter in front of Jordan. He picked it up to feel the weight in his hand. It felt good.

Putting the gun down, Jordan looked the old man

in the eye. "I'll take it." The shopkeeper asked him for ID but instead of showing him any, Jordan said, "I'll give you double what you're asking if you give it to me now." The old man reached up and turned the camera covering the counter to the wall.

"Okay, I can do that, but I'll take that watch you have as well." Jordan undid the strap and tossed the watch across the counter. Next he pulled out some bills and threw them across, too.

"You drive a hard bargain, old man. I want some ammo for free." The man disappeared and returned with a box of bullets and placed it next to the gun.

"Nice doing business with you, son," he said grinning, "Come back any time." Jordan put the ammunition in his pocket, tucked the gun into his belt and headed off with just one destination in mind.

Sam was relaxing on the couch with a cup of hot chocolate. She kept looking at her phone, hoping Billy would call soon and put her fears at ease. Eventually she got up, put some toast on then ran a bath before returning to the lounge to check her phone again. There was a knock at the door. On opening it, she was confronted by the unexpected figure of Jordan Pope. He shoved her back inside and closed the door behind him.

"Where's Dawson?" Sam stood baffled so Jordan asked her again, this time more forcefully. "Where the fuck is Billy?" The outburst snapped Sam out of her daze.

"He... he's gone home, to take a horse back to his folks' place. He'll be back tomorrow." Her voice started to quiver as she spoke.

Jordan shoved Sam on to the sofa then paced back and forth in an effort to think more clearly. He pulled the Jack Daniel's from his pocket, took a few gulps, then slammed the bottle down on the kitchen worktop. When he turned back round to Sam he had an ugly grin on his face.

"Well if your boyfriend ain't here then we can have a little fun, don't you think?" Alarms were going off all over Sam's mind as Jordan had the same look on his face as the two men at the cattle station.

"What kinda fun did you have in mind?" Sam hated herself for talking to him this way, it made her sick to her stomach.

"You know, fun!" Jordan's gaze dropped to Sam's breasts. She took the chance to reach behind him and get a grip of the whiskey bottle. Jordan's hand had worked its way up from her waist and had begun to cup a breast when there was a flash of pain through the left side of his head as Sam smashed the bottle over him hard. She wriggled free and ran for the door but did not make it.

With the remnants of the cocaine running through his veins, Jordan was only dazed by the impact. He slammed into her back and pinned her against the door. The force of the impact knocked the wind out of Sam but she still had enough fight in her to push Jordan away. He reached around and pulled the Colt from his waistband.

"Fucking bitch, if I can't have you no one will." Sam lunged at Jordan and grabbed the gun. They wrestled in what she knew was a life-or-death struggle. It would only be a matter of time before Jordan overpowered her so she bit hard into his face, feeling his warm blood flow into her mouth.

Jordan roared with pain. His finger found the trigger of the gun and Sam fell backward with blood seeping through her top. She slumped against the couch holding her midriff, moaning with the pain.

Using the back of his hand to wipe blood from where Sam had bit him, Jordan looked down at her.

"I never meant to hurt you. I love…" Cutting himself off, he ran from the apartment.

Sam was on the verge of passing out. She crawled across to the table, reached up and knocked the phone to the floor then pressed 911.

"Emergency, what service do you require?" Sam spoke to the operator in a weak voice. "I've been shot in the stomach and…" She passed out. The operator again and again tried to get a response.

"Ma'am, ma'am, can you hear me? Help is on its way, help is on its way."

Chapter Thirty

Billy was glad to be nearly home: he was very tired and needed a rest. He turned off the highway and on to the familiar dirt road that led to the Dawson Ranch. As he pulled into the driveway he could see that a pen had been set up next to Ronin's with a trough for water and fresh hay ready for the new arrival.

Walter opened the pickup door and patted Billy on the shoulder.

"How was the trip, son?" Billy got out and smiled.

"Tiring." They walked together to the back of the trailer and opened the door. Raven turned round from his hay bag for a moment then went back to eating.

"He seems really settled in there," Walter said with a hint of surprise, "Doesn't even have any sweat on him."

"Yeah, he travels pretty well for a mustang," Billy said, "Think we should get him into the pen and let him meet Ronin." Billy undid the lead rope and walked Raven out of the trailer and into his temporary home. Raven went to the trough for a big drink then to the side of the pen next to Ronin where the two horses eyed each other. After a few moments, both returned to their hay and seemed to lose interest in one another.

"Well that was boring," Walter said, "but as I've always said, boring is good." They laughed and headed back to the house. Before going in, Billy parked the trailer and got his bag. Walking back from the pickup, he could see Margaret standing on the porch with the phone in her hand. She called out to him.

"It's Samantha!" Billy's initial thought was, 'Jeez, I'm just in the door and she's looking for me'. He had a secret chuckle to himself then he saw his mother's expression. He knew there was something dreadfully wrong.

Billy flew back immediately and was met at the airport by Frank Hendriks.

"Really sorry to hear about Sam." Billy could only nod his thanks. "They say she's stable but that's all I know." The two men got into Frank's pickup and went straight to the hospital. As they drove, Frank filled Billy in on some details.

"Before they put Sam in a coma she said that Jordan Pope had come to your apartment looking for you. When he found out you weren't there, he tried to rape and kill her instead." Billy's mind raced as he thought of how frightened Sam must have been.

"Where is that piece of trash now?" He spat his words out as his anger built.

"Police searched for him and found his body down by the river," Frank said, "He killed himself with the gun he used to shoot Samantha." The words came as no comfort to Billy. He sat staring straight ahead wondering what awaited him at the hospital.

As they reached the entrance, they could see a few reporters hanging around.

"Thought this might happen," Frank said, "We'll go round back." Turning down a side street, they drew up at some the delivery doors at the back of the hospital. Frank banged on one of the doors three times and was greeted by the night porter.

"We're closed!" he said. Frank smiled at the elderly gentleman.

"This is the boyfriend of the girl who was shot. There are reporters out front and I was wondering…" Before he could finish his sentence, the man ushered them inside.

"I'm real sorry, son," the porter said to Billy as they walked through into the hospital, "Bad thing that's happened to your girl. My wife is saying a prayer at church for her tonight." He directed them to the main reception.

"This is where I have to leave you," Frank said once Billy had been told what ward Sam was in. "It's an awful business what's happened and our prayers are with you. Samantha's a strong girl, let's hope she fights this all the way." Billy watched Frank make his way out of the main entrance then took the elevator to the third floor and walked to the nurses' station.

"Hi, my name is Billy Dawson and I'm here to see…"

"Samantha," the nurse said before he could finish. She told him that she had been operated on and was being brought out of her coma.

"You have just missed her parents," the nurse said, "they were just here half an hour ago." Billy thought about Sam's parents and the hell they must be going through.

"Can I see her?" he asked. The nurse checked with the sister in charge and was told it would be okay, but not for too long.

"You know Samantha kept calling your name before they took her to theatre," the nurse said, "She's in the second room on the left. Remember to use the hand sanitizer before you enter and after you leave."

Billy walked quickly to the room, which smelled strongly of disinfectant. Sam lay on the bed with her eyes closed amid a plethora of tubes and wires. Billy was shocked at her appearance. There was little colour in her cheeks and she looked older. He took her right hand in his and kissed it, then heard his name whispered weakly. He looked at Sam's face: her eyes were still closed but her lips had parted slightly. She called his name again, this time with a little more strength.

"I'm here, honey," Billy said, "I'm here." As he brushed the hair from the side of her face, she opened her eyes a little.

"Hey you, I missed you so much when you were gone." Her voice was barely a whisper. Billy asked if she wanted some water and she said yes. He held the glass to her mouth until she shook her head.

"I missed you, too," Billy said, "I'm so sorry this has happened and I'd give anything to make it go away." Sam raised her hand and placed a finger on his lips.

"You didn't do this, that piece of shit Pope did this. I hope he rots in jail." She coughed slightly and Billy offered more water. After putting down the glass, he told Sam what Jordan Pope had done to himself.

"Fucking coward," she said. Billy was surprised at how lucid Sam seemed.

They stared into each other's eyes for a moment, then Sam said something totally unexpected.

"Billy Dawson, I want to marry you." Billy laughed.

"It's an unusual place for a proposal and isn't it me who should do the asking?" Sam just looked into his eyes waiting for an answer. "Yes, I'll marry you, Samantha Hart," Billy said.

Sam's whole face beamed as the alarms went off on the monitor next to her bed. Billy looked at the machine and back at Sam, whose eyes had rolled back in her head. He held her face and called her name – "Sam, Sam, Sam" – but two nurses rushed into the room and ushered him into the corridor.

Billy watched as a doctor ran into the room. He sat in one of the chairs in the corridor and sobbed openly. An orderly of some sort went into the room and soon emerged with the nursing staff wheeling Sam on her bed. Billy tried to talk to the doctor but was waved aside as they headed for the elevators.

He went to the nurse's desk.

"Do you know what's happening with Samantha Hart, my girlfriend?" His voice was bordering on frantic. It was the same nurse he had spoken to earlier.

"She's been rushed to theatre, that's all we know. Her blood pressure crashed. I'm sorry, I have nothing more to tell you."

Billy went back to his seat in the corridor, exhausted with the turmoil.

Three hours later and Billy had fallen asleep in his chair. He woke with a start when a porter moving an empty bed caught the side of the elevator door. As soon as he had got his bearings, Billy was about to ask the nurse if there was any news when the doctor he had seen earlier headed in his direction.

"Mr Dawson?" Billy nodded. "Would you come with me please?" Billy followed the doctor to a room next to the nurses' station where he was asked to take a seat. His gut churned.

"Mr Dawson, my name is Dr Grey. I'm the head trauma resident who dealt with Samantha when she came in." There was a sombre tone to the doctor's voice. "There is no easy way to say this to you but unfortunately Samantha never regained consciousness during the operation." The world was crashing around Billy. "I'm sorry to tell you that she has died."

Billy was silent for a moment before saying just a single word: "How?" Dr Grey said they suspected that when Sam was shot, the bullet had grazed her aorta which would not have been obvious during the initial surgery. The aorta then ruptured causing massive internal bleeding.

"Because it is an attempted murder, an autopsy is necessary and the coroner will find the cause of death," the doctor said, "Once again, Mr. Dawson, we are all sorry for your loss." With that he left Billy in the room alone.

Billy broke down and cried the tears of a man who had lost a part of his very being. He screamed Sam's name at the top of his voice. One of the nurses came in and sat holding his hand.

After a few minutes he composed himself enough to ask the nurse if he could see Sam.

"I'm sorry, Billy," the nurse said, "but hospital rules will not allow us to do that for you, only the immediate family can grant you permission." Billy just nodded and thanked her for being there for him, then pulled out his mobile and called Frank as he entered the elevator.

Frank said he was in the hospital car park; if Billy waited in reception he would be there as soon as he could. As Billy left the elevator and walked down the corridor, he saw a man holding a crying woman and immediately realised it was Sam's parents. He walked briskly towards them but what happened next stunned him. He made eye contact with Sam's father who looked solemnly in Billy's direction. Sam's mother, however, launched herself at him.

"You bastard, you bastard," she screamed, "My daughter is dead because of you, you and that son of a bitch that pulled the trigger. None of this would have happened if she had not met you, I never want to see you again…" Her words trailed off as she collapsed on the floor. Billy looked at Sam's father for a moment then walked on with fresh tears pouring down his face. The reception was a blur: all he wanted was to get outside. He sat down and in a short while felt a hand around his forearm.

"Billy, Billy, it's Frank." His tutor ushered him out of the hospital and past the pack of reporters.

Billy watched as Sam's coffin was lowered into the ground. He stood next to a tree and waited as the group of mourners grew smaller and smaller until only Sam's mother, father and the men from the funeral home remained. When they too had left, he waited until the cemetery workers had done their job and moved on. Only then did he dare make his way down to where his beloved Sam was interred.

Grief tore at Billy's body like a wild beast desperate

to feed. He fell to his knees on the grass at the foot of the grave and sobbed. Reaching forward with both hands, he grasped lumps of freshly tilled soil until his fists shook with emotion.

"Why did you leave me, Sam? We were going to spend our lives together, now it's like there's no point continuing." As he spoke, his body convulsed. "I wish it had been me, I wish it was me who had been shot and you could have lived with your mom and dad back at the ranch. You are so beautiful, Sam. I remember that first day we met like it had happened this morning. You looked so good that day and..." He fell silent, curled into a ball and rocked himself back and forth.

This was how Frank Hendriks found him, broken and lost, ten minutes later. In the weeks that followed, Billy dropped out of college and gave up the apartment where he and Sam had spent so many happy times. But before he left for his parents' place, Frank spoke with him.

"If there's anything you need or if you change your mind about the job offer, call me." Billy shook Frank's hand then hugged him.

"I owe you so much," he said. With that, the men got in their respective pickups and drove off in different directions. It would be many years before Billy found his way back to town.

Part Three

Chapter Thirty-One

The sign outside the main arena at the Equine Affaire Ohio, one of the premier equine expositions in the US, read: 'Tonite a demonstration in horsemanship by renowned horseman Billy Dawson'. People hurried to their seats and there was a buzz of expectation from all who had gathered to see not only Billy but also several other well-known horsemen and women. Some people had even brought along a copy of Billy's latest book, *Finding a Softer Way*, in the hope that they could get it signed.

As usual with these types of events, there was a lot of glitz and glamour before the demonstration started; this was something Billy tolerated but only barely. Once the lights had stopped flashing and spinning and the main show lights came on, Billy and Ronin stood in the middle of the arena as the crowd whooped, whistled and applauded their presence. Billy's voice crackled into life through the arena's PA system.

"Well hello Ohio, thank you for the lovely welcome." More applause broke out around the arena. Billy waited till it died down before continuing. "Tonight we will be looking at a couple of horses that are struggling to find where they fit into the whole working-with-humans deal. Hopefully with a little encouragement, we can get them moving forward." There were a lot of hoots and whistles and again Billy waited patiently, then spoke one final time before getting the first horse in.

"I will be ably assisted tonight by my constant companion Ronin, who has been my best friend for over twenty years now. We hope you enjoy the show!"

The spotlight crossed the arena and focused on two wooden gates at the far end. A tall thin man held on to a lively young warm blood sorrel, which was running half-circles around him as he tried to manage the long line. As horse and handler manoeuvred themselves to his end of the arena, Billy sat quietly on Ronin then switched on his headset.

"So this young knucklehead has, as we can see, some excess energy and boundary issues. She is a Dutch warm blood called Ruby who has aspirations of becoming a dressage horse."

Billy shared a smile with Ruby's handler as a ripple of laughter spread around the audience. With the introductions done, he got down off Ronin and walked towards the young warm blood's handler.

"I can see that this horse is not one of yours," he said, smiling at the handler who was called Bob. Billy then took hold of Ruby and thanked Bob for his hard work. As soon as Billy had taken over the long line, the horse's energy changed from high gear to low.

"Well, that was a nice little change," Billy said through the PA, "It seems to me that Ruby has been left to her own devices for some time, which we cannot blame her for. It's not the horse's fault that no one has instilled any rules, for want of a better word. She is blameless in this instance." As he spoke, Billy worked Ruby in a small circle around him, changing direction every couple of laps to try and give the horse the proper direction she lacked.

After he had worked the mare for a few minutes, he untracked her hind quarters and halted her quite abruptly. The mare stood panting and her coat was dark and glossy with sweat.

"As you can see, this mare has no fitness but also she's getting a sweat on because there's quite a bit of change going on with her right now." Billy paused before continuing. "I'll let her stand for a while before we get started again." There was complete silence in the arena, something Billy liked as it meant the audience had made a connection to what was happening in front of them.

After a few moments, Billy walked up to the mare and asked her to drop her head so he could rub her forelock, which she did without hesitation. Next he walked along her right side and tracked left when he reached her quarters. As he did this the tension in the line tipped the mare's head towards him and sent the hind end in the opposite direction. Once the mare had completed a small half-circle, she ended up about ten feet behind Billy following in his footfalls.

"As you can see," Billy said, "that little turn I did there sets the horse up to track in behind me and that's all she has to do: follow my feet. If she cuts to the inside or outside I'll quietly redirect her back into position behind me. Doing this takes the pressure off the horse when it comes to making decisions and also gets her to follow my direction. I'll make one thing clear: I'm not going to lead her around like this back at the barn, but I have found that this exercise, along with the next few, really have a benefit in creating a good relationship with your horse and showing them clearly where they are in this shared space."

Billy then passed the line behind his back and into the other hand then turned left. The mare followed without getting out of position.

"Next I'm going to ask for a halt. I will do this by turning and facing Ruby. The important part of this stop is that when I turn, Ruby's first front foot to hit the ground does not get past the other one – and if it does, well I'll ask her to back up, because she has encroached into my safe zone. Also, prior to the stop I'll put my eyes on Ruby to let her know something is going to happen. Watch closely, this is pretty cool!"

Standing in front of the mare, Billy repeated the previous exercise but this time accentuated locking eyes with Ruby, causing her to drop her speed slightly. Once she had slowed he turned softly, bringing her to a nice halt outside his safe zone. There was a ripple of applause which got Ruby on her toes, but still she did not break the invisible barrier that lay between her and her handler.

As the noise dissipated, Billy walked up to Ruby and once again rubbed her forelock then repeated this over her shoulders and down along her flank. The mare's expression had softened quiet considerably since the start of the demonstration. Billy now got ready for the next exercise.

"I'm going to take up the same position as before but with a slight difference this time. I always try to set things up so the horse can get things right, so by stepping out to the right" – he sidestepped two paces – "she has a bigger gap to her right which hopefully will encourage her to choose that direction." Taking the slack out of the line, Billy pointed with his left hand in the direction he wanted the mare to go and she duly obliged.

He then rolled in behind her shoulder roughly level with where the stirrup lay, driving her forward with his right hand which contained the coiled slack from the long line. The mare walked at a brisk pace sending small plumes of dust into the air every time her foot struck the ground. After a lap or two, Billy changed Ruby's direction and kept the mare walking out.

"As you can see," he said, "Ruby is moving out pretty well and I'm only prompting her when I feel she needs it. Basically, it's best to do as little as possible that gets in the horse's way. Now we will see what her trot is like. When I'm asking her to go up a gear, my technique is simple. I visualise what I'm looking for, seeing it in my mind and body, then moving into the mare I speed her walk up." Ruby started to walk faster. "And if at this point the horse is still walking, I could prompt with the end of my line."

Ruby leapt forward into a trot bordering on a canter.

"Well ain't that a mess?" Billy said with a laugh, "Let's see if we can sort this out a little better. Again, as with the walk, the trot has its own rhythm which is a two-beat and this mare is surviving at the moment, so her trot is rather racy. Using myself as a reference point, I will slow down my internal rhythm and see if we can ask her to match it."

Billy went quiet for a moment then his voice came over the PA again.

"I'm changing to a slower rhythm now." The audience watched as the mare's speed gradually began to change, slowing from a 121212 beat to a more balanced 1--2--1--2--1--2. There were a few gasps as the crowd realised they were witnessing something completely different from anything they had seen in the horse world.

"Ain't that the coolest thing you have ever seen?" Billy said, "I never get tired of connecting to a horse on this kind of level, it's a very humbling experience, always gets me right here." There was a quiver in his voice and he put his hand on the centre of his chest.

"And for me that's where all your training should begin, with your heart. If you put nothing of yourself into your horse work then I'm sorry to say you will receive nothing in return. There has to be a connection, be it emotional, physical or spiritual. Without this it's all just mechanics."

As Billy spoke, he stopped Ruby and walked to where she stood. The mare dropped her head and allowed Billy to cradle it in his arms. "Good girl, you did great." He rubbed the mare all over and addressed the crowd one last time.

"All of your horses can get like this. Some take a little training, others take to it like a duck to water, just like this little lady right here. That's the end, folks. If you have any questions or you want a book signed, I'll see you out in the main hall. Thanks for your company and have a nice night." The crowd rose to their feet and applauded vigorously at what they had just seen. There were hoots, whistles and the occasional "We love you Billy" as he made his way out of the arena where, once again, he was met by Ruby's handler, Bob.

"There you go, sir," Billy said, "She's a real sweet

mare, just needs a little work." Billy handed the rope over to Bob who had the biggest smile on his face.

"You know something, Mr Dawson," he said, "I've seen a lot of horsemen over the years but that was in a different league to any of 'em. It's something I know I'll take to the grave with me." Bob reached out his open hand and Billy took it.

"That's very kind of you Bob, but don't be leaving us too soon – the earth's a better place with folks like you on it, not under it." Both men laughed then Billy headed back into the arena to fetch Ronin who was standing quietly where he had been left at the start of the demonstration.

On sensing Billy's approach, Ronin rose from his resting state and greeted him with a soft nicker.

"Come on, old boy, we'll get you bedded down. You'd like that, wouldn't you?" Ronin snorted as if in agreement with Billy's idea.

They headed out to where the trailers were parked. Billy took the saddle off and put it in the tack room at the back of the trailer then took Ronin to the little holding pen on the other side of the truck.

"There you go boy, all you would ever need: hay, water and a bed." Ronin immediately tucked into the hay and Billy headed back to the main hall.

As Billy sat down at his stall there was a line of people as far as he could see. It was going to be a long day. A range spoke to him over the next couple of hours. Some wanted advice about their horse, to which Billy said: "If I can't see the horse in person then I'm afraid that I have no idea what the issue may or may not be".

Others were looking for a better way to be with their horses. Most were simply horse-owners glad to see a softer way to work with their animals.

The line dwindled to the last few and Billy ducked under the table to get another few books. The next person at the stall was a middle-aged woman. She had a book in her hand and sat it gently on the table with the title facing Billy.

"Could you sign it to Ruth please?" Billy's head snapped up with instant recognition and he almost fell off his chair with a mixture of emotion and surprise.

"Ms... Ms Drake?" He scrambled around the table and embraced Ruth. They sobbed into the other's shoulders before Billy broke contact long enough to finish signing the books of the last few people left in the queue. He then took Ruth by the hand and they headed to the canteen.

"My God Ruth, you look amazing, how – where – have you been?" Ruth laughed and took Billy's hand across the table.

"Well, first of all my name is now Collins, I keep Drake as my middle name. My husband was in the air force and died in Afghanistan in a chopper accident." Billy could see the pain in Ruth's face and squeezed her hand.

"We did not have any children," Ruth continued, "as we were planning to do so when he finished his tour. You always think you have time but sometimes life can play cruel tricks." Billy told Ruth about Sam all those years ago. As they consoled each other, one of the canteen staff brought a pot of coffee. She said nothing, smiling politely as she left them to talk about past losses.

Once they had caught up, Ruth looked over to Billy and smiled.

"I always knew you were going to end up doing something very special, and I had an idea it would be with horses after seeing you with them back on the farm." She reached across and took his hands. "You, my boy, have a very rare and special gift. You're just like Walter, you know that, don't you?" Billy laughed.

"Walter's a one-off, I'm just a poor example of a student. I'm sure Dad would laugh if he heard you comparing us." Ruth smiled and looked him straight in the eye.

"Most people would have been crushed by your experiences," she said, "and I'm not just talking about your childhood. You seem to have the ability to turn the most negative situations into life lessons without losing yourself in the process." Billy fidgeted with his coffee cup for a moment before looking back at Ruth.

"I've been lost so many times that I gave up counting. Having the horses was always something I could fall back on but I do carry my share of scars, like most folk do. You may not see mine on the outside but they're there."

He decided to change the subject. "Are you still teaching?" Ruth smiled.

"Once a teacher, always a teacher. I did leave the classroom for a while but got bored and disillusioned and found my way back." She shrugged her shoulders.

"Some things you are just born to do," Billy said,

"I never thought I'd end up being a teacher as well, but here we are twenty years later. Fate." It was his turn to shrug, which made Ruth smile.

They sat quietly for a few moments before Ruth spoke again.

"Are you in town for long?" she asked. Billy sighed.

"Two more days then it's back to the ranch for a break before heading out again. Equine hobo." Ruth laughed again.

"Well I was thinking that if you have time, we could go out for dinner before you leave." Without hesitation Billy agreed, then Ruth stood up and pushed her chair under the table.

"I've taken up enough of your time and we have to save some conversation to reminisce over dinner." With that she kissed Billy softly on his cheek and whispered in his ear. "I'm so proud of what you have achieved."

As he watched her walk away, Billy tried hard to keep a check on his emotions and was doing fine until Ruth turned and called to him: "I still have your dreamcatcher hanging above my bed and I've dreamt of this day for so many years." She smiled and disappeared among the crowd leaving the event.

Chapter Thirty-Two

It was Billy's last day at Equine Affaire Ohio. The event had been good with the horses making some progress, which was always nice to see for all concerned. As he stood in the pen brushing down Ronin after a long day under the saddle, Billy's mind drifted off and latched on to a memory that found him back at his parents' ranch a year after Samantha's death.

Sitting in the old cattle station, Billy took another drink from a bottle of cheap whiskey. He could not remember how or when he had taken to drinking but knew it took the hurt away, for a while at least. He would come up to the station every now and again when he felt like the world was collapsing in on him. Here he could remember all the good times with Sam then wipe away the memory of them as he emptied the bottle.

Walter and Margaret had no idea that Billy drank and he was going to keep it that way; he wanted to suffer alone and did not want to burden his parents with grief. A lot of the time the only ones he could confide in were Ronin and Raven. For their part, all they could do was allow themselves to be conduits for his emotions.

As Billy sat near the front of the barn, he heard the familiar sound of Walter's pickup so he hid the bottle out of sight. He went to the water trough in the paddock and ducked his head fully under in the hope that the cold water would sober him up –it did, but only partially. As the pickup pulled in at the front of the barn, Billy dried his face with his shirttails and walked around from the trough just in time to greet Walter.

"Hi Dad, what brings you up here?" Walter's reply was short and to the point.

"You do." Billy knew by his father's tone that this was not a social call.

"What can I do for you?" A knot of tension formed in Billy's stomach. Walter took a deep breath before speaking, mostly to help him clear his head for what he was about to say to his son, but also to dispel any anger that sat within him.

"I know losing Samantha has hurt you deeply. I can't think of anything worse than losing someone you love and we can only try to support you through the pain." Walter's eyes never left Billy's. "But what I will not allow is for you to drink your life away at the bottom of a whiskey bottle." A cold chill ran through Billy's whole body as it dawned on him that his parents did know about his supposed secret drinking.

"I came up here to keep it away from the ranch," Billy said in an attempt to explain himself, "Here I can lose myself without..." Walter finished Billy's sentence. "Involving us. Did you think we were blind to your grief? Jesus Christ, son, if it hurts you it affects us all, as a family!" The tone of Walter's voice was sympathetic but firm. "Drinking yourself into oblivion will not take the hurt away, it's something you just have to accept and carry with you."

Billy slumped down at the side of the pickup with his head in his hands and sobbed.

"I miss her so much, Dad, so much." Walter knelt

beside Billy and cradled his head against his chest.

"We have already lost a son to the bottle and I won't lose another." The older man's voice finally broke. "We will get through this together, son. We will help all we can but you have to change the way you're coping. Your mother has suggested an external councillor." Through the tears, Billy nodded his agreement to this idea.

Ruth's voice brought him back. "Is there anyone at home and are we still okay for dinner?" There was a hint of humour in her words that made Billy smile.

"Sorry ma'am, I was miles away and yes, I am hungry."

The restaurant was in the university district near the heart of Columbus, the state capital. It was a small family-run business that had a great local following. Billy and Ruth found seats in a quiet corner where their server took a drinks order and left them to mull over the menu. After much deliberation they both decided on the lasagne. It was after placing their order that Ruth dropped a bombshell.

"I've struggled with this for a while," she said quietly, "and I wanted to send word to you but never seemed to get around to it." Billy sat with a puzzled look on his face but let Ruth finish what she was saying. "Becky Brent is dead."

Billy sat still for a moment letting the information process in his head.

"How?" His one-word response put a knot in Ruth's abdomen but she managed to compose herself enough to continue.

"Well it seems that our Becky reaped the whirlwind, to quote an old Arab saying. She got mouthy with the wrong person in jail and…" Ruth shrugged her shoulders to end the incomplete sentence. She looked across at Billy whose expression had softened a little but not much. A flood of emotions was coursing through him but he managed to keep things under control. At that point their meal arrived. Billy and Ruth thanked their server and complimented her on how well presented it was.

The interlude brought Billy's thoughts back into focus. He looked across at Ruth and again spoke one word: "Karma?" Ruth could see no emotion in Billy's face but knew she had done the right thing in telling him about his foster mother's demise. For the rest of the evening, they chatted about their lives, loves and losses, the fun times and how they had both faced challenges.

On leaving the restaurant, Billy took Ruth's arm as they strolled down the sidewalk.

"I dread to think where things would have ended up if you had not intervened to get me out of that hell-hole. I owe you everything." Ruth squeezed his arm tightly.

"What was I to do? Sit back and watch you die slowly? Not on my watch!" They glanced at each other and laughed. Billy was then quiet for a moment. Ruth looked at his face and could see the glistening trail of tears meandering down on to his shirt. She stopped walking and turned to him.

"This," Ruth began, making a circular motion with her arms and eyes, "is your reward for surviving." As Billy's eyes made contact with Ruth's, she reached out and cradled his face in her hands. "Let the pain go Billy, all of it." He knew that Ruth was talking about more than just his time with the Brents. He pulled his teacher close to him.

"I have carried this all of my life," Billy said, "it's almost a comfort at times but you are right, I need to move forward. It's as if all I have inside is grief, with little room for anything else." He held Ruth tight and sobbed softly on her shoulder. Ruth for her part let him cry for a while, watching as passers-by showed looks of brief concern then shifted their gaze so as not to cause embarrassment.

She eased Billy away and stared deeply into him.

"Your cup is full, it's full of the crap you have held on to all these years." She studied Billy's expression. "Live your life and never be afraid of finding happiness, it does not always have to end in heartache. I wanted so much for you back then and you have achieved so much, but all I want for you now is to be happy. Okay?" Ruth's face had moved from one of concern to one of joy, spreading across her whole being.

As he wiped away tears with the back of his hands, Billy smiled back at her. This time there was something different about it. Warmth exuded from every part of him as if his soul had been cleansed. They walked on in silence until they reached Ruth's car, then Billy leaned over and kissed her on the cheek.

"Now you have my number and I have yours," he said, "Call me any time." She smiled and returned her own kiss to Billy's face and whispered in his ear.

"I will always be here for you, you're like the son I always wished for but could never have. Live your life, Billy, find happiness and when you do, let me know."

Ruth turned away quickly and got in her car. As she drove off, Billy could see she was crying but knew it was not out of sadness but hope.

Chapter Thirty-Three

As she looked out of the window, Morag Colquhoun watched the horses standing quietly enjoying the early sun. She smiled then returned her attention to the computer screen. Morag was a creature of habit. Every morning she would get up and tend to the horses and the various other animals that had found their way into her life. Once that was done, she would head indoors for breakfast and spend time on the computer attending to emails, bills and the like.

On this morning, Morag had received an email from her friend Caroline, which simply read: *What do you think of this guy?* There was a YouTube link attached. When Morag clicked on it she saw various clips of a man working with horses that had a whole range of issues – biting, kicking, loading and so on. What pricked Morag's interest was the manner in which the young man went about getting a positive change in the horses, as he seemed to be doing nothing and everything at the same time. She watched the video more than once, mesmerised, before emailing Caroline back.

This guy is amazing. I think I'll go on his website to see if does clinics abroad. Are you up for it if so?

Morag then typed in the man's name and scrolled through his website until she found a section entitled: 'Do you want to host a clinic?' She looked through the criteria, which her own yard met, then went to the contact link and sent a brief message. By now,

Caroline's reply had come in – *Yes*.

After Billy put Ronin in the pen and unhitched the trailer, he headed indoors to see his parents whom he had not seen in a few months.

"Well look Margaret, it's the happy wanderer," Walter joked as he walked over to Billy and gave him a hug. "Good to see you son, we have missed you lots." Billy looked into Walter's eyes and smiled.

"I've enjoyed my own company over the last while," he said, "but thought I'd better get back here to touch base with the geriatrics." Before Walter could say anything, Margaret shouted though from the office.

"I heard that, William Dawson." Billy knew he was in trouble when Margaret used his full first name. He quickly rushed past Walter and made his way to the office where he found Margaret perched on a chair between reams of archived material. He kissed her on the cheek and she let out a little giggle.

"How have things been?" Billy gave his mother a brief update on the events of the last few months.

"You'll never guess who I bumped into in Ohio." Margaret looked at Billy to see if there were any clues then shrugged her shoulders in defeat.

"Who?"

"Ruth Drake," Billy said, smiling broadly, "Can you believe that? She came up after the demo and asked me to sign her book." Margaret was overjoyed at the news and could see immediately how much this chance meeting had had a positive effect on Billy. He told her about Ruth's husband and how she was still teaching, predominantly small children but with the odd class of older kids to keep her senses sharp. Margaret listened intently to the rest of Billy's story then together they caught up on some office work.

"You're pretty fully booked for the next few months," Margaret said, "but I did get an interesting email from a woman in Scotland. She asked if you did clinics overseas and would you be interested in holding one at her place." Billy had never been out of the country to do any work: he didn't need to as there was always enough at home to keep him busy. But as he read through the email, he had a feeling that this might be the right time for him to take a chance and expand his horizons.

Margaret rose and headed for the kitchen.

"I'm making a pot of coffee for your Paw and me, want some?" Billy nodded his approval then typed his reply to Morag Colquhoun. There were already a few thoughts running through his head – what kind of place would it be, what would the horses be like? – the usual things he mused about when sorting out clinics, although Margaret often did this side of things in his absence.

There was a strong smell of coffee in the air as Billy finished his reply and headed to the kitchen. There was something almost primeval about being back home: familiar smells, the comfort of being with his parents again, even knowing that he would get a decent sleep. All this somehow let his worries fade into the background.

"Well did you take the clinic in Scotland?" Margaret sipped at her coffee. Billy was quiet for a moment. As he spoke, Margaret could sense a positivity in her son's words that she hadn't heard in a long time.

"You know, Ruth talked to me about letting go of the past and all the pain that's held within," Billy said as Walter looked up from his horsemanship magazine, "and I feel like a trip to Scotland would be a fresh place for me to move forward with my life." Margaret reached across, rubbed Billy's upper arm and looked him straight in the eye.

"I think that Ruth is correct and I think you feel it, too. Go with your gut but take your brain with you." They both laughed as Walter shouted across from his place at the table.

"Dang it woman, you're stealing all my good lines." Billy poured himself a refill and topped up Walter and Margaret's cups before telling them about all that had happened at his recent clinics.

Morag read the reply email from Mr Billy Dawson.

Dear Morag,

First, I would like to thank for your inquiry, it's nice to get word from faraway places such as Scotland, especially with regard to training horses. I have never held a clinic outside of America so this would be a first for me. I would be delighted, honoured, to teach a clinic at your yard. Eight riders per day max, we usually split them into two-day clinics over here. I see you said there was onsite accommodation which is great and helps keep your costs down. All I need you to do is pay for my flights over, don't bother with business class, it's way too expensive – cheap and cheerful will be fine. My fees *are $600 per day with meals thrown in. I can do private lessons but tend not to if I have a lot of riders. One more thing – I like to be able to ride when I teach so I would need a pretty settled horse to do that, don't want no rodeo during the show if you see what I mean.*

I hope the above is to your satisfaction and look forward to hearing from you in the near future.
Billy

There was a buzz of excitement running though Morag's body as she wrote her reply. Everything seemed to be happening so quickly but she had always been one to go with the flow and follow her instincts. After sending a short acknowledgement, she got to work contacting friends and clients whom she thought would be interested in doing the clinics. Next she posted the event on Facebook with proposed dates and made it public so she would have a larger catchment group. Within a few hours there were enough people to definitely fill four two-day clinics. On top of that, a lot of people were interested in just attending, which was a bonus financially.

With this new information she sat down to write again.

Dear Mr Dawson,

I can confirm that we have enough riders to be able to hold four two-day clinics with lots of interest. I thought it be best to hold two two-day clinics with a rest in between, then the other two. I hope this is to your satisfaction and look forward to hearing from you.

Kind regards,
Morag

Chapter Thirty-Four

In the summer pasture a high wind had taken down one of the old pine trees, which had come to rest, as is common on farms, on top of the perimeter fence line. Surveying the damage, Walter took off his hat, scratched his head then slipped the hat back on again. He turned to Billy.

"Looks like there's only one post that's been broken and a couple of wires that will need re-tensioned. Damn lucky the horses have a little sense and didn't take off to see if the grass really is greener on the other side." Billy smiled.

As he walked over to the pickup, he felt his phone vibrate in his back pocket. He took it out and saw he had a message but simply texted back:

Sorry whoever you are I don't have time right now to reply, got some lumberjacking to do. He took the chainsaw from the truck and the two men made light work of the fallen tree. As a bonus, there were now a few more logs for the wood store.

As they returned to the ranch and entered the kitchen, the smell of home cooking hit their senses almost to the point of salivation.

Margaret appeared from the living room.

"You boys ready for some lasagne, my own recipe?" Walter and Billy both nodded their approval. "And strawberry cheesecake for afters?" Again, the men nodded.

"You know something, Mom," Billy said, "this is what I miss the most about being away." He walked across and gave Margaret a big hug. She stuck her tongue out at Walter then smiled as if she were the chosen one.

"So much for boys sticking together," Walter said, "or am I too old for you to hug me?" He stood with arms outstretched with his bottom lip sticking out. Billy laughed.

"Aw Dad, you know I love you, too." He gave Walter a hug as he had with his mom before Margaret broke up the embrace.

"If you want any of this here delicious food you had better wash your hands and help set the table." Walter and Billy duly obliged then fetched plates from the cupboard and put out the cutlery. Billy went upstairs to change out of his work clothes, giving Walter the perfect opportunity to sneak up behind Margaret and put his arms around her.

"Do you know how happy you make me, wife?" He squeezed her gently and kissed the back of her head. Margaret reached around with her hands and squeezed Walter's rear ever so softly.

"And do you know how much I love you, husband?" She leant back and allowed herself a brief moment to enjoy Walter's body heat next to hers, then whispered: "Hey handsome, I can't serve dinner with you attached to me the way you are, so get your cute ass over to the table and give Billy a shout."

Margaret retrieved the lasagne from the oven and cut it into manageable pieces. Once he returned, Billy helped her to set out the bowls of potatoes, carrots and peas. After the main course and then the cheesecake had been eaten, there was the usual post-meal small talk before Billy headed to his room for a nap. He checked his phone and remembered the message that had come in while he was fixing the fence. It was from Morag.

Dear Mr Dawson,

I am delighted to tell you that I have provisionally secured enough riders for you to be able to hold four two-day clinics at my yard. There will be onsite provisions for your good self and all meals will be supplied by me, that is if you like home cooking. I do have a horse that should do a good job for you, he is an older boy now but still loves his work and I'm sure you will get on fine with him, his name is Brogan. I will be back in touch with regards your flight details and look forward to seeing you in late July.

Kind regards,
Morag

Billy smiled: he liked this girl's no-fuss attitude. He typed out a polite response then read it over a couple of times, made a few grammatical changes, then pressed send. Walking back into the kitchen, he let Margaret know that his schedule for July would be full.

"Looks like I'm off to Scotland. I can't believe the girl over there has got this sorted out so quickly." He poured himself a mug of coffee and sat down next to his mother.

"Sounds like a girl after my own heart," Margaret

said, "Need to get her over here to help out in the office." Billy laughed then asked where Walter was.

"Your old Paaaw" – she emphasised the words for comedic value – "is out tending to your horses, no less. I told him you would do it but you know what he's like." Billy jumped up and pulled his boots on.

"The old coot's got no patience, likes me to feel bad for not looking after my horses properly." He laughed as he said this and Margaret knew he was not really mad at Walter, though he was a little.

Although he was away a lot of the time, it had not escaped Billy's attention that his parents were getting older. He had realised that he increasingly thought about this when he was touring, knowing that at some point they would have to hire help. But his father was a proud man and the last thing Billy wanted was to make him feel useless.

In the weeks leading up to the trip to Scotland, Billy spent a lot of time working Ronin and Raven to keep them in shape. Although Raven had progressed well in his training, there was still a long road for him to travel to reach the standard of connection that Billy had with Ronin. When Billy sat in the saddle with Ronin underneath it was as if their bodies became one being. Often at clinics Billy would have people come up to him and say something like, "I see the horse responding but for the life of me I can't see what he is responding to that is coming from you". When this happened, Billy would smile and say, "That's the fun part, it's all internal".

Most folks would laugh and shake their head but on

occasion someone would quite openly check his tack for electronic aids and, finding none, would stomp off with a perplexed look. Billy just usually shook his head when this happened and let the mild insult go. Ronin for his part knew only this: that when he worked with Billy, it was how Billy made him feel that made the difference. He would do anything for his two-legs friend.

Chapter Thirty-Five

The big day had arrived and Walter drove Billy to the airport.

"You're pretty quiet, son," Walter said after a few miles, "Anything you wanna share?" Billy paused before answering.

"I'm just apprehensive about this trip. It's quite a journey and my first flight overseas, you know things get inside your head and…" He left his thoughts hanging in the air.

"Look son, things will be just fine and you'll have fun meeting new people and experiencing their culture. And as for the flight, well there's one change at O'Hare then it's direct to Glasgow. All you have to do is sit back and enjoy the movie." Billy laughed. He loved the way Walter could play things down in any situation.

"Guess you're right, Pops. Who knows, I might even enjoy myself!"

The connecting flight from Billings to O'Hare was eventful. It was the time of year when a lot of thunderstorms kicked up and today was no exception. There was a slight delay on departure due to an active weather cell moving through but it passed quickly. It had, however, left some rough air in its wake and when the captain's voice came over the PA it was to ask passengers to keep their seatbelts on.

There was a tangible air of apprehension throughout

the plane. Some people spoke in whispers while others talked of the bad service the airline had provided on previous flights. Billy sat with his nose buried in a book trying to block out the buzz of anxiety. He had flown extensively throughout the US and had been caught in a few hair-raising situations here and there. About a half an hour into the flight, things settled down enough for the cabin crew to start their service.

O'Hara International in Chicago arrived without further incident. On the flight to Glasgow, Billy once again buried his head in his book and disappeared into the world within. A jolt from some turbulence woke him suddenly and the book landed on the floor. As Billy reached down to grab it, he hit his head on the food tray on the back of the seat in front, much to the amusement of his fellow travellers. He smiled with embarrassment then looked up at the map showing their progress across the Atlantic. To his surprise he saw they were only an hour out from Glasgow, having made good time due to a tailwind. He must have been more tired than he thought.

Soon he could see the lights of Glasgow below. He always found it amusing and slightly terrifying that a machine this big and heavy could go so slow yet still maintain altitude. There were the customary whoops and hollers as the plane became an earthbound machine and taxied to the arrivals gate. Billy was soon through customs then with relief saw a woman with a sign that read 'William Dawson'. He let out a laugh.

"What's the big joke, Mr Dawson?" Morag asked in a rather flat tone and with a perplexed look on her face.

"I'm really sorry, Morag," – Billy pronounced it as

Mawrag – "One, it's been a long flight and two, the only person to call me William Dawson is my mom and usually she's pretty peed off when she does." Billy put out his hand and Morag shook it gently but with a firm grip.

Billy was immediately aware of how beautiful she was: a nice physique and fine facial bones framed by straight auburn hair. What most caught Billy's attention were her blue eyes, which accentuated her other features. For a brief moment everything stopped around them, as if he had been locked in a moment in time with Morag still holding his hand.

"Did you have a good flight?" The words snapped Billy back into the present.

"Just the usual several hours stuck in a tin can with a bunch of folk you don't know and with the ever-present threat of disaster." Morag laughed.

"You know something, Billy, that's exactly how I feel about flying. Come on, I'll get you home and we can have something to eat." He nodded his approval and they headed for the main entrance and out into the cold Scottish air.

"Did you sleep well?" Morag was at the cooker as Billy entered the kitchen.

"Like the dead," he said, "it was great. That little wooden house has a really good vibe in it, makes you feel right at home." He walked over to the kitchen table and sat down.

As he waited for breakfast, he looked around the small but beautiful farm kitchen and loved that Morag was using an old range to cook the food, which smelled amazing. There were photographs of horses on the walls and flat surfaces. One picture which caught Billy's eye was what looked to be a draft cross thoroughbred jumping a cross-country fence at a flat-out gallop.

"Is that you?" Billy pointed at the photo hanging on the wall. Morag looked over her shoulder then back to the frying pan.

"Yes. Not very good form but my mare Bruja was not one for stopping once she got the bit between her teeth, so to speak. It was taken at an event not far from here and was one of only three occasions when I was brave enough to compete in eventing. After that I focused on dressage working hunter show classes, but my main passion was professional show jumping. I competed in that for years."

Billy listened intently to what Morag was saying. He was interested from a trainer's point of view but also because he loved her soft Scottish accent, although the speed it came out of her mouth was like being shot at with a verbal machine gun. As he looked at a few more of the pictures he noticed Morag had gone very quiet and there was a shift, ever so slight, in the atmosphere in the kitchen.

"It's never easy losing a good horse," Billy said, "It feels like part of your soul has been taken from you." Morag turned and looked at him, tears welling in the corners of her eyes. When she spoke, he noticed how shaky her voice sounded.

"How did you know she had passed? I never told you that!" Billy walked to where Morag stood then wrapped his arms around her in a gesture of support.

"We had an old horse, Toby," he said, "who I learned to ride on..." He went on to tell the story of a very difficult decision he had once made.

Toby's body convulsed to and fro as he tried to free himself from the pain that tore at his intestines. His body shone brightly in the early sunlight bathed in a film of sweat that covered him from head to hoof. The herd looked on as they grazed close by, their ears and eyes alert for any predator that might be attracted by Toby's spasms.

Ronin had stood guard at his friend's side the whole night, occasionally nuzzling the older horse's neck in an effort to get him to his feet but to no avail. Finally consumed with hunger, he had given up his vigil and gone with the herd to graze, but he still kept a close watch on his old companion. On hearing the sound of the two-legs' approach, Ronin rushed towards their voices and pawed frantically at the gate. The colt could feel the anxiety emanating from the pair of two-legs and stopped pawing but continued to call out in an almost frantic manner.

As the men approached, they could see that the colt was in a state of high alert, moving cautiously towards him before hurdling the fence. Ronin ran to where Toby lay outstretched on the ground then looked back to where the men stood. It did not take them long to cover the distance to the older gelding and they immediately worked on getting him to his feet. The younger two-legs then went back to the gate and returned with a tether, which he quickly passed to the older one who secured it to Toby's head. They walked Toby back and forth for what seemed like an age but as much as the two-legs tried, Toby kept on going to ground until he simply had no energy to get back up.

The younger two-legs disappeared for a while, returning with two things. One was a cover that the horses used when it got cold or rained hard, and the other thing was new. Ronin could not tell what it was but it smelled odd. The younger one came over to where he stood and cradled his face then stroked his forelock, which always settled Ronin when he got worried.

After a while, Ronin was led to where the other horses stood grazing. As the young two-legs walked back to where Toby lay, there was a crack like a thunderclap which caused all the horses to run to the far end of the field. After the noise there was a stillness that seemed to blanket the very earth where the horses stood. Ronin looked to the far end of the pasture where he could see the two figures kneeling beside Toby who had gone very quiet.

The two-legs then walked over to the gate and disappeared into the foliage. Once they were out of sight, Ronin walked forward on his own until he stood next to Toby. His body smelled different as if the life force had been drained from him. It was at that moment that Ronin remembered where he had encountered that scent before. It had been the way his mother was all those years ago.

One by one, the horses came to where Toby lay and then, as it is with nature, they made their way to the farthest end of the field to put distance between themselves and the corpse.

By the time Billy had finished telling his story, he and Morag were both in tears. After a little while she sat down and briefed him on the horses he would be working with the next day.

Chapter Thirty-Six

Morag had been up early getting things ready for Billy's first clinic. As she went about her work, she could not get the thought out of her head of how comforting his embrace had been the day before. It had been a while since she had let anyone into her world and for the last few years she had enjoyed the solitary life. 'He's a visitor and it's a professional relationship', she told herself, 'and you're acting like an adolescent schoolgirl who's just had her first kiss'.

She was confused emotionally but managed to put things to the back of her mind as Caroline pulled up in her car.

"Morning Caroline, how are you? Hubby taking care of the boys?" She smiled as her friend made her way across the yard.

"Hubby knows that when I'm stressed, do not question me or my life choices." The women hugged and walked back to the house. "So missus, how's your new guest settling in, well I hope?" Morag paused for a moment before answering.

"Yes, he's fine…" Her words trailed off for a second. "Can I tell you something in confidence?" Caroline took Morag's arm and stopped her near the back door of the cottage.

"You haven't slept with him, have you? I mean, not that I'm against sleeping with rugged cowboy types, but that would be a record even for you!" Being of German descent, Caroline was always straight to the point with her observations on life.

"No, no, nothing like that." Morag blushed and she knew Caroline could see it. "It's just something happened yesterday and I'm still trying to get my head around it." She told Caroline of the conversation she had had with Billy and how he had known that Bruja her old horse had died.

"Is that all?" Caroline asked, "I mean, it's hardly *Fifty Shades of Grey* and you know some of these horse folks are very intuitive…" She in turn let her sentence tail off just as Billy stepped out of the back door. Morag jumped with fright.

"Jesus Christ, Billy, cough or something to let us know you're coming!" He laughed and extended his hand.

"And you must be Caroline?" She shook his hand firmly then turned to Morag.

"Did you tell him I was coming or is this more of that intuition we were talking about?" Morag blushed again, Billy frowned and Caroline laughed before ushering everyone into the kitchen for coffee.

"Mary had a little lamb, its fleece was covered in – yeah, it's working fine." Billy switched off the headset control for the PA system and looked quizzically at the four horses and riders milling about at the far end of the arena. He glanced down at his watch: 8:55am, just a few more minutes before they would start.

Morag appeared with a couple of bottles of water, which she passed through the fence.

"Well thank you kindly, ma'am," Billy said in a

drawn-out southern accent. "No, thank you." She made her hand into the shape of a gun and pointed it at him. They both laughed and Billy switched the PA back on with an audible click.

"Good morning everyone, glad you all could make it here today. My name is Billy Dawson and I'm a horse trainer, you may have already worked that out." He waved his hands up and down, signalling to people to look at what he was wearing. There was muffled laughter.

"Now, people try to sell my style of horsemanship as 'natural horsemanship', but to be honest with you there ain't nothing natural about it as far as the horse is concerned." He paused for a moment. "Like dogs, horses have been domesticated for hundreds of years and also like dogs, we have cross-bred certain gene pools to create horses for specific tasks. The drawback to this is that we have also bred weaknesses into our equine companions, weaknesses that are physical or temperamental. That being said, most folk get along fine with their horses, but every now and again they may get stuck at some place and need the help of a trainer like yours truly." The audience laughed a little louder, which settled Billy's nerves somewhat.

"In the States, I have a reputation for my work with horses and some of you folks here may have seen some of my methods on the internet." There were a few head-nods. "And put simply, what I do is to let the horse find the solution to whatever is holding it back while I act as a support mechanism to that change. Sometimes I have to do the same for the human that owns or rides the horse, and in the process I try to do it with as light a heart as possible. So let's get this show on the road, Caroline."

Billy spent the next few hours working with the first group of riders. There then came a lunch break ahead of working with the next group, a system that would be repeated the next day. At lunchtime he went into the kitchen where Morag was busy.

"What's on the menu, Mo?" She had allowed Billy to use the short form of her name.

"Gypsy stew," she replied, "but only free-range Gypsies, I don't use farmed ones." This made Billy laugh just as Caroline walked in and asked what was so funny. Morag explained that she had told Billy about the Gypsies. Caroline said it was an old German recipe for stew and no Gypsies were used in the preparation, not that she knew of, anyway.

As they ate, Morag told Billy that the afternoon class included a couple of very experienced riders who should keep him on his toes. Billy thanked her for the warning and asked if it would be okay for him to ride Brogan in the afternoon session.

"No problem," Morag said, "I'm sure you'll get on all right with each other, he's a really sweet-natured old boy." Morag locked her gaze on Billy for the briefest moment then smiled and looked away.

"Is Brogan that fine liver chestnut skewbald that I saw in the back pasture? What a nice-looking horse, is he Clydesdale cross?" This time it was Billy's turn to gaze at Morag. She smiled and said he was correct in knowing the horse was Clydesdale.

"The breed is from this area. The farmers needed a

strong and well-built draught horse for ploughing the steep fields that are a feature of the Clyde Valley."

Billy thanked her for extending his knowledge of the horse then stood up, put on his hat and let Morag show him the way to Brogan's stable. She brushed the horse off and quickly saddled him ready for Billy to ride.

As in the morning clinic there were four riders warming up their horses at the top end of the arena. Billy walked in with Brogan, closed the gate and checked his horse's cinch was tight enough. Once he had done that he slipped his foot into the stirrup and eased himself into the surprisingly comfortable saddle. Looking around the arena, the crowd seemed to have doubled in number. "Word must have got out," he said quietly to himself. He moved Brogan around in a walk then asked him to halt then walk again, with some lateral work on both sides and finally a little trot to halt. 'This horse is well-schooled', he thought. Looking out of the arena, he locked eyes with Morag. "Mo, you have done a great job with this one, what a great little guy," he called out. Morag smiled and a flush of embarrassment spread across her cheeks, which Billy found endearing. Then he turned his attention back to the riders, one of whom was having trouble with her mount.

"Okay, the lady with the little bay horse, just ask her to do some small figures-of-eight while we get to know each other." This was a tactic Billy often used. He would give the rider a simple task and talk to them at the same time, causing the rider to separate their focus between the two tasks. It took their attention away from what the horse should not be doing and let them relax.

After the woman, Jill, got her horse into a nice rhythm she at last turned her full attention to Billy.

"Sorry about that," she said, "I think your PA is freaking her a little bit, it's her first time at something like this." Billy walked Brogan up alongside and circled in the same figure-of-eight pattern while talking to her.

"Well for one thing, that is a pretty brave thing you are doing to bring your mare to a deal like this as her first big outing. I'm glad you chose me." Jill and the audience laughed and Billy watched the tension in her body slowly subside. "Jill, in a minute I'm going to ask you to take – sorry, what's your mare's name?"

"Iona," Jill replied.

"Well that is such a sweet name for this little girl," Billy said as he reached over from Brogan and rubbed the mare's forelock. "I'm going to ask you to ride Iona down near to where the PA is sitting. The moment you feel her getting tense, break away still in the walk, as if you had asked her to do a twenty-metre circle. I'll demonstrate." With that, he rode down the fence line and let Brogan roll off the fence into a gradual curve then back up the other side of the arena.

"Just like that, but only if you feel her tense up, okay?" Jill nodded and set off. Billy watched as she rode down the rail. As he did this, he told the audience the story of the first time he tried to saddle Ronin. He used this as a way of gauging how much the PA was really bothering the mare, as well as giving a bit of light entertainment to show that even cowboys have to start somewhere.

The audience watched Jill and Iona grow in confidence to the point where, after a few laps, the PA became just another part of the horse's education. When he thought that both horse and rider had done enough, Billy asked Jill to join him in the middle of the arena.

"What a great job, guys," he said, "Just give your horse her head as a way of rewarding her for facing up to her fears." Jill did as instructed and Iona dropped her head down and worked her jaw a little then cocked her back leg and relaxed.

"Did you see Iona work her jaw when Jill let loose with the reins?" Billy said to the audience. A few heads nodded. "That's one of the ways she can physically let go of any tension that might have built up during this little exercise. We're the same, we get tense and lock our jaw, then when things calm down we wiggle and sometimes yawn to get rid of our tension." More nods of agreement.

"Now what I do see a whole lot of is that when a horse gets worried, the rider gets into a wrestling match with them and that's what I call 'shaking the champagne bottle'. Ah, I see that you know all about champagne," Billy said as the audience laughed at the analogy, "You shake and shake that bottle and there is only one option for the liquid inside: it blows the cork. And once that cork goes, well let's say in horse terms you may have to explain yourself to your equine companion."

Billy by now felt he had the connection to the audience that he wanted.

"If we look at the way we got Jill to open herself and her horse to something totally unfamiliar, the PA, we explained it a whole lot better to the horse than just getting into a fight with her. We listened and when the horse got worried, we turned away and gave her relief.

Most of all, though, we said to her 'I'm here for you buddy and nothing is gonna hurt you'."

Billy now asked Jill to work on some walk-halt transitions at the top of the arena and asked for "the next victim" to make their way out to him. He watched the second rider walk up and noticed that she was very rigid, almost regimental, as was her horse, a gun-barrel grey gelding.

"Good morning, ma'am, what can I do for you?"

"I was thinking exactly the same thing," the woman replied, "What can you do for me?" Billy knew by her tone that she was going to be a live one. He carried on and asked her name and the name of her horse.

"My name is Celia and this handsome boy is called Leonidas, or Leo for short." Billy then asked her to walk around so he could look for any areas that might need work.

As he watched, Celia started to pick out all her horse's faults and describe them to him.

"You see how he is stiff through his shoulder on the turn and he doesn't track up behind – and look at his trot, I mean, it's hopeless!" Celia brought the horse back to walk and sat facing Billy in an almost defiant manner.

"What I see in your horse, Celia," Billy said, "is a lot of tension, so before we do anything I would like you to dismount." She did as Billy asked and he likewise dismounted from Brogan. He handed the reins to Celia and took Leo's from her.

"If you look at this horse," Billy said through the PA, "he is way too tight, which is easily seen in his high head carriage. I'm going to release his poll and front legs and you guys tell me if you see any difference." As he worked on Leo, the horse's expression throughout his whole body changed quite remarkably. Once he was finished, Billy asked Morag to hold both horses while he spoke with Celia.

"Now Celia, I need you to trust me a little here, okay?" Celia nodded. "I'm going to take your arm in a manner that will show you how much tension you're holding in your body. Okay, you ready?"

"I am," she replied. Billy grabbed Celia's forearm hard enough to make her wince.

"Now that's roughly how much tension you are taking to the horse," Billy said, "What I was hoping to show you is how much we can have an effect on our horse's performance."

The exercise had been an eye-opener for Celia to the extent that she became tearful at the thought of the potential damage she was doing to her horse. Billy walked over to where she stood and without switching off his microphone, he hugged her as he spoke.

"Don't be ashamed of your tears because they belong to you and your horse. They show that you understand what's been going on and you are here because you realised that you needed to change." Celia gave a rather muted thank you then fished a tissue from her pocket to dry her eyes.

Over the next few minutes, Billy gave her a few exercises in how to relax her body before riding her horse. He then asked her to mount up and see how things were. The change in them both was enough to make the audience burst into applause. Billy then asked Morag to take Brogan as he felt he had done enough work for the day.

The rest of the session went along the same lines with positive changes in horse and rider, and soon it was time to finish.

"I hope everyone has had a good day and will be here again tomorrow," Billy said. The audience clapped him all the way out of the arena and a few came over to ask him to sign copies of his book.

He was about to leave when a voice called him back.

"Mr Dawson, do you have a moment?" It was Celia but something had changed in her appearance: she looked elated. "I just wanted to thank you for your help and to apologise for what I said today at the start. I have been riding for over thirty years and have learnt more in my time with you than in any of that. You have given me and my horse a platform to start anew and I thank you from the bottom of my heart."

Billy was so taken aback as to be momentarily left speechless, even more so when Celia planted a kiss on his cheek.

"Well… well thank you, ma'am," he said, "and I'm so glad things are working out for you." Celia disappeared into the stable block just as Morag walked forward to rescue Billy from any more attention.

"You have a new fan, I see," Morag said. Billy smiled.

"Is that a twinge of jealousy I hear in your voice, Morag Colquhoun?" She again smiled and blushed at the same time.

"You wish!" They both laughed and headed back to the cottage where Morag needed to make a start on the evening meal.

Chapter Thirty-Seven

"Oh my God, Mo, this smells amazing – more Gypsies?" Billy sat down at the kitchen table.

"No, tonight you are having steak, and not just any steak: *hielan coo* steak. I have a friend who works on a beef farm and they send their animals to a local abattoir which is very humane in its treatment. If you have never tasted this meat, you're in for a treat." She tossed the first steak on to the grill and there was a loud hiss as the raw meat made contact with the hot metal.

"I have not had the pleasure of consuming a *hielan coo*," Billy said, "but they sure do smell good. Do you need a hand with the prep work?" As a rule Morag would do everything herself but tonight she felt like a change.

"You could set the table? Plates are in that cupboard, knives and forks are in that drawer. There is bottled water in the fridge and the glasses are over there."

Once he was finished Billy asked,

"Anything else, ma'am?" Morag laughed.

"Your mum has trained you well. You can take those over, too." She nodded in the direction of a large bowl of cooked vegetables that sat on the worktop.

As Billy squeezed past, he placed his hands on her waist in a way that made her move closer to the range. Billy apologised then lifted the bowl. Morag turned to him as he was about to squeeze past for a second time.

"No need to apologise, Billy." Her eyes locked on

to his and for the briefest moment she felt like leaning over to kiss him, but a little voice inside said "not yet". Instead, she turned around and gave her full attention to the steaks which were now almost ready.

The moment had not been lost on Billy, however. He had not felt this way around a woman for a long time, not since Samantha. There was something special about his host but he didn't want to rush into anything feet first. He sat the bowl of steaming vegetables down on the table and poured two glasses of water.

"How do you think the first day went?" he asked. Morag put both steaks on a serving plate and sat down at her side of the table.

"To be brutally honest…" Billy's heart sank a little. "I have never seen anything like that before, it was amazing." He let out a small sigh of relief.

"I've worked in the horse world for many years," Morag continued, "and never seen anyone with your approach, it's so eye-opening." As Morag spoke, Billy cut off a piece of steak.

"Thanks Mo, those are very kind words. And this steak is amazing, I have never tasted meat so tender." She smiled.

"Thanks, told you they were good." She paused before continuing. "I was brought up in a world where if the horse didn't do what you asked, you would make it do what you wanted." Billy nodded and put down his cutlery, realising that Morag needed to speak about this.

"I've done a lot of good things for my horses," she said, "but more that I'm ashamed of. Then I saw a documentary on natural horsemanship and it was as if a light had gone on in my head. This was the thing I had been searching for all those years. I made a decision right there and then to try and work with my horses, not just make them do my bidding." Tears formed in the corners of her eyes and Billy reached across and took her hand.

"Look Morag, we have all made mistakes, done things we are not proud of, but we have to forgive ourselves for those mistakes, errors in judgement or whatever you want to call them. What is important is you are here now, you have survived. An old friend told me that the worst thing you could do in life was to hold on to pain and regret. They just hold you back from all the good things that can come into your life." Billy gave Morag's hand a squeeze. "Now eat your damn steak woman, it's getting cold."

It was the small hours.

"Dang, Morag, it's way past my bedtime and I have to be up early for day two. If I don't get a good sleep I get a little cranky at breakfast." Morag laughed.

"I don't believe that for a minute." They headed for the door and Billy was surprised that Morag followed him over to the annexe.

"Thanks for the great meal, Mo, tasted delicious not to mention your lovely company, it's like a home from…" Before he could finish his sentence, Morag had put her arms around him and was kissing him passionately. Billy looked down into her blue eyes.

"Can't say I haven't been thinking about that but doing it is sure better than thinking." As she looked up at him, Morag pulled him close until they were locked in a lovers' embrace.

As quickly as it started, they both broke contact and smiled at each other. She kissed him softly on the cheek and slowly walked back to the cottage. When she reached the door, she turned and gave him a little wave then disappeared inside. Billy's head was spinning.

Once inside the cottage, Morag walked about talking to herself. "What are you doing? What are you doing? You barely know him!" She admired Billy through watching his teaching videos and through the way he had written to her by email. There had been a connection right from the start but she had not really realised how strong it was until Billy arrived in person.

Morag had only had a few meaningful relationships and one in particular had been very violent. She had managed to get out of that situation and since then there had only been a couple of casual flings. This, however, felt different. The last thing she wanted to do was to drive Billy away by acting like some love-struck teenager. As she got ready for bed she resolved to rein back her feelings and see how things developed.

At the same time, Billy sat on the couch in the annexe wondering what to do. He made a coffee then sat back down to think things through. He could not deny a physical attraction to Morag but there was also a connection he had known only once before. Again, his thoughts were drawn back to Samantha.

He didn't know if it was guilt that put this doubt in his head or if he knew it was time to move on with his life. Part of that would mean letting go of the memory of his first true love. He drank the last few mouthfuls of coffee and headed to bed feeling more confused.

There was a soft knock on the kitchen door and Billy walked in.

"Good morning," he said, "Did you have a good sleep?" Morag turned to him.

"Billy, I've been hurt in the past and I don't know what happened last night. It just felt so right and I'm sorry if I offended you…" Before she could continue, Billy had crossed the space between them and was holding her tightly in his strong arms.

"Morag, what happened happened. I'm not ashamed of it and neither should you be. Like you I've been hurt, but with you there's a chance to feel something again."

He told her about Samantha and how things had ended. Morag listened intently to the pain Billy must have suffered. After he had regained his composure, Billy thanked her for being so understanding and for allowing him to unload his heavy burden.

"You must really like me to share such a personal event in your life," Morag said, "and I'm honoured it was me you chose to confide in." She reached across and once again, like the night before, they kissed – but this time it was different, more passionate.

Then they heard a car pull into the yard and sat back to see who it was. Caroline walked into the kitchen and asked cheerily if anyone fancied a Danish pastry. Neither Billy nor Morag could contain themselves and burst into laughter. Morag got up and gave her friend a hug.

"That's just what we were wanting. Anyone for another coffee?"

Chapter Thirty-Eight

Day two of the clinic followed the same pattern as day one. There were more people and all the riders went away with homework. That evening in the cottage kitchen, Morag, Billy and Caroline sat exhausted from the day's events. It was then that Morag made an announcement Billy was not expecting.

"As a treat for all your hard work over the past few days, Mr Dawson, Caroline has very kindly offered to hold the fort while I take you for a day's sightseeing up in the Highlands. If you get changed quickly we can head off as I've made reservations at the Loch Leven Hotel in North Ballachulish." For a moment Billy was taken aback. Then he got his senses back and agreed to the deal.

Morag was carrying an overnight bag to the car when Billy appeared from the annexe. He had shaved and by the look of his wet hair he had also showered. He put his bag in the boot and got in the passenger side. Morag popped her head through the driver's window.

"I've just got to speak to Caroline about a few things, back in a moment." She smiled and disappeared into the house where she found Caroline sitting on the couch going over some notes.

"Can't thank you enough for this," Morag said, "We'll be back Friday night." As she went to leave, Caroline called to her.

"So Ms Colquhoun, is this the guy you've always been waiting for?" Before Morag could speak, Caroline continued. "All I've ever wanted for you is to see you happy, and if he can do that for you then let it happen." Morag rushed over to Caroline and embraced her.

"Thank you so much buddy and I think, fingers crossed, that Billy is the guy I've been waiting years to find." She kissed her friend on the cheek and waved goodbye as she went back outside.

As she got into the car, Billy noticed she had been crying.

"Is there anything wrong, Mo?"

"No Billy, everything is just fine." She started the car and they headed out of the yard and turned north.

Rock faces rose steeply on both sides of the road. Large swathes of forest clung to the almost vertical slopes much like on the mountains of Montana. Billy never tired of being in the high country and this was no exception. As the sun hit the treeline, colours seemed to burst into life, a patchwork of green and gold along with the rainbow colours of the wildflower meadows.

As they travelled, Morag and Billy talked about their lives and even here there were signs that they were meant to meet. They had both known hard times but they both had a spirit of endeavour, never giving up. As the mountains gave way to some rolling flatlands, the scenery changed from one of beauty to somewhere that felt like you always had to be on your guard. Mile upon mile of open heather was interspersed with the occasional small lochan and off to the left there was a great cone of dark rock.

"Where are we?" Billy asked. His tone was one of bewilderment, which made Morag laugh.

"We are about to enter Glen Coe. We've just driven across Rannoch Moor and that big fellow on the left there..." Morag pointed out of the window at the conical peak set back off the road, "...that is the Buachaille or to give him his full title, Buachaille Etive Mor, the great herdsman of Etive."

Billy looked up at the peak with awe. He had often been in the mountains back home but this felt different. As they drove on the walls of the glen closed in, so much so that it felt quite claustrophobic in places. On the right Billy could see a pile of stones stacked on top of one another. Again, he asked what it was.

"That is a cairn to the Clan MacDonald," Morag said, "whose bloodline was nearly severed in a dark time in Scottish history. They say that when the clans went into battle each man would take a stone which, if he lived, he would then bring back. It was a crude way of knowing how many were lost. If you want to know the story, I will tell you later." Billy nodded.

Even deeper into the glen on the right was a continuous ridgeline. On the left, great peaks seemed to rise defiantly skyward. Between each peak there was a narrow valley eroded by a river that ran through its centre.

It was to one of these valleys Morag pointed.

"That's our destination for tomorrow." Billy's eyes followed Morag's direction, a very narrow valley between two of the taller peaks. "That trail leads to the Lost Valley," she said, "It's such a beautiful spot but quite a climb to get there. It's said that the Clan

MacDonald would stash their stolen cattle up there away from any prying eyes, a bit like they would in the Wild West. In fact, there were a lot of Scots who ended up on the plains and mountains of America. Some of the MacDonald descendants have links to the Sioux nation."

They drove down to the foot of the glen past the beautiful village of Glencoe and on towards Ballachulish. The Loch Leven Hotel sat on the north side of the old ferry crossing that linked Glencoe to Fort William and all points north. Once inside they were greeted by a young woman at the reception desk.

"Good evening, do you have a reservation?" She spoke with an eastern European ascent – probably Polish, Morag thought.

"Yes, we do. It's in the name of Colquhoun." The woman took the key from the closed wall cupboard behind where she sat.

"You're in room twelve, which is on the first floor. It is a lovely room and looks out over the loch." Morag and Billy followed the receptionist upstairs and along the corridor. She opened the door, made her usual speech to new guests, then left Morag and Billy to settle in.

It was a pretty room with a great view, as promised. It had not gone unnoticed to Billy that there was only a double bed in the room. Before he could say anything, Morag spoke.

"I didn't think we would need a twin!"

In the morning, Billy looked across the bed at Morag's sleeping form. He watched the rhythm of her breathing then tenderly brushed away the hair that had fallen across her face sometime during the night. She awoke slowly and greeted him with a soft "good morning", to which Billy just smiled and kissed her forehead.

He got out of bed and headed for the bathroom, showered and returned still wearing his towel. Morag was sat upright in bed checking her phone. Billy sat on the end of the bed and had got his jeans and socks on when Morag shuffled down behind him and wrapped her arms and legs around his body. She kissed the back of Billy's neck as he caressed her arms then legs, before turning her all the way around so she sat naked on his lap.

They kissed passionately, his hands moving slowly up and down her back as she moaned her pleasure. Then they looked into each other's eyes. It was Billy who spoke first.

"I can't stop thinking about last night, it was like a dream. I'm so glad we met this way, Mo. Karma." She smiled.

"Some things are meant to be and I think you choosing to do your first clinic abroad at my place was no accident. Fate has brought us together, Billy." She leaned in and kissed him again then stood up and headed for the shower. They went down for breakfast and then their appointment with the Lost Valley.

As they walked along the footpath, Billy was in awe of the scenery. Morag pointed up the glen at the streams they could see rushing down the mountainside.

"We call them 'mares' tails' because that's what they

look like as they fall down off the hill." They reached the main stream, which could only be crossed thanks to a bridge built by the army some years before. Billy paused halfway across to look down at the clear water that ran underneath.

"The only time I have seen water that clear," he said, "was the run-off from a glacier in Canada. It's so beautiful."

At the far side of the bridge stood a steep rockface they would have to climb before reaching the path beyond. Morag showed Billy where to put his feet and in a couple of minutes they had reached the trail that would take them to the hidden valley. About a third of the way up there was a high stile in the deer fence, which they crossed carefully. The support posts must have had some heavy snow on them during the winter and this had made them slack.

Every now and then they would come across some fellow walkers and exchange a quick hello, then walk on further up. The terrain levelled out but the path narrowed across one of the steeper sections. Again, they carefully negotiated the obstacle, only for Morag to tell Billy on the other side that a woman had fallen to her death here just a year before.

"Thanks for the heads-up, Mo!" She laughed.

"I didn't want to scare you before we crossed." Billy asked if they had to come down the same way. Morag simply shrugged her shoulders and smiled, at which Billy let out a long sigh.

They continued deeper into the glen and the terrain changed once again, this time to a boulder-strewn gorge. Some of the larger stones were the size of a small house while others leaned against each other as if they could topple with the slightest of sounds.

As they walked through the boulders, Billy found himself tiptoeing through some of the smaller gaps and even held his breath once or twice. They pushed on until they came to a ford in the stream where Morag refilled her water bottle and drank from it in large gulps.

"You could not do that back home," Billy said, "A lot of our water system is tainted by the wildlife."

"Well up here you can drink your fill," Morag said, "It's the best water on the planet." Billy followed her lead and filled his flask then took a few tentative sips before drinking the whole bottle.

"You're right, Mo, it's amazing!" He refilled again then they crossed the ford and followed the path which once more started to climb.

At the top, Billy looked ahead in wonder as a long valley opened up in front of them leading all the way up to what was left of the snowline.

"Jesus, Morag. I know you said it was beautiful, but…" His words tailed off as if he could find no explanation for the sight. Morag put her arms around him and kissed him softly on the cheek.

"Worth the climb then?" Taking his hand, they walked along the path until the ground flattened out. To their right was a huge boulder that stood like a sentinel watching all who entered the valley. Finding a nice spot to rest, they took off their packs and sat down for some food, their backs against a large flat stone which warmed them as it had been in direct sunlight for some time. Billy let out a sigh.

"Mo, you sure can pick them, this is going to stay

with me till I'm gone." He stood up and handed Morag his phone. "Could you take my picture so I can show my folks how beautiful this place is?"

"Smile for Mom and Dad," she said and Billy pulled a cheesy grin as the image was captured for posterity. He then set the timer and rested the phone on the rock where they had been sitting.

"Thank you for bringing me to this wonderful place," Billy whispered into Morag's ear as the camera clicked, "I could not think of a better person I would want to be in this moment with." He kissed her softly on the lips then ran off to climb one of the big boulders that littered the valley floor. As he reached the top, Morag shouted out to him. "You're gonna break your bloody neck ya big show-off, and then come crawling to me when you do!" Billy suddenly lost his footing and disappeared backwards behind the boulder. Morag ran fast to where he had fallen, a knot of anxiety gnawing away at her. When she reached the spot where Billy should have been, there was no sign of him. At the same moment a pair of hands grabbed her waist from behind.

"Gotcha, my fine Scottish maid!" Morag spun around, slipped a leg behind his right knee and with the lightest of twists sent him to the floor.

"You fucking idiot," she said, "You could have been hurt!"

As Billy lay on the ground winded, all he could say in reply was, "I think I already am".

She helped him to his feet and rubbed his back. After a few moments, Billy apologised for having been an idiot.

"Yes, you are an idiot," Morag said, "a very cute

and sexy idiot but one nonetheless." They laughed and held each other until Morag said, "Right mister, are you ready for the descent?" Billy nodded. "Good. I'm going to take you to meet a friend of mine out on the road to Oban." Billy narrowed his eyes.

"Does this friend have a horse? I'm not on the clock." Morag laughed.

"No, he does not own a horse but he is good with his hands." They headed back down the trail leaving the scenery as they had found it.

Chapter Thirty-Nine

The sign on the white stucco wall read Columba's Bay. They pulled off the road into a car park and stopped outside a small single-storey building. Morag's friend John met them at the door of his café.

"Hey honey, how are you doing?" Morag hugged John then looked over at Billy who was waiting to be introduced.

"John, this is Billy Dawson, a trainer friend of mine from the good old United States of America." John reached out his hand and shook Billy's firmly.

"Nice to meet you Billy, what part of America are you from?" There was a warmth about John that Billy liked.

"I'm originally from a small town called Estes Park up in the Colorado Rockies but I now live with my parents in Montana." John smiled and ushered them inside. The café was small and compact but very well presented. There were a few customers inside so John left Morag and Billy with the menu while he attended to them.

"Do you recommend anything?" Billy didn't look up from the menu as he asked for Morag's opinion. Her response was one word:

"Everything". John soon came back to the table with his notepad.

"What can I get you guys? I can put a steak on for you, my Glasgow butcher got me some nice Angus sirloins."

"Sounds like a plan," Morag said as she put the menu to one side.

Once John had disappeared back into the kitchen, Billy looked across the table at Morag. "How long have you known John? He seems a really nice guy." Morag smiled.

"The family came up to Oban on holiday many years ago before my parents passed away when this place had a different owner. I was passing by one day and got talking to John – and once you taste his food, you'll realise why I come back any time I'm in the area."

John returned with a salad starter, some cut bread, two small bowls of olive oil and what looked to Billy like balsamic syrup. John was just about to leave when Billy asked what was in the olive oil.

"Balsamic syrup," John said, "Trade secret." Billy laughed.

When John looked perplexed, he said, "Sorry John but your secret's out, my mum has been serving me and my dad this for years!"

"You don't say," John said, also now laughing, "That's incredible. You know Tesla invented radio but Marconi was a better salesman and got credited with the idea?" John winked and headed back to the kitchen.

The food was just a simple salad but John had seasoned it to perfection and in a few minutes both plates were clear. By now the other customers had settled up and left. John appeared with their steaks.

"If they taste as good as they smell…" Billy's mouth was watering as he spoke.

"I know you will love it," John said, "Enjoy." Billy looked at Morag, said "wow", then they ate their fill until John returned from the kitchen.

"That was one of, if not *the* best steak I have ever had," Billy said, "You must give me a copy of the sauce recipe for my mom." John blushed ever so slightly.

"Now coming from a man who lives in cattle country I will take your compliment." Billy pulled out his wallet to pay for the meal but his host stopped him. "Your money is no good here and anyone who is a friend of this little lady is a friend of mine." Billy stretched out his hand and John shook it with a warmth that seemed to ooze from every cell of his body.

"Where you guys off to now?" Morag replied that they would probably head back to the hotel and chill out for the night, maybe stopping at Kilmartin on the way home.

On opening the car door, Morag waved and shouted back to John,

"Thanks for the meal and say hi to Liz for us." They drove off and continued waving until John and Columba's Bay disappeared behind them.

After checking out of the hotel the next morning, they turned south and followed the signs for Kilmartin and destinations beyond. The coast road down through Argyll was a mix of spectacular scenery and large established forests which looked over the sea lochs that cut into the landscape. Kilmartin consisted of a few rows of cottages and larger houses and a church with a museum and café attached.

The graveyard in the southern corner of the church

grounds contained headstones purported to mark the resting place of Templar knights: it was to these that Morag and Billy headed. Morag said the church had been built in the 1500s and the whole of Kilmartin Glen was peppered with Neolithic and prehistoric sites of importance. It was common for the church to build on sites of previous pagan worship in an effort to wipe away the memory of what they considered to be improper religious practices.

Billy and Morag took great care not to stand on any of the graves old or new. They entered a low-roofed building and were greeted by two rows of large headstones that ran either side of the room and rested upright against the walls. Morag said there were questions as to the authenticity of the stones but they were believed to be of great importance to Scottish history. Billy looked at the intricate carvings, a mixture of flora and fauna, swords, and skulls and bones.

After a while they drove further along the glen. "It's not often you get this place to yourself," she said. They walked down a small path and over a bridge. In the field in front of them was a group of large upright stones. Billy was taken aback.

"This looks similar to Stonehenge," he said, "I never thought I'd visit a place like this!" He held Morag closely and kissed her. "Thanks Mo, for all of this." She smiled at him.

"You're welcome, honey." Billy had never thought he would hear that term of endearment again, not after Sam. He took Morag's hand as they walked further into the site. There were the remains of a burial tomb and more big stones that lined up with the ones at the entrance. Morag looked excited.

"If you think this is good," she said, "wait till you see what's next!" They walked through a field of sheep, stepped over a stile and walked along a narrow road until reaching a sign to Temple Wood beside a small grove of trees. There was a circle of stones measuring roughly twenty metres wide. Inside the circle there were individual stones piled in a similar fashion to the ones they had seen at the MacDonald cairn, except in a gentler gradient. Billy read the information board and learned that this site had been built by archaeologists from the ruins found when it had first been uncovered. After taking a few photos he turned to Morag.

"I never thought I'd ever see anything like this, Mo, not in my life." She reached over to take his hand and they stood in silence for what seemed like an age, then carefully picked their way back through the stones and headed for the car.

As they drove off, Billy took a last look back over his shoulder. Then they started the long drive back to Glasgow and the final two horse clinics before he would fly home to the States.

Chapter Forty

Caroline greeted them as they got out of the car. "Did you guys have a good trip?" Morag threw her arms around her neck and whispered:

"The best, just the best." The friends looked into each other's eyes and smiled.

There was a thump as Billy closed the boot of the car then walked toward them with a holdall draped awkwardly over both shoulders. Caroline announced that there was a pot of tea brewing in the kitchen so it was in this direction they all walked, chatting as they went.

"You know, it's nice going away," Morag said as they sat down, "but you can't beat a good cup of tea in your own chair." Caroline laughed.

"Speaking of that, I'd better get back to rescuing my long-suffering husband from the clutches of the terrible twosome which are our offspring." Before she left the room, Billy thanked her for letting him and Morag have their time together.

"I never knew that your country had such a rich tradition and history," he said, "not to mention the breathtaking scenery." Caroline blushed slightly, something Morag had never seen her do before.

"It was no trouble at all and I'm so glad you both enjoyed each other so much. I mean, enjoyed your trip together." Morag and Billy both burst out laughing at Caroline's slip of the tongue, which she took in good humour. She then gave Morag a run-down on the horses that had arrived for the next clinic before bidding them both goodnight.

Later as they lay wrapped in each other's arms, Billy said: "You know something Mo, I'd love for you to come over to my folks' place. I could show you around, let you see some of our scenery and history. I think you would love it." Morag pulled in close.

"I'd love to do that. Maybe next year?" There was a hint of sadness in her voice as she knew all too readily that their time together was coming to an end.

"It's not that long," Billy said, "and there's always Skype or email!" A smile crept across Morag's face and she kissed Billy softly on the lips, then tucked her head against his chest as they gradually fell asleep.

There was a knock at the door as they sat eating breakfast. Caroline entered with a bag of goodies.

"I hope you don't mind, Mo, I brought some fresh bread, tomatoes and cheese – thought we could have a ploughman's for lunch if you have some pickles?" Morag clapped her hands.

"You're an absolute angel and yes, I have some pickle dressing." Billy, still a bit confused by the Gypsies, sat bewildered wondering if the girls were speaking some foreign language.

"What's a ploughman's?" Morag and Caroline laughed in unison then Morag explained.

"It's a meal that farmers used to have which consisted of bread, cheese and a savoury, usually chutney, which is a topping of chopped savoury pickles." Billy poured himself another coffee.

"I'll look forward to lunch, then." With that he headed across to the annexe.

Caroline sat down next to Morag. "Penny for your thoughts?" She smiled and patted her friend's leg.

"It's nothing," Morag said, "just that Billy will be heading home soon and I feel things are just getting started for us." Caroline could feel Morag's emotional turmoil and put her arm around her.

"Listen, you once told me that distance is nothing when we are working on our connection with horses. It's no different with humans. If this is meant to be then it will be and no distance in the world will stop you." As Caroline spoke, Morag realised there were tears running down her face and she wiped them away with the sleeve of her sweater. When her eyes cleared she could see Caroline's face beaming back at her.

"I've never seen you like this with anyone," she said, "Is he that special?" Without hesitation Morag said, "Yes". Caroline put her arms around her.

"I'm so happy for you, it's been a long time coming and you so deserve someone special in your life."

Billy walked back in.

"Excuse me ladies, should I go out and come back in?" Morag and Caroline both threw cushions at him.

"Was it something I said?" Billy asked, "or is this another weird Scottish custom?" More cushions were fired in his direction, one of which managed to dislodge his hat.

"Now there's a lot that I will tolerate," Billy said, "but knocking a cowboy's hat on to the floor is just damn disrespectful."

Morag stopped laughing and searched Billy's face

for any signs of humour: there were none. He reached down and picked the hat off the floor, and as he sat it back on his head a smile rippled across his face.

"You should see how ashamed you guys look," he said. Morag ran across and slapped him across his chest.

"Billy Dawson, that's just not fair, poor Caroline is mortified."

"Speak for yourself," Caroline said. Billy rubbed his chest where Morag had hit him.

"Jesus Mo, you have hands like shovels." She stuck her tongue out at him as he walked to the door. "I'll go check the PA, see if it's okay and will catch up with you guys later." Morag blew him a kiss.

Two days later they rose early as Billy's flight was at 9.30am. The final two clinics had gone without a hitch and he was already booked in for more in the future. Morag had done a good job promoting him.

Over breakfast neither said much, just the usual pleasantries you find anywhere on the planet at this time of day. Billy went to fetch his bags and to tidy up. Back in the kitchen, he sat holding hands with Morag until the headlights of Caroline's car snapped them out of their melancholy state.

As she entered, Caroline didn't say much either, just a quick good morning. Morag took down the car keys from their hook and walked hand-in-hand with Billy out to the car. He opened the boot and swung his bags inside. It was at this point that Morag could no longer hold back her emotions.

"Billy, I don't want you to leave." They held each other tightly.

"Mo, I truly don't want to leave you either but we never expected this to happen and we'll just have to work at it as best as we can." As he spoke, Billy never took his eyes off her – it was as if he was searching in her eyes for some last-minute reprieve where she would say that she was going with him.

They got in the car, headed out of the yard and drove towards Glasgow and the airport. There were surprisingly few people in the terminal building apart from the odd traveller waiting for a connecting flight to take them here and there. Morag escorted Billy upstairs to the overseas departure gate.

"I never thought I'd feel this way again with anyone," Billy said, "but here we are." Tears ran down his cheeks and Morag reached up to brush them away as he spoke. "I know this is just the beginning for us and no matter what it takes I'll make it work."

"We're like two halves of something that was broken being put back together again," Morag said. Then as if it had been choreographed, they both spoke at the same time: "I love you." They kissed for what seemed like an age then stopped and looked up to check the time on the board.

"You had best be going," Morag said, "or I might steal your passport." Billy slowly walked towards the check-in area then turned and gave one final wave before disappearing from sight, leaving Morag wondering if she would ever see him again.

Chapter Forty-One

Walter sat impatiently in the arrival zone of the airport waiting for Billy to appear. Finally after about twenty minutes, the familiar sight of his son's hat bobbing along in the crowd brought a smile to Walter's face.

"Did you have a good flight?" Walter helped Billy lift his bag into the back of the pickup.

"Aw the usual, Pop," Billy said, "just counting the minutes till we landed." There was a sense of melancholy in his voice which Walter picked up on but did not pursue.

"Your mom tells me your trip went well and the clinics were a success." Again, Billy sounded a bit far-off with his reply.

"Yes Pop, Morag did a real nice job at organising things over there. She's a nice girl and I think you guys would like her." Walter tried to cheer up his son.

"Well, we could come with you the next time you go to Scotland, I hear it's a beautiful country and if my memory serves correctly we have family over there that go way back." Billy smiled and eased himself into the passenger seat.

"That sounds great. I'm sure you guys would love it."

Walter told him to put his head back and catch up on some sleep. It did not take them long to get home. Billy woke as soon as the pickup hit the track running up to the ranch, as he knew every bump even with his eyes closed. As they pulled up, they could see Margaret out feeding some kitchen scraps to the chickens. She stopped and rushed to see Billy, wrapping her arms around him hard.

"Hey Mom, you're gonna snap a rib." She slackened her grip and kissed him on the cheek.

"Can't a mother show affection to her son who has been gone for a while?" Billy nodded his agreement. Walter meanwhile had taken the bags from the vehicle and was standing with arms outstretched, waiting for his hug. They ignored him and headed inside, much to his amusement.

Billy headed straight upstairs. Walter entered the kitchen and Margaret kissed him on the forehead.

"You know you're my one and only," she said but noticed he was thinking about something. "Penny for your thoughts?"

"I'm sorry, honey." Walter kissed her on the cheek. "Billy's been funny since I picked him up, kinda like his mind is still back in Scotland." Margaret rubbed Walter's back.

"I'll have a talk with him once he's unpacked and settled in, okay?" Walter nodded in agreement but was still worried. He headed out to the yard.

Margaret didn't have long to wait until Billy came back down for his customary homecoming mug of coffee. He walked into the kitchen with some envelopes that Margaret had left in the bedroom.

"Look at this," he said, "junk mail, I wish there was some way to just get rid of it." Margaret sensed there was more than the usual frustration in her son's words.

"There is, honey, you use it to get the fire going in

the wintertime." Margaret then took a gamble. "So, was Scotland a good thing?" Billy smiled and looked straight at her.

"In more ways than one," he replied.

"In what ways, son?" He fumbled with the pile of mail.

"The clinics were great and Morag had done a brilliant job organising the events..." Before he could finish, Margaret interrupted.

"You have feelings for Morag and it's more than just friendship, I'll hazard a guess?"

Billy looked up from his mail and saw a smile on his mother's face.

"How did you know that?" Margaret came around the table, sat in the chair next to him and took his hand.

"Billy, you're my son and you've always worn your heart on the outside, which is a wonderful gift. And sometimes you forget I'm a counsellor and we're trained to look for the little things, imperceptible changes in a person's being." Billy let out a laugh as he squeezed his mother's hand.

"Can't hide anything from you, can I?" He told Margaret all about the trip and his feelings for Morag. By the end he was a bit emotional and Margaret did her best to comfort him, but she always found it best to just sit, listen and let Billy get things out of his system. They drank their coffee for a few moments before Margaret spoke again.

"My mother, God rest her soul, used to say, 'if something is meant to be, it will be'. And no force on this earth will stop that from happening, especially in matters of the heart. You know, as I've grown older I see it happening more and more. The modern world is so small that love has no barriers anymore. There are so many ways to stay in touch – social media, Skype – Jesus Christ, most of us carry our office around in our pockets these days." Billy listened intently and felt better the more his mother spoke.

"What I'm trying to say," she continued, "is don't give up on it, son. I'm sure if Morag feels as strongly as you do then you will both make it work somehow." Billy leaned over and kissed her on the cheek.

"Thanks Mom, you're right." With that Margaret stood up, washed her mug, then asked Billy to fetch his dad for lunch. Billy went to the back door and shouted that if he didn't hurry up then his lunch would be forfeited. Walter heard the change in his son's voice and smiled. He knew Margaret had sorted out the problem.

In the weeks that followed the clinics, Morag found that work kept her occupied through the day but she felt loneliness at night. She had been in frequent contact with Billy by phone and email but she longed for the time when they would be together again.

Morag had asked Caroline round for dinner one night.

"Okay, Colquhoun," her friend said, "what is it this time?" Morag blushed slightly.

"What do you take me for, can't I have you over for dinner without there being some ulterior motive?" Caroline laughed.

"No!" Then they both laughed.

"I've decided to fly over and visit Billy," Morag said, "and I was wondering if you would look after the place for me. It won't be for at least a month but I thought I'd run it past you now." Caroline was quiet for a moment, thinking.

"I'll have to clear it with Scott but it should be okay." The friends hugged and cried.

"Thank you so much," Morag said, "you're a star. I don't want to let this opportunity slip away, know what I mean?" Caroline smiled.

"I know how things were with Scott and myself and I'd have done the same for him. Well, you do when you're in love!" The women talked late into the night, making plans and sorting out schedules.

After Caroline left, Morag lay in bed thinking about the journey ahead and what might come of it.

Chapter Forty-Two

Leaning on the field gate, Billy watched the horses go about their daily life and in particular Ronin. It had been on the last clinic run that he had made the decision to retire Ronin from work. Although it was a tough decision and pained him, it was in the horse's interest, which for Billy was of paramount importance. Ronin had simply grown old. He could still do the work but his sharpness had slowed. This coupled with the onset of arthritis in his hocks meant it would have been a disservice on Billy's part to force him to continue.

As Billy watched Ronin in the field, he knew the right choice had been made. With this thought still in his head, he started down the track that led back to the ranch. The trees were shedding their leaves, which blew here and there on the sharp easterly that usually signalled winter's imminent arrival. On walking into the yard, he saw Walter slumped over against the barn wall and immediately ran towards him.

"Pops, what's wrong?" Walter was almost grey in colour and very short of breath but was able to speak.

"I was chopping some logs and took a dizzy turn, tried to make it back to the house but didn't have the strength." Billy ran and got one of the picnic chairs and sat Walter down, then fetched a horse blanket and draped it round his shoulders.

"I'll be back in a moment, okay?" He hurtled back to the house and shouted for Margaret. She ran out of the door, leaving him to call the ambulance.

Walter was propped up in bed looking like some caged animal at the zoo. Margaret and Billy sat next to him unable to help with his pleas to let him get up.

"Dad, what happened yesterday was a warning for you to slow down," Billy said, "Depending on what the cardiologist says it will determine what you can and can't do back home and that's that." Billy knew he had to stand firm or his dad wouldn't listen.

Just as Walter was about to reply, the door opened and a tall man with salt-and-pepper hair entered the room: Dr Smith, the senior cardiologist.

After a few brief pleasantries, the doctor got to the point.

"Mr Dawson, we have looked at both the ECG that the paramedics took and the ones you have had here and we think you are suffering from a condition known as atrial flutter. This means your heart gets out of its natural rhythm and goes into a higher cyclic rate. We have prescribed beta blockers which will hopefully keep things working just dandy, but we will be running more tests on you in the near future. Any questions?"

Walter tried to speak first but Margaret beat him to it. "What causes it?" The doctor smiled.

"Wear and tear. Your husband has been a very active man all his life and although that has had its benefits, there are, on occasion, some health consequences which go with that lifestyle. Mr Dawson will just have to start taking things easy." The doctor looked over at Walter then back to Margaret. "Or next time it could be a full-blown heart attack and, excuse me for being blunt, it's a lottery as to whether or not he would survive that."

Margaret thanked the doctor for being so honest.

"Now you are free to go home, Mr Dawson," he said, "but you will be back here in a couple of weeks for a few more tests to see how you are coping." With that Dr Smith left the room. Billy looked at his dad.

"Pop, I've spoken to Frank Hendriks at Montana State and he's going to see if some of the students can come along and help out on the ranch, under your supervision of course, just till we see where things are going with this. Okay?"

He could see reluctance in his father's face so was surprised when he agreed to the suggestion. They then had to wait for Walter's catheter to be removed before he could get dressed and head back to the ranch, back to normality.

Nearly a month had passed since the incident and Walter had been given the all-clear, although he would be on medication for life and could only perform light duties around the ranch, much to his displeasure. True to his word, Frank had provided a few students who could help out on the ranch. This would also count towards the work experience needed for their course completion.

It had been a while since Billy had been at Montana State but he felt the need to go and thank his old tutor in person. Walking through the campus brought back many nice memories of his time there and, of course, of happy days with Samantha. Billy had arranged to meet Frank over lunch and as he approached the campus restaurant, he could see him sitting at a table just inside the main door.

"Hey, great to see you again," Frank said with a smile, "Been a while. How's your father doing?" Billy filled Frank in on the latest goings-on and apologised for not having come to visit sooner.

"You've got nothing to be sorry about," Frank said, "With all that's happened I'm surprised you're even here, but glad of it." His thoughtfulness filled Billy with warmth and made things easier.

"Thanks, time's a great healer so they say." Billy shrugged his shoulders as he spoke. "And anyway, I know this ain't much but it's a small token of appreciation for your help with Dad." He handed Frank a bag which contained a bottle of Jura single malt.

"You didn't need to do that," Frank said, "you know if I can help then I will. But thank you." The two men talked for a while then Billy shook his friend's hand.

"You have an open invitation to come out to the ranch, just show up any time." Frank smiled.

"I'll take you up on that because I have to assess those young fellows who are helping your folks." As Billy walked away, Frank shouted after him. "Don't leave things so long next time!"

After leaving the campus, Billy found himself heading towards the cemetery where Samantha lay. Without hesitation, he swung his pickup into the grounds. The last time he had been here Sam's headstone had not been in place, so for the first time he read the inscription her parents had placed there: *Our beloved Samantha will never grow old. She will never suffer the ravages of time, for she is safe in the arms of our Lord Jesus Christ.* A lump grew in Billy's throat as he looked at the old flowers that filled a small vase at the side of the headstone. He sat down beside the grave and began to speak.

"You were my first love and I'll never forget your spirit and beauty. We had so very little time together but that which we had I will cherish till the day I die. I love you, Samantha Hart."

He was just about to leave when he heard a voice.

"And she loved you too, Billy Dawson." As he turned there was a grey-haired woman standing directly behind him. He searched her face for some sort of recognition then it came to him: she was Sam's mother. His first instinct was to leave but something in the tone of her words made him wait. She looked at him with tears in her eyes.

"Those things I said to you at the hospital were wrong and I was bitter. I wanted to lash out at the world for snatching our daughter from us and instead I struck out at you, the one person who had brought so much joy to Samantha's life. I have waited years for you to come back and now here you are." She broke down in tears, Billy walked over and held her in his arms.

"I'm so sorry you lost your daughter," he said, "I blamed myself for so many years but eventually I healed and moved on. Maybe it was fate, me coming here today, but I'm so glad I did." He slackened his grip and stood back so he could look Sam's mother in the eye.

"We all lost something beautiful that day," Billy said, "someone precious, that's what I carry in my heart's memory of her. I carry Sam's love for me and mine for her. No one can take that away from us, ever." Sam's mother reached up and brushed his cheek with the palm of her hand.

"Thank you, Billy, for being so understanding but most of all for loving my little girl, Samantha." With that, the elderly woman turned to the grave and laid some fresh flowers. Billy walked slowly back to his pickup then drove into town and took the highway that would take him home.

As he drove, he felt a sense of peace, a feeling of being cleansed of a heavy burden. He smiled to himself and switched on the radio. It was playing *Thunderstruck* by AC/DC. Billy tapped the steering wheel in time to the beat and pressed the accelerator.

Chapter Forty-Three

"How's she coming along?" Walter made his inquiry as Billy worked the little Appaloosa mare on the line.

"Summers? She's coming on fine, Pops, loves to please the handler and that's always a bonus." He walked to the middle of the pen and took off the mare's halter, hanging it on a post next to the gate before fetching her some hay.

Walter waited for Billy to finish.

"Are you taking her on this clinic run? She would be good company for Raven." Billy put his arm around Walter's shoulder as they walked back to the house.

"Yes, I am going to take her. It will be good experience for her and as you say, Raven can have a travel buddy. And anyway, I might need a stand-in if anything happens." They reached the porch where Margaret greeted them with a smile.

"I swear you two have cameras rigged so you can see when the food is ready." The men laughed and walked inside.

Over the past few weeks Margaret had switched the lunch meals from wholesome to healthy on the advice of the cardiologist. Walter to his credit took to the new menu with vigour, as did Billy. Today's meal consisted of homemade tomato soup followed by a light salad with vinaigrette. After they had eaten, Billy went to pack a few things for his clinic in Florida then lay on the bed and sent a message to Morag. She did not reply immediately, which was common for both of them as they did not live by their phones.

The Florida clinic run would be Billy's last for the year. Although he loved teaching and working with the horses, he did need time to recharge his batteries and spend time with family. The Florida clinics consisted of a day here and a couple of days there, and Billy always enjoyed his time in the south as it gave chance to feel the warm sun on his back. Montana in the winter, although beautiful, could be pretty inhospitable to human and animal alike.

There had already been a few small snowstorms but nothing like the ones that would come late in the year and at the start of the following year, which was when ranchers really earnt their stripes. This year would be slightly different for all of them as there would be extra help provided by Frank Hendriks' students.

Billy picked up a couple of bags and headed out to the truck then returned to print out his schedule. With Summers being a clinic novice, Billy thought it better to leave a day earlier than usual as he always liked to make more stops with the new horses. It would normally take two or three days to get to where he was going and with the extra day this journey would be a long one.

Back in the kitchen, Walter sat at the table going through some papers.

"You got a minute, Pops?" Walter looked up at Billy and put his papers to one side.

"Sure thing, son. What can I do you for?" Billy always smiled when his father gave this reply.

"I spoke to Frank and there's a young fella called

Ben Carson coming over for the two weeks while I'm away." Walter nodded. "He is supposed to be a pretty decent rider, sympathetic and all, so I thought if you wouldn't mind you could you keep an eye on him." Walter sat a bit straighter in his chair.

"Sure, son, I'll keep a bead on him for you, maybe teach him a trick or two!" A smile spread across Billy's face. As he had hoped, this request seemed to lift his father's spirits by giving him some responsibility.

Billy then returned to his room and found to his delight that Morag had replied to his message. She had lost one client and gained another two, which was the way things went at a livery yard. There had been a couple of horses booked in for her to train, bringing a little extra money and providing a welcome distraction from the daily grind of running her own business. He told her about the Florida clinics and apologised in advance if he was not as frequent in his messages to her. She forgave him his sins. Later, Billy lay in bed thinking about Mo and how they could make their long-distance relationship work.

Billy didn't know it, but Morag had just finished booking her flights when he replied to her message. A coil of excitement spun inside her as she had arranged her surprise visit to coincide with the last day of his clinic run. There was a real sense of urgency to her days now: she pushed herself to the limit physically and at times mentally. It had been a long time, if ever, since she had felt so deeply for another human being. At times her feelings consumed her every waking thought.

Gradually, if ever so slowly, the days tumbled off

the calendar until there were no red crosses left. Morag stood at the departure gate in Glasgow airport waiting anxiously to board the flight that would set her heart free of its current constrictions. On leaving, Caroline had given her one piece of advice: "This may only happen once in a lifetime. Look forward at what might be, not backward to what was."

As Morag recalled the words, a voice crackled over the PA. "Would all priority boarding for BA flight 2816 to Orlando please make their way to the gate, thank you."

Morag slung her rucksack over her shoulder after retrieving her passport and boarding pass from one of the side pockets. "This is it," she whispered under her breath.

There was the usual bustle in the queue but none of it really bothered her and soon she was sitting in the business class section of the plane. She had chosen to pay extra for the peace of mind it gave and with it being such a long flight she could, she hoped, sleep through much of it. She made herself familiar with the in-flight entertainment then settled down to read a book she had picked up on her way through the terminal. The captain wished everyone a pleasant flight and everyone waited for the roar of the engines.

Morag put the book to one side and closed her eyes. She was not a fan of take-offs or landings and chose to lie back deep in her seat. Gradually the nose lifted, contact with the ground was broken and the plane pitched steeply upward into the clouds. She watched as Glasgow disappeared below then picked up her book again. Her flight plan was to read, eat, then watch a movie until it made her fall asleep before waking up in Orlando.

Everything was set. She had booked a rental car complete with satnav and she had the address of the last clinic Billy would be teaching. Every now and again she sneaked a look at the map showing the flight's progress, but the last few times she had done this the plane seemed to be hovering in the same spot beyond the coast of Ireland. As if by some divine intervention, a stewardess appeared and Morag ordered a salad starter followed by chicken and chips.

Fifteen minutes later the meal arrived and it all looked edible. There had been previous flights when the food had not been up to her standard of what she liked to describe as 'good nosh'. Morag finished the meal, put on the movie and fell asleep ten minutes into it. When she woke it was only a couple of hours until they landed. A small smile crept across her lips and she pulled the book out and began reading again.

Chapter Forty-Four

After he had bedded down the horses for the night, Billy took time to thank the clinic hosts and have a final meal with them before leaving the next day. There was the usual post-clinic banter, which always meant that the event had gone well. Then with a long drive ahead, Billy wished everyone goodnight and walked back to his trailer where he poured a glass of water then sat down to take the weight off his feet.

His phone rattled into life on the countertop startling him, so much so that he knocked over his glass of water. He could see that it was Morag calling so he hurried to answer.

"Hey honey, how are things in bonnie Scotland?" Morag smiled to herself.

"Ah, Scotland is great, if a little cold at this time of year, and it won't be long before the horses are off the pasture. How did your tour go?" Billy paused for a moment before answering.

"Yeah it went well, had a couple of knuckleheads to straighten out but nothing worth writing home about. I sure do miss you, though. Any idea when you'll be able to make it over here?" Morag almost laughed but managed to stifle it.

"Well, with winter coming on there's little chance of me going anywhere till spring." She now had to bite her lip to stop herself from laughing. "Did I hear a knock at your trailer door?" Billy was about to say no when his door was knocked three times.

"Yeah, you were right. Hold on and I'll see who it is." He reached for the handle and pulled. The light from the trailer spilled out to reveal Morag standing with a huge smile on her face.

"Surprise!" Billy stood dumbfounded with the phone still at his ear. After what seemed to be an age he put the phone in his pocket and rushed outside to take Morag in his arms.

"How did you manage this? I thought it would be next year before we would have time together." She took his face in her hands.

"Love has no boundaries," she said. They kissed passionately and went inside the trailer. The initial shock was wearing off as Billy sat next to her on the small couch.

"God Mo, I've missed you so much. When you said it would be next year before I could see you my heart sank." She kissed him softly, her eyes never leaving his.

"I couldn't wait, Billy, it's been hell back home without you there so I booked a one-way ticket and here I am."

They sat enjoying the physical touch of the other and every sense of tiredness left them.

Billy got up and put the coffee pot on. "Fancy a cup?" Morag nodded her agreement and headed towards the door.

"Be back in a moment, just getting my bag." With that she disappeared out to the car. When she returned, Billy had set the mugs on the table. Morag picked up hers and took a big gulp.

"That tastes like heaven," she said. Billy smiled and

put his arm around her as she sat down. They finished their coffee and headed out to check the horses that were in a pen behind the trailer. As they approached, both horses stop eating the hay and nickered in their direction, a sound that any decent horseperson loved. For Morag it instantly brought thoughts of home. She looked in the pen and saw a stunning mustang gelding and an equally pretty Appaloosa mare.

"Where's Ronin?" The question made Billy laugh out loud.

"You don't miss a thing, do you? He's back home as I made the decision to retire him from the clinic runs, but he can still earn his crust helping Mom and Dad with their therapy work." Morag smiled.

"So who are these guys?" They stepped inside the pen and it was the mustang who came over first.

"This guy here is Raven aka El Diablo," Billy said. Morag frowned a little at the second name as Billy continued, "I know – great name for a black horse! And the shy one over there is Summers. One of my clients had a kid and that didn't leave a lot of time for the horse, so…"

They walked towards the mare which immediately made a direct line for Morag, who ruffled the horse's forelock and kissed her nose, much to Billy's amusement. "I think she likes you," he said. With the introductions over, they left the horses for the night and headed back to the trailer.

Morag woke and reached out to touch Billy but he was not there. It was then that she caught a whiff of bacon being fried and the sound of whistling in the next room. She slipped on a pair of jeans and a T-shirt. As she opened the door to the living area, Billy asked how she liked her bacon done and did she want an egg?

"I let you sleep," he said as he kept an eye on the cooking, "Hopefully it will let you recover from your flight. I'm going to be heading home to Montana today, fancy tagging along?" Morag jumped up from the couch and hugged him tight around the waist.

"Yes, yes, yes!" Billy smiled at her and set the frying pan to one side.

"I think my folks are going to love you but not as much as I do." He kissed her hard before they took their seats at the table. Morag said that all she had to do was to drop the rental car off at the nearest branch, after which she was free to go anywhere.

Once breakfast was done, they finished packing the trailer and mucked out the pens. It was about ten o'clock when they started the long journey to Montana where both of their lives would be changed forever.

Chapter Forty-Five

Time seemed to fly on the journey north. They made good time and the horses seemed to be coping well, especially Summers. Once again, Billy turned on to the dirt road that led to the ranch and home. Pulling in, he noticed that Walter had brought the horses down from the pasture for the winter and as he and Morag stepped out of the pickup he could feel why. There was an east wind blowing that caused even Morag to put on another layer. They quickly got Raven and Summers into their respective paddocks and had just started to put away some of the equipment when Walter and Margaret appeared on the back porch.

"William Dawson, have you no manners? Are you not going to introduce us to this lovely young lady?" Billy knew by his mother's tone that what she said was in jest – mostly.

"Mom, Dad, I'd like you to meet Morag, who pulled a surprise visit on me down in Florida and now on you guys here in sunny Montana." Morag made her way towards the porch and climbed the steps to be greeted first by Margaret then Walter.

"We'll leave Billy to put his things away," Margaret said, "Why don't you come into the kitchen out of the cold and I'll make us a coffee, sound good?" Morag nodded in agreement then turned and stuck her tongue out at Billy as they headed indoors. Before Walter could offer any assistance, Billy looked up at him.

"No, it's just a couple of saddles and a bunch of washing. I'll be fine but thanks for the offer." Walter gave a wave of his hand and went inside to join the others for coffee. There he found Margaret already deep in conversation with Morag.

"So your clan still holds ownership over the lands of Loch Lomond? That's amazing. And do you live far from there?" Morag took a sip of her coffee.

"It's about a forty-five minute drive away. Most of it has been turned over for the tourist sector: hotels, log cabins, golf courses, you know the kind of things." Margaret nodded in agreement then turned to Walter.

"Did you hear that, old man?" Walter sat down at the table next to the women.

"Yes, I heard everything, my heart may need a service but the ears are still okay." They all laughed, then it was Morag's turn to ask the questions.

"Is this your family home? I mean have you always lived here?" Before Margaret could say anything, Walter answered.

"No and yes." Morag looked puzzled as he continued. "It is our family home but it's not inherited. We both have farming backgrounds and wanted somewhere to call our own, and besides that we both have kin that still work our old family farms. We bought this place back in the late fifties, has everything we need." There was a joy Morag could see in Walter's face that reminded her of her own father, who had died a few years earlier.

She smiled and just at that moment Billy stumbled through the door with too many bags, one of which he dropped on the floor, spilling its contents for all to see. Morag could only laugh at this clumsy entrance while

Walter and Margaret sat shaking their heads.

"Some things never change, do they Walt?" But before he could answer, Margaret continued. "Billy Dawson, do you ever on your travels by any chance think of visiting a Laundromat?" She got to her feet and started to gather Billy's things and put them back in the bag. Billy just stood there looking at Morag for sympathy, which he did not get.

"Ah, the joy of being back home," he said. "You know Mom, you're right, I should take my dirty drawers and wash them myself, note to self." Morag walked over to help him with the bags and Billy steered her in the direction of the stairs.

Billy's parents watched as the young couple disappeared upstairs out of sight.

"You know something, Walt?" Margaret said.

"What?"

"I really like that girl and she reminds me in so many ways of Samantha." Walter put his arm around her and they stood in silence looking at the top of the staircase.

They had come to the end of the trail where sunlight spilled over a large expanse of lush green pasture. Morag could see a small group of horses off in the distance.

"You see the dun on the far left?" Morag nodded as Billy spoke. "That's my old boy, my first horse." Morag could see how proud he was of his horse and at the same time sad about him.

Billy climbed on to the top rail of the fence and whistled three times. There was a slight pause then every horse's head lifted and looked in their direction.

Ronin led the charge but was quickly overtaken by the younger and more sprightly members of the herd. They arrived at the gate with chests heaving and nostrils flaring, but once the herd realised their visitors were only interested in Ronin they sought out more sustenance at this end of the pasture.

Ronin was the centre of attention and he kept nuzzling Morag's hair and shoulder, causing her to laugh.

"I think he likes you," Billy said.

"Yeah, I kinda thought that myself," Morag said, still laughing, "Is he always this fresh with people?" Billy thought for a moment.

"Now that you mention it, he is usually friendly, but what he is doing to you is bordering on assault." They laughed. Morag continued to give her attention to Ronin until finally he grew bored with his human companions and walked away to where the rest of the herd were grazing.

With the horses checked, thoughts turned to what Margaret had put in the picnic basket, which had been set aside as they entered the field. Billy lifted the bag of goodies and put his free hand around Morag's shoulder.

"Wait till you see this nice little spot," he said, "it's so peaceful and there are meadow flowers everywhere." She smiled and wrapped her left hand around his waist as they entered a small open area where the sunlight broke through the branches. There were flowers of all colours and at the far end a stream cascaded down over the rock with an almost hypnotic tone. It was as if they were the first people ever to rest there.

"My God Billy, this is so beautiful and a perfect

place to have a picnic." He was glad she liked it as there was no better place to tell her what had been in his thoughts for some time.

As usual, Margaret had excelled herself with her home cooking and they barely ate a quarter of what she had prepared.

"Your mom can sure cook," Morag said, "Do we keep the rest for later or squirrel it away somewhere as it's almost winter?" Billy laughed.

"Usually I take it up to my room and devour it slowly over a few days." Morag laughed too and it echoed around the glade, so much so that a couple of quail flew out of their roost and disappeared further into the woods. Packing up the picnic and walking down the path, they stopped at another small clearing within view of the main ranch house. Billy put the basket down.

"Mom and Dad had always said this would be a good spot to build my own place, what do you think?" Morag looked around. It was relatively flat and would not cost a lot for him to get amenities in place. There was the bonus that he could be near to his parents as they got older.

"Yeah, it's a great spot," she said, "Close enough to your folks but far enough away that you have your own privacy."

There was an excitement growing within her that was almost instinctive but it wasn't until Billy turned towards her that she had a real idea of what was going on. She could see tears forming in his eyes but at the same time he had the biggest, dumbest smile on his face. He looked straight at her, inside her soul, and as he spoke her whole world seemed to light up brighter than the sunniest day of summer.

"Mo, would you like to share this place with me? I mean…" Billy's voice broke but he continued with what he had to say. "There is no one else in the world that I want to share my life with other than you. What I'm trying to say to you is, will you be my wife?" The words rang in Morag's ears and she watched Billy's hand as it slipped into his pocket and brought out a small dark circular object – a ring braided from horsehair.

"I only had the courage this morning to ask you," he said, "and there was no time to go get a proper ring and all, so I made you this just in case you said…" Morag cut him off before he could finish.

"Yes, Billy Dawson, yes I will marry you and I don't want a fancy ring because what you made for me with your hands is worth more than any precious jewel. I love you with all my heart and I want to be with you till we are old and of no use to anyone." Laughing and kissing, they held each other with the power only genuine love can bestow.

Once Billy had got over the initial shock, he spoke again.

"Let's go tell the good news to the folks." Forgetting the picnic basket, they ran the short distance to the house and found Walter sitting at the table rummaging through a tin of old nuts and bolts.

"Dad, do you know where Mom is?"

"In the office catching up on accounts, I think," Walter said, not looking up from his task. Billy shouted through to Margaret, at which his father shook his head and continued looking for the holy grail of the nut world.

"Did you enjoy the picnic?" Margaret asked as she appeared at the kitchen door. Immediately she could see a change in Billy and Morag so she sat down next to Walter and gave him a gentle tap in the ribs.

"Yes, very much," Billy said, "Mom, Dad, we have something important to tell you." Grins spread across the faces of his parents as they knew roughly what was coming next but were polite enough to contain their emotions. "We are going to get married to each other."

Walter burst out laughing.

"Well, it is customary to get married to each other and not elope and get married to yourself." He rose to his feet and took his son's hand. "I'm so happy for you both." He looked across to Morag then back to Billy. "Your mother and I knew this was coming, didn't we darling? You just have to look at you guys to know you want to spend your lives with each other, just like us."

Walter reached out and embraced Margaret, kissing the top of her head as he did. They all hugged, kissed, cried and congratulated each other. Billy ran out the door, saying "I'll be back in a minute" as he went.

"What's that all about?" Walter asked Morag,

"You're not pregnant, are you?" Morag smiled.

"No not yet. I think he's just remembered that he left the picnic basket back on the trail." Once again they all laughed then waited in the kitchen for Billy to return.

Chapter Forty-Six

Morag had insisted on one thing. "If you want me to come and live with you here, then I want to be married in Scotland." Without hesitation Billy agreed then wrapped his arms around her.

"Where in Scotland do you want to be married?" Morag's face lit up as an image came into her head.

"Home." A puzzled look ran across Billy's face.

"You want to get hitched in the horse yard? I mean it's pretty and all, but…" Morag placed a finger on his lips.

"No, ya twit. I would like to be married at Luss parish church on the banks of Loch Lomond – it is after all the seat of the Colquhoun clan." She had the look of a bride not to be messed with so Billy capitulated once again and Morag squealed with delight.

They then got down to working out who would be invited to the wedding. They immediately agreed that there would have to be a get-together on this side of the Atlantic for those who could not travel all the distance for one reason or another. Their respective lists were soon drawn up and were not too long, as neither had a large group of friends and likewise there weren't many on the family side of things. Billy gave his list to Walter and Margaret who added a couple of names.

As they thought about where to hold the stateside reception, Margaret had a suggestion.

"Why not hold it here? Then you're not tied down to

booking some place. We could get external caterers and a marquee, make it an old-fashioned barn dance." They all fell silent for a moment.

"I think it's a brilliant idea," Morag said, "What about you, honey?" Billy looked across at his parents and smiled.

"If you guys are up for it then let's do that."

Over the next few days, Morag booked the church and contacted her friend Laura who ran a carriage business, booking an open-top carriage to take her to and from the church. She was also inspired by Margaret's marquee idea and booked one for the Scottish end of things, asking permission of a nearby venue to put it up on their land.

The catering would be provided by her good friend John, who offered it for free by way of a wedding gift. Morag tried to negotiate a price but John held his ground until Morag yielded. For Billy's part it was less complicated; all he needed to do was to turn up. One very important person was required, however: a best man.

He watched Walter sitting on the porch looking out at the horses in the pens opposite, something he did often now that a lot of the ranch work had been taken off his hands. Billy came across and sat next to him.

"Do you have a minute, Dad?" Walter looked at Billy's face and saw it had a rather serious expression.

"Sure thing, son. What's on your mind?" They sat quietly for a moment.

"I was wondering, and you can say no if you want,

there's no pressure to do it – would you be my best man?" Looking away from Billy for the briefest of moments, Walter had tears welling in the corners of his eyes.

"You know, son, when our boy Daniel died there was a time between his death and the funeral when I was in a kind of limbo you might say. I would sit and see him go through college and find someone to settle down with and I'd get to walk down the church aisle and stand by my son on the day of his wedding. All of that disappeared as I laid his coffin into the ground."

Billy had never heard his father talk about this.

After a pause, he continued. "Then you came into our lives and gave us the second chance that we both had already given up on." He paused again. "Son, it would be one of the proudest days of my life to stand by your side on the day you wed that beautiful girl from Scotland." The two men hugged each other. Then with his arm around Walter's shoulder, Billy walked his father and best man into the kitchen to tell the girls the good news.

The drive to the airport was long and slow. Winter had finally let loose its first serious snowfall and caused chaos with the traffic. Morag and Billy had talked a lot about their plans for the wedding, but as they pulled into the airport car park the most daunting fact was that they were about to be separated once again. Billy took Morag's bags and they walked slowly in the direction of the terminal building.

"It won't be long before we're together in our own place," Billy said, "Just think of that, Morag – us married." She tried to put on a brave face.

"I know. You know me, I always want everything yesterday, even my husband." Billy smiled at her.

"Got a nice ring to it, if you'll pardon the pun." Morag looked puzzled then understood what he meant.

"Aw you mean 'husband', yes it does." She looked up at the board and it was time to go. With a final embrace they went their different ways, both looking back repeatedly until they were out of sight of each other.

On the drive home, Billy felt an emptiness inside him, as did Morag on her flight east.

Chapter Forty-Seven

The snow came and went then came back again, as is its wont. The evergreen trees held the only colour in a world almost exclusively shaded in greys and white. Then as midwinter passed there came a hope, along with the lengthening days, that the warmth of the sun would bring back to life everything that had lain dormant as winter yielded its grasp on the land.

On the ranch they had lost two of the older mares. When horses pass their prime, the cold eats deeper into them and, as so often in nature, the old and weak fall victim to time and the seasons. Whenever the Dawsons lost an animal it would be buried on the land where it once roamed. As Billy sat in the office, on the wall to his left were nameplates and braids of tail hair from every horse that had passed on the ranch, including the two lost recently. It was a solemn reminder not just of his responsibility to the animals but also of how fragile life can be.

He turned his attention to the computer keyboard and typed Morag's name into an email.

Hey Mo,

Hope all is well with you. I can't wait to see you at the end of the week, it's been a long hard road but we're finally nearing the end. Thanks for booking the folks into the hotel for me, I'm sure they are gonna absolutely love it. I love that photo you sent of the venue, it looks amazing as does the setting. The church is beautiful and I'm sure there will be many memories of this day for us to look back to in the future (when we're two old farts that are no use to man nor beast). I love you so much and can't wait to hold you in my arms again.

See you soon honey xxx + xxx = ?

PS: Can't wait to get into my kilt and let it all hang out LOL

He hit send and the message was gone. At that moment he heard a car door bang shut and went to the kitchen to see who was there, bumping into his parents as they came in by the back door. Startled, Billy let out a "Jesus!" Walter laughed.

"Hey son, this wedding business has got you a bit jumpy." He smiled as did Margaret.

"Don't pay no mind to that old crow," she said, "he's just a little cranky because they had to let the pants out in his one and only suit." She pulled a face in Walter's direction. Billy laughed.

"Did they manage to squeeze you back into it, Pops?" His father put on a look of distain.

"Old age comes to us all son, with the exception of your mother, who is as pretty now as the day we met." She blew him a kiss from the far end of the kitchen then started to put away the things they had bought in town. Billy smiled to himself and quietly hoped that his marriage to Morag would be as happy as that of his folks'.

"Mom, Dad," he said, "I'm going to do some more work on Morag's surprise, give me a shout in for lunch." Without waiting for confirmation, he left through the screen door and headed out across the yard.

Morag had asked Caroline to be her maid of honour and on that pretext had invited her out to lunch to discuss the arrangements. They discussed the times of day that the carriage needed to be at the farm and had a last check of the seating plan. Then just as they finished their main course, Morag sprang her surprise.

"Are you any further forward with your plans for your own yard?" Caroline almost choked on her wine before replying.

"I thought you were a horse trainer? Not a comedian. No, I have not got any further with that dream. I think it will sit on the back burner for a while as I make sure that the boys grow up sane, unlike their mother." They laughed together for a moment then Morag spoke again.

"Would you like your own yard? I mean, would you like to have my place?" Once again Caroline lost control of her mouth and this time managed to spray Morag with house white.

"You're serious, aren't you?" Morag nodded. "Why?"

"I'll tell you why, honey," Morag said, "because you have always been there for me through everything. Because you're my friend who I love and also because I know what it feels like to have a dream." After a few moments Caroline regained her composure.

"I don't know what to say, Mo. This has been my dream for a long time but I never in my wildest imagination thought it would ever become a reality." Morag took hold of her Caroline's hands.

"Well, now it is," she said, "I have one more favour

to ask you, though. Billy still would like to come and do clinics here in Scotland, and since he is already established at the yard we thought it would be good for you and him to continue the relationship. It also means we get to see each other regularly." Morag squeezed her friend's hands gently then let go. Caroline was still in a state of semi-shock.

"Of course you guys can hold clinics," she said, "Jesus Mo, this is all too much for me, I feel very overwhelmed." She caught the waiter's eye. "Excuse me, can we have a bottle of the house champagne please? We're celebrating."

When the meal was over, they spent the rest of the day sorting out the finer points of changing the ownership of the yard into Caroline's name, which was relatively simple as the mortgage had already been paid off.

As they headed to their respective taxis, Caroline shouted across, "Hey Mo, you're one in a million."

Morag called back in reply,

"Ditto."

Chapter Forty-Eight

For the Dawsons, and especially for Walter, the flight over to Scotland had been a long one. They made their way through the usual airport checks and headed out into the arrivals lounge where Morag and Caroline waited to greet the three of them. When the bride and groom-to-be embraced and kissed it brought a barrage of good-natured abuse from their companions, in response to which they continued in a more comedic manner until giving up in fits of laughter.

Morag and Caroline dropped Walter and Margaret at the hotel then Caroline headed home to rescue her husband from the terrible twins. Morag and Billy then had chance to catch up on the latest events. Morag told him about her gift to Caroline and Billy in return said there was a surprise waiting when she got back to Montana. This led to her pestering him for information on the rest of the journey home, but Billy stood his ground and did not divulge any details, even when threatened with a wedding call-off.

They reached Morag's house, took Billy's suitcases up to the bedroom, then spent some time getting reacquainted with each other before going downstairs for supper.

"Do you think we should call the hotel to see if Mom and Dad have settled in?" Even before Billy had finished his sentence, Morag was shaking her head.

"Billy, your parents are grown up, we can see them

in the morning." He smiled at her.

"You're right. It's just that I've become a little over-protective of them since Dad had his heart scare. Which brings me to something else I wanted to discuss with you." Billy took a sip of his coffee. "You know Mom and Dad run therapy courses, mostly for kids that are disadvantaged or needing help?" Morag nodded. "Well, they were wondering if we would like to take over the running of the courses, under their supervision initially, but gradually we would be given full control of the curriculum with freedom to add to it." Morag leaned over to kiss him on the forehead.

"I think that's a great idea and it's something close to your heart." He returned her kiss.

"You're one in a million, you do know that?" She smiled.

"Of course!" With that out of the way, Morag informed him that she had organised their kilts and he and Walter would have to go along for a fitting.

"Why don't we go round in the morning to see how your folks have settled in," she said, "then go along to the kilt shop and get you guys fitted out?" Billy laughed.

"I'm not sure the world can cope with my exposed knees, and as for my dad…" He let his sentence tail off. It was Morag's turn to laugh.

"Big strapping cowboys like you and your paaaw." She emphasised her point with an American twang. "And anyway, these are modern times and it's okay to expose your naked knee for the entire world to see."

As Walter knelt on the floor inside the kilt shop he complained about, as he put it, his 'damn arthritis'. The fitter chuckled to himself.

"This is the most accurate way of correctly fitting you for your kilt, sir."

Morag had picked the Flower of Scotland tartan for Walter and Billy as it was the one that most closely matched her own clan pattern. Once the fitter was finished, he ushered both men to the changing area where they would be kitted out in their full wedding attire. They had been gone for some time when the fitter heralded their reappearance.

"Ladies, I present to you the groom and the best man." Morag and Margaret let out gasps as Walter and Billy entered the waiting area.

"You guys look amazing," Morag said, "don't you think so, Mrs Dawson? Sorry, Maggie?" Margaret looked at Walter.

"Yes, such a handsome pair." She planted a kiss on the end of her husband's nose and stood back to look at him once more. Billy seemed a bit unsure.

"So I take it that the kilts are a hit, ladies?" The women each slipped a hand under their respective men's new purchases.

"You'll have to lose the underwear if you want to be a true Scotsman," Morag said. Everyone laughed before she settled the bill and the two men left the shop with their wedding attire draped over their shoulders.

With the wedding only hours away, it had been arranged that Billy would stay at the same hotel as his parents as his way of keeping with tradition. Morag and Caroline would spend the morning having their hair and make-up done then travel by limousine to the venue before switching to the carriage for the short distance to the church. Caroline's boys were to be the ring-bearers, the rings themselves having tail hair from Ronin and Brogan incorporated into the design with the main body being white gold. Morag's friend John would walk her down the aisle.

At the hotel, Billy paced back and forth. "Dad, what time is it?" Letting out sigh, Walter looked at his watch.

"Five minutes later than the last time I told you." He shook his head. He had never seen his son as wound up as this. In an effort to distract him, he reached under his kilt, removed his boxer shorts and threw them at Billy's feet. "Are you man enough to be a true Scot and go commando?" Looking down at his father's discarded underwear, Billy let out a laugh.

"That's it, son," Walter said, "Release all that tension. You're going to remember this day for the rest of your life so make the memories happy ones." With that, the two men hugged. As they headed to the door Billy stopped, slipped off his shorts and smiled at his father.

"You only live once," he said.

Chapter Forty-Nine

The limo driver approached the door and was intercepted by Caroline.

"The bride will be a few more minutes," she told him, "and anyway, it's traditional for her to be late." The driver shook his head and walked back to the car. Caroline returned to the kitchen just as Morag appeared in the doorway.

"You look absolutely radiant, Mo," she said, "he's a lucky man."

"Shall we do this then?" Morag asked with a grin. Her friend nodded and they made their way to the car.

"Looking lovely, ladies," the driver said as he guided them into the back seat, "I'll get you there in jig time." Caroline took Morag's hand and gave it a soft squeeze.

"I'm so, so proud of you Mo, you've waited a long time for this. Let's make it a day to remember for the rest of our lives."

As they reached the venue, Laura was waiting with the carriage, which was to be pulled by a young draft mare called Misty.

"Mo, this is for luck," Laura said, handing over a beautifully wrapped package which Morag quickly opened to find a chrome-plated horseshoe. The women hugged one more time then climbed into the carriage. Laura gave Misty a command: "Walk on".

The ornate gateway of Luss parish church had a

small roof which covered the wrought ironwork of the gate itself. The steepled church gave the impression of being small inside but there was ample room for all the guests. Walter, Billy and Margaret got out of the car and were ushered to the gateway by the photographer.

"This way folks, Mr Dawson junior in the middle." The usual wedding sets were taken and they then headed into the church itself. Walter turned to Billy and echoed what Morag had said to Caroline earlier.

"Well my boy, will we do this?" Billy had a smile on his face.

"Why not, Pops?" The two men walked up the central aisle, which had been adorned with white ribbons on the end of every pew and on each side of the altar there were more flowers. Billy looked to the side and nodded to people he knew.

The further down the aisle they walked, each face became more familiar until almost to his disbelief Billy saw Ruth Drake. She was with a blond-haired man whose face looked familiar and he realised it was Sam Quinn, who gave Billy a thumbs-up.

Next he saw Frank Hendriks and his wife, while Anne Rea stood with tears running down her face as she dabbed her eyes with a tissue. Billy had to fight to control his emotions.

Then he was standing at the front of the church.

Walter leaned across and whispered, "Are you okay, son?" Billy nodded, fearing that if he tried to speak he would break down in a sobbing mess. The two men stood there waiting for the bride.

The carriage made its way around the last corner

and the small church stood resplendent in the spring sunshine. Caroline let out a little cry.

"We're here, honey." Morag beamed at her friend.

"I know, isn't it beautiful?" The carriage halted and Laura came round to the nearside door.

"Take your time," she said, "I've got to go and do a quick change." Morag and Caroline got out then Laura climbed back in and took the carriage round the next corner. As with Billy and Walter, there were the photographs to be taken – more in this case. After several minutes spent standing there and posing, Morag whispered to Caroline.

"I think Laura will have plenty of time to get in her seat." The photographer heard this and gave them a stern look.

When they were finally able to enter the back of the church, John stood waiting for them. Caroline wished them good luck and headed up the aisle to one of the front pews.

"You look radiant, my dear," John said as he looked at Morag, "It's an honour for me to give you away." He gave her a gentle kiss on the cheek then the sound of Mendelssohn's wedding march announced their approach along the aisle.

At the altar Billy waited patiently, not wanting to turn around for fear it would bring bad luck. Finally, he looked and saw Morag standing beside him in a white lace wedding dress with a bodice adorned with her clan tartan. A thin ribbon of tartan held her veil in place. Before he could say anything, the minister, who had waited quietly to one side, came and stood in front of them and asked if they were ready to proceed. The smiles on their faces were the only answer he needed.

"Dearly beloved, we are gathered here today to witness the wedding of this man and this woman…" As the minister spoke, Morag and Billy never took their eyes off each other, both so lost in the moment that no one and nothing else mattered. Morag heard her name being called as if from afar.

"Morag and Billy will now pledge their commitment to one another by placing rings on each other's fingers as a sign of their love."

Caroline's two boys appeared, escorted by her, each with a single ring on a velvet cushion. Walter took both rings and handed them to the minister. He took the smaller ring and gave it to Billy, who in turn held Morag's left hand.

"William John Dawson, do you take Morag Anne Colquhoun to be your lawful wedded wife, to have and to hold, to love and to cherish, in sickness and in health, till death do you part?"

Billy said, "I do" and slipped the ring on Morag's finger. Then it was Morag's turn.

"Yes, I do, with all my heart," she said, then placed the second ring on Billy's finger.

The minister looked over his glasses and smiled.

"It is with great pleasure that I now pronounce you husband and wife." He turned to Billy. "And as is traditional at this point, you may kiss your bride." Billy said thank you then leaned across and kissed Morag softly on the lips.

"I love you so much Mo, and I'll try to be the best husband there can be." She laughed as tears rolled down her cheeks.

They all walked to the church office to complete the necessary paperwork, with sobs of joy from some of the congregation and calls of good luck.

Chapter Fifty

The carriage took the happy couple to the venue, where the white marquee stood reflecting the sunlight in what had become a lovely spring day. There were more wedding photos, but once inside Billy and Morag finally got a chance to mingle with their guests. Almost immediately Billy excused himself and went in search of Sam Quinn and Ruth. He found them standing in a corner with glasses of champagne in their hands. He hugged Sam tightly.

"Man, it's good to see you. How long has it been?" Sam looked at Billy and smiled.

"Too long my friend, too long." Billy turned to Ruth.

"I'm so glad you could make it – and with a nice surprise, too." Ruth was beaming with pride.

"William Dawson, you've come a long way." Billy put his arms around both of their shoulders.

"I would like you to come and meet my wife," he said, walking across to where Morag was standing with John, who stretched out a hand.

"You're a very lucky man, my friend," he said, "I wish you both all the happiness in the world." Morag then asked Billy who his friends were.

"Mo, this is my teacher and saviour, Ruth Drake."

Morag took her hand, saying "Billy speaks of you very highly", at which Ruth blushed.

"And this handsome youngish devil," Billy continued, "is my other saviour and friend, Sam Quinn."

Again, Morag reached out and took his hand.

"Billy has very fond memories of your time together, especially your field goal." Sam looked perplexed for a moment then realised what Morag was referring to.

"Seemed like a good idea at the time," he said, and they all laughed.

Soon everyone was ushered to the tables for the meal, and it was only now that the newly-weds had the chance to spend some time with Billy's parents. Walter took Morag's hand as they sat down at the top table.

"You guys are the perfect couple," he said, "and Mo, we both are in awe of your dress choice, beautiful." Morag blushed a little.

"It was mainly my mother's wedding dress, but I wanted something different that showed our heritage – and what better than our clan tartan?" Margaret touched her hand and said it was the perfect choice.

They all then ate, before Walter tapped a wine glass to catch everyone's attention. He told a few stories about Billy and his early days as a horse trainer, including the one about how he tried to put the first saddle on Ronin, before raising his glass and wishing the bride and groom "health, happiness and a great deal of patience for each other's mood swings".

When Billy rose to his feet he was met by loud whistling.

"Thank you, Frank," he said, "I now have tinnitus. First of all, we would like to thank both Caroline and this old cowboy sitting next to me for being maid of honour and best man respectively." After a burst of applause, Billy continued. "Before I sit back down, I'd also like to say thank you to a few folks who mean a whole lot to me. My parents for their constant love and support, to Anne Rea for putting me back together," – he felt his voice start to break a little as he said this – "and to Sam Quinn for being my first real friend. And Frank, you know me better than most folks and you're like a brother to me."

Frank shouted back, "Ditto", and again people laughed.

"And before I get to this lovely lady here beside me," Billy looked down at Morag, who was smiling back at him, "there is one other very special lady in this room who quite literally saved my life, her name is Ruth." He gestured to where his former teacher was sitting.

"Morag and I, you could say, had a whirlwind romance – or was it a tornado? We met, as most of you know, through our shared love of horses, and that in turn blossomed into a love of each other. I know there will be good and bad times ahead, but one thing I'm sure of is that we will face them together, till death do us part." With that, Billy lifted his glass and toasted his new bride. He then leant over and kissed her.

After the meal there was a short interval that allowed the room to be reconfigured with a dance floor for the ceilidh. The bride and groom started things with a waltz to the tune of the Skye Boat Song, then as the floor filled they returned to their table for a break. It was at this point that Sam caught Billy's eye and beckoned him over.

"I'm married as well," Sam said, "with two lovely kids, both adopted. My wife and I felt there are so many children in care that even though we could have had our own it was a no-brainer to adopt." Billy smiled at Sam's enthusiasm. "Your folks tell me you're having a barn dance when you get back," Sam said. "Would it be okay for me to bring the family?" Without hesitation, Billy said

"Yes."

He returned to Morag and they walked out of the marquee to a smaller tent where they found bags with a full change of clothes. They then walked across to the limousine, which would take them to Rossdhu House, a hotel on the shore of Loch Lomond. As they climbed into the car, everyone came out to bid them farewell and to toast their happiness. The driver set off at a slow pace until the marquee was just a dim glow in the Scottish dusk.

Chapter Fifty-One

It only took Billy and Morag ten minutes to reach the hotel, which had soft lighting set into the shrubbery at the foot of its grand walls. The doorman took their bags and escorted them to reception, then to the bridal suite on the third floor. Once the solid oak door had closed behind them, they looked around the neo-Jacobean style room, where three full-length windows each had at least twenty small panes. The bed, which dominated the middle of the room, was a reworking of an older four-poster design done in deep red mahogany. The rest of the room was fitted out in golden gilt and styled for the wealthier visitor.

Lying on their backs, they found themselves looking up at a tapestry of a unicorn.

"Well now, Mrs Dawson," Billy said, "I claim my right of *prima nocta*, it's my duty as your laird to spend the night with you." He spoke using a very bad Scottish accent with far too many Rs.

"If your bed technique is as bad as your accent," Morag said, "you can stuff it." He laughed and rolled on top of her. They looked into each other's eyes, then Billy leaned down to kiss his new bride.

Come morning, they ate a full breakfast then called a taxi to take them back to the farm from where they would leave for the US the next day. Although the wedding had been a joy-filled occasion, there was something weighing heavily on Morag's mind. When she moved away to a new life there was a big part of her home that she was going to miss: her old boy, Brogan. As she leaned on the rail that bordered the field, tears tumbled down her face as she called his name and waited for his response, which as always was to look up and gradually make his way to the top of the field where she stood.

It had been a painful decision not to take Brogan but given his age and wellbeing the upheaval would probably have been his undoing. It was decided he should stay with Caroline, with his herd and his home. Morag took some comfort in knowing it would not be the last time she would see him, as she planned to come over whenever Billy had clinics booked.

On reaching the top of the field Brogan greeted his owner, as usual, by blowing air through his nose on to Morag's face. The 'air kiss' only compounded her sadness, and as she spoke to him – "Hey old man, you're such a good boy, you know that" – the tears ran freely down her face and were caught on the horse's nose.

"I have to go," Morag said, "but your auntie Caroline will take great care of you when I'm gone." She looked deeply into the horse's eyes, searching for some emotion that said it was fine. Brogan lifted his head and gently let out a huge breath of air as if to tell her it was going to be okay.

When Morag stopped sobbing into Brogan's shoulder and lifted her own head back up, she reached into a pocket and pulled out a small red apple, his favourite. As a rule, Morag never hand-fed her horses, but today was an exception. She stood there until there was nothing left on her hand but Brogan's saliva. With a final kiss on his nose she turned and walked back to the house and onward to a new beginning.

Chapter Fifty-Two

As they drove home to the ranch, Billy was keen to let Morag in on his secret but had to be patient for a little while longer. She had fallen asleep almost as soon as the car had hit the freeway, and Billy hoped things would stay that way until they got home. His wish was granted, and it was only as they pulled into the driveway that Morag stirred.

"Jesus, I must have been tired from the flight," she said as she woke, "That was turbulence I will not forget." Billy laughed, but there was something in his eyes that Morag could see. "Billy Dawson, husband, what are you up to?" He put on his serious face, or as good a one as he could manage.

"I haven't a clue what you're talking about, Mo." She searched his face for any signs of falsehood and could find none, so she just let out a "hmmm" and stepped out of the pickup.

Walter and Margaret joined them for coffee in the kitchen. Walter told them about some of the students from Frank's course who had been gaining work experience at the ranch in their absence. Margaret then gave Billy a chance to let on about his secret.

"Billy, didn't you have something to show Morag?" Billy feigned surprise.

"Aw yes. Totally forgot about that, thanks Mom." With a wink he took Morag's hand and they went outside across the yard to the end of the stable block.

Here Billy stopped Morag and asked her to close her eyes. When she asked why, he said he wanted to hear her first thoughts on something.

With Billy behind her, they walked a little further then stopped. "Remember, I want your honest opinion," Billy said. Morag nodded and opened her eyes. It took her a few seconds to adjust to the light.

"My God Billy, is this our new home?" She sat down on the grass in front of the cedar wood cabin that Billy and a local contractor had built over the winter. There was a covered deck and a large bay window that would capture the light in summer. Next to it was a paddock for horses with a double stable and summer shelter.

As she got to her feet, Morag threw her arms around Billy. "It's perfect," she said, "thank you." He kissed her and took her hand as they climbed the steps of their new home.

Inside had been furnished but not finished, as Billy thought that was something they could do together. Morag jumped up and down as she saw the kitchen with its beautiful colours of wood that had been used for the counter tops.

"I made this myself from some dead-fall we had," Billy said, "and the drawer handles too, just so it would all match." Morag hugged him, then they went over to the kitchen window, which overlooked the paddock where a horse was standing in the shade: Raven.

"This is my final surprise," Billy said, "I'm giving Raven to you, and he still has some work needing done on him but..." He didn't get to finish the sentence as Morag kissed him firmly on the lips.

"I love you so much, Billy Dawson," she said,

"You're the perfect husband." He blushed and they kissed again.

On coming back out to the porch they were met by Billy's parents.

"Glad to get you kids out of the house and into your own place," Walter said. Morag ran down the steps and hugged both Walter and Margaret before turning to Billy.

"I really like our new neighbours," she said, "don't you?" Billy laughed.

"Just love 'em, honey, just love them."

It had been almost a year since the wedding. Morag was getting to the end of her citizenship application, just in time for that year's course. She and Billy were settled into the cabin and had furnished it to their tastes. One of the things they saw every day was the chrome horseshoe, received as a wedding token and now nailed above the kitchen sink to remind them of that special day.

Walter and Margaret had started to take a back seat with their courses, but kept active in a supporting role, recognising that retirement was an idea rather than a law. Dr Rea had put them in touch with a qualified therapist who would help with running the courses that were for children, and also a new project inspired by Ruth Drake's late husband: equine-assisted courses for the armed forces. Ruth herself would come out on occasion and help with some of the schooling, plus she simply liked being around the ranch with her friends.

Sam Quinn had brought his family out for visits and Morag was teaching the children to ride whenever the chance arose. As an addition to the courses, Billy had come up with the idea of refurbishing the old cattle station with a bunkhouse and teaching the children – and the adults – how to live off the land and also how to work in a team environment. It was at one of these gatherings that something happened which brought back some memories for Billy.

The sound of children laughing always brought a smile to his face. Their laughter was so joyful and honest that it made his soul calm. As he looked around the barn, there had been a few changes. It had been re-boarded, as it now doubled as a classroom if the weather turned, and all the pens had been replaced with new metal ones that needed less maintenance. There was also now a large main arena that could be used for course or stock work, and finally the old ranch house had been restored as a bunkhouse annexe. Morag fitted in as if she had always been there, becoming almost inseparable from Raven, although it would still take time for the bond to become as close as with Brogan.

On one of these course days Billy noticed one of the kids sitting off by himself. He motioned to Morag to continue without him, then carefully he made his way over to the young boy and hunkered down beside him.

"Hey there," he said, "what's your name?" After a few moments the boy replied in almost a whisper:

"Billy, my name is Billy." There was a lump in the older Billy's throat as he spoke to the boy.

"Well that's a coincidence, because my name is Billy, too, but so we don't get mixed up with each other, you can call me Bill, is that a deal?" Again, there was a pause before the boy responded.

"Okay." Billy smiled and stuck out his hand.

"Shake on it?"

The boy looked up at Billy then down at his hand, and ever so slowly reached out and took it.

"Do you want to meet an authentic wild American mustang?" Billy said. This time when the boy looked up there was something different in his eyes.

"Yes please," he said. Billy smiled inwardly as he took the boy's hand and led him across to where the dun horse stood beside the water trough.

"This here horse is a genuine wild American mustang," Billy said, "and his name is Ronin." The horse reached down with his muzzle and let the young two-legs stroke his forelock. The boy smiled and so did Billy.

Lightning Source UK Ltd.
Milton Keynes UK
UKHW040820090222
398402UK00002B/266

9 781914 560040